Lock Down Publications and Ca$h
Presents

FOR THE LOVE OF BLOOD 5

SURVIVOR'S GUILT

By
JAMEL MITCHELL

First Edition 2025

Printed in the United States of America

Lock Down Publications
P.O. Box 944
Stockbridge, GA 30281
www.lockdownpublications.com

Like our page on Facebook: Lock Down Publications
www.facebook.com/lockdownpublications.ldp

Stay Connected with Us!

Text **LOCKDOWN** to 22828 to stay up-to-date with new releases, sneak peaks, contests and more…

Like our page on Facebook:
Lock Down Publications

Join Lock Down Publications/The New Era Reading Group

Visit our website:
www.lockdownpublications.com

Follow us on Instagram:
Lock Down Publications

Email Us: We want to hear from you!

Acknowledgements

First and foremost, all praise is due to Allah and Allah alone. I thank you daily for this talent and the blessings you give. Alhamdulillah . . . I also thank want to express my gratitude to my lovely family for their constant advice, patience and support. That shit is very much appreciated. I know I get on ya'Il nerves, but shit I mean well. Lol. I love y'all unconditionally. I don't know what I would be if I didn't have y'all in my comer. Tah'Keem . . . Ke'Mante . . . My twins . . . man I love you niggas more than I love anything else in this world. I hope you know how deep my love for you guys run, real shit. Words can't express how much I love you lil niggas. Ya'Il my best friends. I live for y'all. I can't make up for lost time, but I promise to make the ill est memories, ya heard. Stay dangerous!

Momma . . . Jameela . . . Dewayne . . . Lynitrah . . . Jamey . . . Jordy . . . King . . . Empress . . . Journey . . . You know I ain't gone forget my baby this time. I love you Katie, please don't ever forget that. You know we forever locked in momma. Auntie Puda, I love you, beauty. I know you and lil momma be beefed out, I've learned many times over in this bitch, family is all we got. With that said, someone has to be the bigger person auntie. I know her evil ass missing you. LMAO Munchie my nigga, my brother, man you know the vibes, I love you my nigga forever ya heard, I hope by the time this shit touch the press you free. My apologies for just saluting, a nigga mind be everywhere when it's time to do these thank you's, real shit. But please forgive me you know it's all love gang. Tap in fool. Janiece, I love you, Ma. 'Bout time we link back up lil nigga. Donnell, I hope you proud of a nigga big bro. Who would have ever thought . . . You one of the strongest men I know, I tip my hat to you. Keep that shit up man, I wish I could have been half the man you were, to my babies. Nigga you short from amazing. I love you big bro. Free my Evil Twin Joshua Meregildo . . . Nigga every book I write I'm gone scream free you until we make that shit happen. Word to my dead. I love you, nigga. You greatly missed that's for sure. COURTLANDT OVER EVERYTHING.

Dedication

This Book is dedicated to the Memories of ...
Granny Polly . . . Nya Marie Terry . . . Katelynn Berger

To my fans I am sorry for the delay. The things that goes on behind these walls is no different than what goes on out there. But thank you for your patience and understanding. I hope y'all didn't count a nigga out. I hope y'all enjoy this as much as I enjoyed writing it.

Chapter 1

The rain cascaded down from the dark, melancholic clouds above, hitting the black and gold casket as the pastor gracefully lead Gloria's soul into God's heavenly gates.

Carlos sat reserved, listening to the beautiful words the pastor spoke that described his **most precious jewel—his daughter, Gloria Rayne Rivera. Carlos sighed and took a deep breath. To say that he was stressed would have been an understatement. Death felt more promising than anything life could currently offer.

Carlos swiped at the water running down his face carelessly, wiping away any evidence of tears and emotion. He looked to his side and saw his ex-wife's mascara running in streaks along her face. He felt for her. Their pain was different, but one in the same. He bit his bottom lip and looked toward the ground in shame.

"I promise I'm going to kill the people responsible for this, momma. If it's the last thing I do on this earth," he scoffed, whispering to himself, thinking of ways to exact revenge.

Carlos looked at what he had left of his daughter and thought vividly about the memories they shared. Though there weren't many, the ones that he had saved in his memory bank seemed to flow in repeat across his eyes in small flashes. The glory days of raising Gloria, he called it. It was all he had left of his baby girl.

Thoughts . . . fucking thoughts . . . all I have left is thoughts, Carlos said to himself, thinking of Gloria's light being faded at such a young age. His hurt only seemed to build.

Carlos shut his eyes tightly trying to suppress his emotions. He was trying like hell not to break down, but damn, it was almost impossible.

How? How could this have happened?

Carlos just couldn't shake his mind of it all. He was so confused. How the fuck could this have happened to his daughter?

He had meticulously scrutinized the wars he played parts in, making sure that no enemies came back to haunt him and his family. He couldn't think of no one. Carlos hadn't had a problem in the streets for years. He had no enemies. He rubbed his temple, his thoughts fueled by anger, confusion, and hurt.

Carlos wiped the water from his face again. The rain finally began to slow as the pastor came to the end of Gloria's eulogy. Carlos looked around the cemetery at the people in attendance and screwed his face up. The teenagers that were present in support of Gloria were questionable, to say the least. They wore bandanas of all colors: red, black, brown, blue, and burgundy. Carlos wasn't too familiar with the exact meanings to the colors, but he was educated enough to know that the bandanas were in correlation to having gang ties.

Carlos made a mental note to check into the players in attendance on his daughter's behalf, because he knew nine times out of ten, one of the teenagers present knew the who, what, when, where, and how surrounding the situation behind Gloria's death. And in due time, he would make sure to press the masses for that particular information.

But right now, on this present date, he wanted Gloria to be celebrated as the Princess that she was. He wanted the memories of Gloria's last days on earth to be that of grace and celebration. Carlos knew he would have time to act accordingly to his feelings and emotions.

Other than Juan—his bodyguard—and a few members of his ex-wife's family, he did not know no one in attendance. The relatives Carlos did know on Carmen's side of the family were no longer among the living. So damn near every face besides Carmen and Juan's was unfamiliar to him.

He looked at each person apprehensively. Everyone was suspect at this point. Carlos knew the killer could very well be among them, lurking, mingling, trying their hardest to fit in.

It would not be the first time a killer showed up to the funeral of their victim to admire their work—or to show remorse. Carlos was a realist. Sometimes people deserved death. Carlos wondered to himself if this was one of those times.

Did my daughter deserve this? Was Gloria one of those people that deserved their demise? Or was it just her time?

The questions ran rapid through Carlos's mind, not really giving him the time to think of any conclusions. What hurt Carlos more than anything was this: he did not know if Gloria's death was due to his karma . . . or her own.

He surveyed the crowd in hopes of finding a killer in the midst. He knew exactly what to look for, because he had once been the same kind of mu'fucka—pulling up to the funeral of the man he put in the ground.

So Carlos knew the vibe all too well. He was a snake looking for another snake.

When Carlos realized that the crowd was made up of nothing but mourners, his suspicion shifted to jealousy. Many of the people had one thing he didn't—time. They had spent real time with Gloria, laughed with her, cried with her. Meanwhile, he had barely managed to piece together moments. He wasn't privileged enough to be around his daughter like that. He had let the streets snatch away the loves of his life.

Carlos was a boss; that's all he had ever been. And in being that, he let his home life fall apart. It came at a price—a heavy one.

Gloria had been just six years old when Carmen packed up and left, taking her to live with her older brother in Edgewood, Maryland. Carmen gave Carlos an ultimatum, one that he wasn't too fond of. He needed the dope game to take care of his family, but he needed his family more. Carlos wanted to choose his family, no doubt about it. But the lure of being a boss was just too strong. He couldn't go cold turkey.

When Carmen found out he had not changed, she bounced for good and never looked back. Carlos searched high and low for Carmen and Gloria, but every lead led to a dead end. Now, after finally finding and making a bond with Gloria, she was snatched away from him. Permanently. The hurt was unbearable. The only way Carlos could find peace was to erase the entire bloodline responsible.

Carlos's eyes glistened from the buildup of raw emotion that coursed through his body. He made a promise to himself and his lost love that all involved with his daughter's death would pay dearly. Carlos felt a tap on his shoulder, startling him. He looked up into the eyes of Carmen Rivera, his ex-wife. The look he gave her was of pure disgust. He wanted to spit on her, but he held his composure for the sake of Gloria. He didn't want to cause a scene and act out at Gloria's funeral—he didn't want people to remember Gloria in that light. Carlos pinched the bridge of his nose as he tried to calm himself. He inhaled deeply, then exhaled loudly. He took his hands from his face and looked into the beautiful eyes of his ex-wife.

"Yes, Carmen?" he asked in a flat, unfriendly tone. He wasn't going to fake the love just because his daughter was gone. He wanted Carmen to see the hate that he had bottled in his heart for her. Carlos wanted her to know that he hated her with his whole heart.

Carmen stood in front of him as the tears ran down her face. The big black Dolce & Gabbana glasses that Carmen wore did a good job of concealing the majority of her emotions—just not all. The grief was evident. Carlos looked at her and felt no remorse. Carmen was hurting; Carlos could clearly see that. They both had lost their only child. Carlos couldn't help but lighten his heart a little when a lone, black, mascara-filled tear rolled down her face.

Carmen's emotion was of the rawest kind. Chills slid down Carlos's spine as he shook the love from his memory and blackened his heart. He had loved Carmen more than he could ever love himself—he thought that she was the one who got away. But as he sat and looked at her on this day, all he could feel was pain. Carlos wholeheartedly blamed Carmen for Gloria being in that black and gold casket. The decision she made all those years ago had cost them their beloved daughter.

"I don't know what you keep crying for. This is all your doing," Carlos thought aloud.

No sooner than the words seeped from his lips, he regretted them. Carmen slapped him as hard as she could. Carlos's face stung from the hit, but he stood there unfazed. He couldn't blame her, because whether he was right or wrong, the words shouldn't have been said.

"What are you going to do to me? Hit me?" Carmen stepped closer to Carlos, fear and anger etched across her with each movement of her lips. Carlos sighed and breathed deeply, trying to suppress his growing anger. Carmen was taunting him—she wanted a reaction, one that he wasn't willing to give. At least not on this date. Carlos was trying to refrain from doing anything that he would later regret, so he continued to remind himself that the time and the place just wasn't right.

Carlos pulled Carmen into him forcefully. She flinched, awaiting pain. When none came, she opened her eyes. Carlos whispered into Carmen's ear firmly—no one needed to hear what he had to say.

"It was you who kept me away from my daughter, raising her in all these hoods around all these damn niggers. Now you take your happy-and-go-lucky ass and find out who's responsible for murdering our daughter in cold blood. Please take this conquest seriously, Carmen—your life may depend on it. I loved you, and you left. Your choice, not mine. Now you have to live with your fucking decision to crawl from under my blanket of protection and put your big-girl panties on. This is the one and only time I'm asking for your help. Do you hear me, Carmen? Am I making myself clear?"

When he felt his ex-wife acknowledge him with a simple nod, he released her from his grip and kissed her forehead. He nodded to his bodyguard that he was ready and walked off without saying another word.

Carlos didn't know when the drizzle of rain picked back up, but he welcomed it. The perspiration mixed with the gentle droplets of rain concealed his tears. Though he knew he shouldn't be concerned with such trivial shit, he was. He still had an image to uphold. As Carlos continued his walk through the graveyard, he could feel Carmen burning a hole through his back, but not once did he falter his stride. He kept his head held high the whole way to his customized limousine—a 2006 Mercedes-Benz, the one he rented just for this juncture. Juan pulled the door to the limo open, holding it in place for Carlos to hop in. Carlos placed his right foot into the luxury, but stopped and stared across the graveyard at Carmen. They locked eyes before he disappeared into the limo.

The stare Carlos gave her said it all—Carlos wasn't playing, and she knew it. Carmen knew if she didn't find out who he was looking for and prove to be useful, he would have her killed. Or would he? Carmen asked herself: *Is my ex-husband really capable of ordering my murder?* She didn't have the answer. But she did know that the man who stood in front of her was just a shell of the man she once called her husband. The man she saw today was hurt, callous, and determined.

Carmen removed her glasses and swiped the water from her face. She got herself together mentally and emotionally before approaching the awaiting crowd of mourners. They had a life to celebrate—plus, they had to put to use all the money Carlos had spent to make sure the day was memorable for everyone in attendance. Carmen showed the fakest of smiles as she mingled and took in the love that Gloria's friends showed. *My baby was loved by so many*, Carmen thought, as she was embraced and hugged lovingly by all in attendance. Carmen knew Gloria like no other—Gloria was her baby, her one, her only, her heartbeat.

And she knew if Gloria could speak from the grave, she would cuss the crowd for their somber mood. The thought alone made Carmen smile tearfully. Her daughter was just so special. *Why did this have to happen to my child?* Carmen hated her thoughts now, because she simply couldn't run from herself. It was hard, as a loving mother, to not ask the questions that stung the most.

How? What did I do wrong? Carmen tried not to beat herself up with the questions, but she just couldn't help herself. The tears rolled down her face unwillingly. Carmen wiped her eyes—this time with a smile—and addressed the crowd.

"Thank you all for coming to celebrate my daughter's life. The repast will be held at my home in an hour. I encourage you to go home, freshen up, and change into something a little more comfortable. Being sad stays here. I won't be able to handle the tears and shit. So, I beg, please leave the tears and all the other sad shit here. She was my daughter—and believe me, if I can hold it, so can you. Let's enjoy one of my baby's last days of remembrance. In the words of Gloria Rayne: it's time to turn up! See you guys there. If you need directions, text me."

Carmen raised her hand and waved as she walked off, her heart breaking piece by piece the farther she got from Gloria's final resting place.

Chapter 2

Fatty Man pointed his gun at Darla, sweat dripping from his head profusely. He wasn't expecting for Santana to bring the static like he did.

Bitch ass nigga kicked bruh's candles. On my soul he gone die about that, Fatty thought as he eyed Darla up and down.

"Darla, sit the fuck down. I'm not here to hurt you," Fatty Man assured Darla before turning to the men with him.

"And lil' nigga, you shoot that muthafuckin' gun in this bitch again, I'm gone leave you in this bitch stinking," Fatty stated coldly, looking his newest addition FB Gleek, square in the eyes. The only reason he wasn't already dead for the stunt he just pulled was because if it wasn't for his gun, Fatty might have not made it out his Impala in one piece. Santana was proving to be a problem, and though Fatty wanted him dead, he had to admit that claiming Santana's body was going to be harder than he anticipated.

"Fatty, just leave, please! How did this lead to my doorstep? This shit has nothing to do with me, Ronald. Why are you here? What the fuck do you and Santana got going on that got you all in my house with these dingy-ass niggas waving guns around in my face? Huh? Answer me!" Darla screamed in pure desperation. She was scared, hurt, and confused. Darla wanted answers, and she wanted them now.

Fatty looked at her in contempt. He had nothing to say. He was there for one reason and one reason only—Santana.

"Leave me and Melquan out of this! We don't have shit to do with this fake-ass street shit y'all niggas got on. I don't want my son to see these niggas in here with their guns drawn when he gets back from the movies with Sofiya. I'm serious, Fatty. I'm begging you," Darla pleaded, tears streaking down her beautiful face.

Fatty Man ignored Darla and walked to the living room window. Precautiously, Fatty stepped to the side and used his Glock to look out the curtains. There was no movement whatsoever outside of Darla's home.

Where the fuck is this nigga at? Fatty thought, letting the curtain fall back into place. Fatty looked at Darla with a look of pure disgust. Out of all the niggas in Charleston to choose from, she chooses to fuck with an out-of-town nigga. Fatty hated her kind.

"Fatty! Please," Darla pleaded yet again. She knew that this was going to get out of hand, and she wanted to stop it before it actually did.

"Why him, La? Why you choose him? That nigga killed Breeze, ma, and you sitting in this bitch playing house with that nigga. How? Why? I just don't understand this shit. Rayo turning in his gra—"

Darla cut his words short.

"Keep my baby daddy's name out ya mouth, nigga," Darla replied venomously as she wiped the tears from her face.

Fatty Man sighed deeply before rubbing the cold steel of his Glock .17 against the side of his face. He looked like a madman. A man possessed. Darla knew the look all too well, because it was a look that Santana wore often.

"Why the fuck you fall in love with this nigga out of all niggas? What the fuck, man! Let me think, let me think."

Fatty wanted to let her live for the sake of his love for her baby daddy, his lil' nigga Rayo. Rayo was killed in a drive-by only months after Melquan was conceived.

How could I let this bitch live? She real live rocking with the opposition.

Fatty just let his thoughts run wild as he paced the floor back and forth. And truth be told, the longer Fatty had time to think, the more he leaned toward walking out of Darla's house and leaving his beef in the streets. He knew if the tables were turned, Lil' Rayo wouldn't have his baby mother hemmed up over some bullshit.

"Man, let's—" One of the doors to the back room creaked open, stopping Fatty in mid-sentence. He stopped talking for a second—he wanted to make sure he wasn't tripping. As he surveyed the room, the looks on his soldiers' faces assured him that he wasn't hearing shit. They had heard it too. The floorboards creaked as the person began to get closer.

"Fatty, please, it's just Melquan. He was in the back room sleep. Please don't hurt my baby! Rayo would never have—" Darla's words were cut short as Fatty looked down the hall and saw Melquan walking down the hallway in his pajamas, rubbing sleep from his eyes. Darla knew she had to think fast, because the look on their faces screamed disbelief.

"Mommy," Melquan said lowly in his usual sleepy voice.

FB Gleek raised his gun and pointed it at the opening of the hall.

"Nooooooo!" Darla hopped from the couch as Melquan came into view. She bent down and scooped him up. FB Gleek fired his weapon, hitting Darla in her shoulder blade and neck.

"Arrrrgggghhhh!" Darla screamed as she fell to the ground unconscious, forcing Melquan to the floor with her limp body.

Fatty Man looked up at Gleek and raised his gun. "Nigga, what the fuck!" Fatty screamed in frustration as he looked down at the blood seeping from Darla's body.

"Fatty, I didn't—" Gleek tried to plead.

Fatty Man squeezed the trigger without remorse, hitting Gleek in his face twice. Fatty walked over Gleek's lifeless body and fired two more shots into his head as he walked out, confirming the kill.

Fatty Man was pissed. He knew Santana would most likely come for Darla—now he'd have to catch him in another setting. He sighed and stepped over Darla on his way out.

Fatty's soldiers looked on in disbelief as they followed Fatty in silence. Fatty felt bad, but he couldn't let it eat his soul.

"Come on! This stupid-ass nigga, man," Fatty said as he ran out the back door. His goons followed suit.

Melquan wiggled from under his mother and pushed her over onto her back. Her warm blood scared him. He started to cry.

"Mommy! Mommy! Get up, Mommy! Mommy!" Melquan shook her. Darla groaned in pain as she opened her eyes.

"Mommy!" Melquan said excitedly. He hugged her. His innocence was crazy. He was so pure and full of love. It was all Darla could think of as she went in and out of consciousness.

"Call 9 . . . 1 . . . 1 . . . Mel . . . qua—" Darla coughed blood from her mouth.

Melquan wasted no time. He hopped up on his little legs and ran into the kitchen, where the house phone was located. The phone was too high for him to reach, so he grabbed a chair from the dining table and climbed it. Melquan grabbed the receiver and hit the three numbers his mother taught him to dial in case of an emergency.

"911, what's your emergency?"

"My mommy hurt!" Melquan yelled into the receiver.

"Help is on the way. Is she—"

Melquan dropped the receiver and climbed back down off the chair. He ran back to his mother's side. Her eyes were barely open, but she was holding on.

"I wuv you, Mommy. Mommy? Mommy? Mommy, wake up, pwease . . . Mommy? Pwease, Mommy, wake up." Melquan started crying. He shook Darla until she opened her eyes wider. He smiled slightly.

"Mommy, I wuv you, you hear me? I promise I be a good boy, I promise. Pwease, Mommy, wake up." Melquan pleaded.

Darla lifted her arm and grabbed Melquan, pulling him closer to her.

"Mommy loves you too . . . b . . . aaa . . . b . . . y." Darla coughed, and blood flew from her mouth.

Melquan laid in her arms and cried, waiting on help to arrive. Darla whispered in his ear until she lost consciousness.

***

Santana sped down the highway with Rasheed in the passenger seat. The silence was awkward, but it was needed. Santana couldn't fathom losing another person he held dear to his heart. It was his karma. *Why does someone else have to feel pain for the shit I do?* he asked himself over and over again, praying that Darla and Melquan was okay.

"Bruh, slow down. What already happened, you can't change. And getting killed before we get there definitely not gone help neither one of us," Rasheed said as he held on tightly, watching Santana weave in and out of traffic like a NASCAR driver.

"Blood, I just heard my baby's mom got shot. Enough, please. Let me think," Santana stated as patiently as he could muster. Rasheed tried to keep his comments to himself, but he was lost, so he had to speak on what was floating around in his mind.

"Ya baby's mom? Okay, now I'm lost as shit. I thought you said you was fucking with Lil' Rayo BM, Darla. Who you got a baby by?" Rasheed asked cluelessly. Santana looked over at him with the stupidest look.

"Darla, my nigga, Darla. Now please shut up and get them cannons together," Santana replied frustratingly. He was getting agitated by all the Q and A's. It was already a task to have the unknown stranger tagging along, and now with him asking so many questions, he was beginning to get annoyed with Rasheed's presence. Santana pulled on to the ramp that led to Charleston's West Side.

Santana pulled up to Darla's home and his heart dropped. The police and ambulance were everywhere. He hopped out of his truck and ran to the gate that led to Darla's front door.

Fuck it, I need to know what the fuck is going on, Santana thought to himself as he lifted the yellow tape and ran into the house. Santana searched the house with his eyes until he locked eyes with Brian Williams, a detective of Charleston Homicide Division. Detective Williams sighed and rose from the dead body in Darla's living room. Santana noticed his frustration. Santana looked around the rest of the room. Blood was everywhere. There were streaks of blood, as well as small foot prints of blood throughout the house.

Melquan? Where is Melquan?

It was the only thing that Santana could think about. He looked back at the detective as if he could read his mind. The look of sorrow washed over his face.

"Where is my girl?" Santana asked the detective, eyes misting.

"She's been shot pretty badly, Santana."

The detective's reply weakened Santana. He had to grab hold of something to keep from falling. Luckily, the love seat was close. He grabbed on to the arm rest and sat down.

"Son, what the hell do you got going on out here, that all the people around you are getting either shot or killed?"

Santana ignored the detective's snide remark.

"Is she going to die?" Santana asked, rubbing his eyes as the tears fell.

Detective Williams looked at him and momentarily felt for him. He knew the feeling all too well—losing someone to violence brought on by someone else. It was the story of his life.

"I don't know," Detective Williams answered solemnly.

Santana looked at the scene again. He searched the face of the deceased for recognition. He came up blank. He had never seen the kid before—or so he thought. He looked around the scene a second longer and saw the small footprints for the second time. This time, it set off an alarm in his head.

"Where is my son? Oh shit, where is my child? Was he harmed too?" Santana's anger rose as he wiped his face for the last time. It felt like his world was beginning to crumble right before his eyes.

"Calm down, calm down. He's fine. He is in my unmarked car, under the air condition. I wanted to pull him away from all this. A child his age doesn't need to see this. God knows what he did witness will—"

Santana could care less about what the detective was talking about. All he wanted to do was hold Melquan in his arms—he needed to make sure he was okay.

"Aye!" Detective Williams yelled after Santana.

"What, nigga? This shit is your fucking fault. You wanted to start a fuckin' investigation into me about some shit that I'm innocent for, so now niggas want my fuckin' head. Give me my child so I can get to the fucking hospital. Don't you think you've done enough?" Santana was livid, and he did nothing to conceal that fact.

"Hold on, who told you that? I—never mind—"

Santana snarled at him, nose flaring.

"Everybody and they momma know, my nigga. You put a damn target on my back for it. So please, all I ask is that you give me my son so I can see how my lady is doing. I'm wasting time tongue-boxing with you. Make this shit right and get my child out your car."

Santana walked off. He started to search each car parked awkwardly around Darla's home.

Santana looked into one of the unmarked cruisers that was running. He saw Melquan curled up into the fetal position, sucking on his thumb. The bloody clothes he had on broke his heart. It meant that he was present the whole time, and most likely saw his mother get shot. It was also obvious he was the person who found her.

Santana knocked on the window.

Melquan looked up. When he realized who was knocking on the window, his frown disappeared. He smiled big and jumped up. He was extremely happy to see Santana's face.

"Tana! Tana! Tana!" Melquan yelled excitedly.

"Hey, baby boy. Are you okay in there? I'm going to take you home with me until mom get better, okay?"

Melquan's smile faded at the mention of his mother, and his eyes began to water.

"Aye, what I tell you? Not here, okay? Don't let them see you sweat. I love you. I'll be right back. I gotta get this door open, okay?" Santana said before walking off in search of the homicide detective.

"Tana?"

Santana turned back around to face him. The built-up emotion was getting to him.

"What's up, lil' man?"

"I wuv you."

He smiled and sat up with a new sense of hope. Santana smiled.

"I love you too, killa."

Santana had to hurry up and turn around. He didn't want Melquan to see the tears threatening to fall from his eyes. Santana only took one step before he was stopped by Detective Williams.

"Damn," was all the detective could say.

He had watched the whole conversation transpire through his own eyes. He knew Santana wasn't the boy's biological father—he knew Raymond "Rayo" Myers was. He also knew Myers was killed in a drive-by years prior, in a case of mistaken identity—or so the file said.

Brian Williams was fighting a war inside himself at the moment. He knew releasing Melquan into Santana's custody was against the law, but his judgment was screaming something totally different.

He thought for a second. He was gonna have to follow his heart on this one.

He walked past Santana and opened the door.

Detective Williams watched Melquan run full speed into Santana's arms. It was at that moment that he changed his view on what he thought about Santana. Detective Williams wasn't looking at this from the eyes of a detective. He was looking at this current situation from the eyes of a father. And he was satisfied with the outcome.

Santana picked Melquan up and held him in his arms.

Detective Williams reached out and grabbed a hold of Santana's shoulder before he had the chance to walk off.

"Please don't make me regret this."

Santana looked up, partial smile on his face.

"I won't. Come on, little man. We have to see how Mommy doing."

"Okay. But put me down. I'm a big boy now, Tana—remember?"

Santana laughed as he let Melquan slide down his body to the ground. The pair locked fingers and walked off, hopping into his mother's Tahoe.

Detective Williams took note of the bullet holes that riddled the body of the truck. He made a mental note to revisit that fact on a different day. He walked back into the home of Darla Collins and looked around, trying to piece things together.

He needed so desperately to figure out what happened that left one dead and another fighting for their life.

Chapter 3

Santana walked hand in hand with Melquan into the ICU ward, with Rasheed in tow. The waiting room was packed with Darla's family and friends. Santana sighed heavily, getting ready for the backlash that he knew was for sure to come. He saw Sofiya pacing back and forth, rapidly talking into her phone.

As Santana approached the waiting area, he locked eyes with Sofiya, stopping her dead in her tracks. She smiled, cupping her hand over her mouth in pure shock. The tears that rolled down her face broke his heart—it reminded him that he wasn't there for Darla and Melquan when they needed him most.

Sofiya hung her phone up and opened her arms. Santana let Melquan's hand go, and he took off into his auntie's arms. Everyone just looked at Santana—they were weary of his presence.

Sofiya could see the building tension between her family and Santana. They needed someone to blame, and he was the perfect scapegoat. It didn't make it any better that no one really knew him, but that was Darla's doing.

Darla really didn't rock with her family like that, and Santana knew this, so their looks came as no surprise. The only person he really knew was Sofiya, Darla's younger sister. Sofiya was his road dawg. She had showed him on many occasions that she was team.

Sofiya genuinely loved Santana. She loved the way he treated her sister and nephew. He was truly heaven-sent;

Santana had single-handedly brought the spark back into Darla's life. And Sofiya was extremely thankful for that. So watching her family condemn him was not okay. She had to speak.

"Why the looks? Family, this is Santana. Santana, this is my family." Santana looked around and nodded at everyone in attendance.

"What they saying about wifey?" Santana asked, wasting no time on pleasantries.

That made Sofiya smile even harder. *I hope I find me a nigga like this one day.*

"She still in surgery," Sofiya responded, biting her bottom lip nervously.

"But is she good?" Santana asked frantically.

Sofiya could feel Melquan looking up, waiting on the answer also. Sofiya kept her game face on as she answered the question.

"Yes. Mommy is okay. She is a soldier—you know that. The doctor said she will be back to normal in no time." Sofiya pulled Melquan closer. "You gone have to be a big boy when she does finally come home. Can you handle that?"

Melquan nodded in agreement.

"I'm going to hold you to that, baby boy. Go make sure Nanna's okay—she was worried about you," Sofiya stated as she rubbed her hand across Melquan's head.

"Rasheed!" a pretty brown-skinned woman called out in confusion, interrupting the conversation between Santana and Sofiya.

He looked over at Rasheed and sighed. Santana laughed because he knew the look all too well. Rasheed was not happy to see whoever the girl was.

She walked up to them with that famous ratchet Black girl attitude and laid into Rasheed.

"So you can't return my muthafuckin' calls now?" the beautiful woman spit venomously, rolling her neck and eyes at the same time.

Santana couldn't help but burst out laughing.

The girl looked up, annoyed, at Santana.

"Ummmm, excuse me, and you are?" the woman asked as she yet again rolled her eyes and neck all in the same motion.

Santana smiled as he put his hands up in surrender.

"I'm nobody, Ma. I'm just here to make sure my girl straight," Santana replied with a smirk plastered across his face.

Her eyes grew wide.

"Ohhhhh, so you the nigga that got Charleston in an uproar? That nigga Fatty—"

Before the girl could finish her sentence, Rasheed interjected.

"There you go, always in someone's muthafuckin' business. Fuck Fatty and the rest of them dick-eating ass FB niggas. Stay the fuck out of shit that don't pertain to you or my muthafuckin' child. Do I make myself clear?"

Rasheed walked up to his baby mother and gripped her face.

"Aye, bruh!"

Santana looked back at the voice and saw a man rise as if he were about to intervene.

"Aye bruh, what?" Santana asked, lifting his shirt with the swiftness, showing the man the butt of his gun.

Without any further argument, the man stood down. How Santana was feeling at the moment, he was liable to do anything. So he was glad when the man retook his seat and let Rasheed—and who seemed to be his baby mother—finish their conversation.

"Baby . . . pay attention, please. Stay. The. Fuck. Out of people's business, because if you get hurt for running your mouth, you already know what I'm on. So please to save me that case, just stop. Fuck!" He leaned in and kissed her lips passionately, then let her face go. "Please," Rasheed pleaded sincerely.

"I promise. Can I get another one of this though? That shit made my coochie wet."

Everybody in ear distance busted out laughing.

This bitch crazy, Santana thought to himself as he let them have their privacy. He walked over to where Sofiya and Melquan were and noticed that the older woman holding Melquan was a spitting image of Darla. It didn't take rocket science to notice that the woman was Darla's mother. Santana never broke his stride as he approached the lion's den. This would be their first time meeting each other, and the only thing he could think about was the timing.

What a time to meet the Queen of the pack. He sighed and shook his head from side to side.

Santana walked up to Melquan, arms opened wide. It was the only way he felt comfortable enough to even approach the trio. Darla's mother locked eyes with Santana. He could tell that she was studying him as he approached. Sofiya looked at Santana, then back at her mother. She loved the fact that her mother accepted Santana without the usual bullshit, because if she felt some kind of way about him, you could believe everyone in the hospital's waiting room would have known by now.

"Mommy, this is Santana. Darla's boo." Sofiya chuckled.

"Husband, Ma. I'm Darla's husband." Santana corrected Sofiya, a smiled plastered across his face.

"Oh, okay, my bad, my bad. Man, I love you. Any wayyyyyyzzzzz, Santana, this my mother, Momma Collins."

"So you must be the infamous Santana Vasquez that I hear so much about." Darla's mother offered him her hand. Santana smiled and took it happily.

"The gesture is nice, but I would love to give you a hug instead. You look so much like my wife, that hugging you would make me feel connected to her. That's if you don't mind," Santana replied sincerely

"Not at all," Darla's mother replied as she rose from her seat, letting Melquan down and pulling Santana into her arms. Santana rested his head on her shoulder and cried. The emotion took Darla's mother by surprise, but she understood his pain. Momma Collins knew the feeling all too well.

"It's okay, baby, God got her. She's going to be okay. You just sit with us and I promise God will make sure she comes back to us. Have faith. Do you have faith?"

Santana grew silent, letting the words hang heavy in the air. Then he said quietly, "Thank you. The kid needed that." He wiped his eyes. All eyes were on him, especially Melquan's. Santana laughed at Melquan's famous face when he was about to call you out on some shit.

"Tana, you said never let'em see you sweat. Get it together. I wuv you."

They all started laughing at Melquan's smart but innocent comment.

"What?" Melquan looked around trying to figure out what was so funny.

"I love you too, lil' man," Santana replied and gave Melquan a high five.

The bond between him and Melquan was unbelievable. A blind man could see the love radiantly shine between them. It was a bond only a father and son would have. It brought tears to the eyes of both Darla's mother and sisters as they watched Santana interact with their most precious jewel.

Melquan seemed to be in his highest height of happiness when around Santana and Simfany. What Melquan had been missing his whole life, he finally had.

The smiles that brought them temporary happiness faded as a doctor approached. The doctor's face held no emotion, so the news coming laced them with fear.

"Anyone that is here for Darla Collins, please gather together so I can say this one time—please and thank you."

The doctor waited until everyone came into hearing distance and spoke.

"Good evening, everyone. My name is Doctor Patterson. Ms. Collins is slated to make a fast and speedy recovery. The bullet that hit her shoulder went in and out. Now, the neck wound will be the most uncomfortable, but she survived—hurt, but alive. The good news I do have: her baby is still healthy, so no worries there. Ms. Collins is still very much sedated; you can see her once she wakes. Before I forget, I will be keeping Ms. Collins in the ICU ward due to her pregnancy. I want to be able to monitor the baby's responses to this kind of trauma. Does anyone have questions?"

When no one responded, the doctor took that as his cue to depart.

"Okay, thank you for your patience. I pray you have a great night."

"Thank you, Doc. We appreciate the help. Please keep me posted about that child growing inside my wife." Santana extended his hand to the doctor. They shook hands firmly, and the doctor walked away.

Ms. Collins and Sofiya looked at Santana with that *what-you-got-to-say* face. Santana looked away and scratched his head. He couldn't contain his smile.

"What?" he asked innocently.

"What? Nigga, you know what! How long have you known? And I swear that ass bet not lie." Sofiya raised her hand playfully as if she was about to back smack him.

"Santanaaaaaaaa . . ." Sofiya started to cry. He could tell that she was happy hearing the news. Ms. Collins, on the other hand, didn't seem too enthusiastic about it. But they both listened intently to him as he answered Sofiya's questions.

"I've known since Heem's funeral. Darla didn't tell me either, so don't feel no kind of way. I knew. I watched her get thicker right before my eyes. I figured she was pregnant. Plus, she had a glow on her skin that was radiant—you know, different. I don't know, it's hard to explain. I just knew something was different. I don't know why she held it from me for so long. Maybe she was fearful of my reaction. Why? I have no clue. I just . . ."

"It's just what us women do, Santana. We are skeptical. More men than you could ever imagine leave behind women telling them that they are pregnant," Ms. Collins interjected as she hugged herself subconsciously.

"Don't get me wrong, Ma, I'm scared as hell. But I'm not on no shit like that. I love your daughter—I love Darla with all my heart. Leaving isn't an option for me. Secondly, telling you or anybody else about her pregnancy isn't my place. So please don't be mad at me." Santana looked in the eyes of both women.

"Are you ready for that? Are you ready to take care of not only one, but two children? It gets hard, baby. You do a good job—I see that already—with my grandson. But are you here to stay, Santana? That's the real question," Momma Collins asked with a stern look on her face.

"I'm here. My heart would stop beating before I leave or abandon mine. I'm dead-ass serious—please know that. I love your daughter and grandson more than I love myself. Give me a chance, please. That's all I ask."

Darla's mother opened her arms yet again, and Santana happily walked into her embrace.

"You're a big baby," Momma Collins said.

Santana laughed. He knew she was right, but he needed all the love he could get at the moment.

"Do right, please. Darla has been through a lot, Santana."

"I got you, love," Santana whispered back in reply.

"Daddy, I want hug too," Melquan said as he reached his arms up for Santana.

Sofiya covered her mouth in complete surprise. Her tears fell unwillingly—she couldn't suppress the joy and the fear that came with Melquan's words.

Darla's mother released Santana so he could cater to Melquan.

"Hop on, Quannie," Santana said and outstretched his arms.

"Mommy is going to be okay, all thanks to you. I love you so much, you hear me? You saved our queen, baby boy. Thank you."

Melquan giggled when Santana tickled his stomach.

"Okay, okay, Tana . . . ahhhhh! Okay, okay. Daddy, stop! Ahhh . . . Fiyaaaaa!" Melquan laughed, squirming in his arms.

Everyone in attendance smiled. The love was pure—that, everyone could see.

Ms. Collins looked on. She silently prayed that Santana was the real deal and not just another person who would come into their family breaking hearts.

***

Santana walked into the hospital room that Darla was being kept in. He turned his nose up as he looked around. The hospital smell was the worst of the worst. The lingering smell of piss, feces, medication, and bleach took his breath. But it was the smell of death that, ironically, killed him the most. It was evident and present 24/7.

Hospitals were definitely not a place for any loved ones of his—that was for certain, even if it was for the smallest of reasons. He hated the thought, period. And for Santana to not know how long Darla would be cooped inside CAMC angered him even more. He knew, at the moment, Darla needed the medical assistance, so being angry and uncomfortable was all that his feelings would be able to amount to.

Santana sat and watched Darla's chest rise and fall to the rhythm of her heart. He was very happy that she was still amongst the living.

All praise is due to Allah. Thank you for protecting Darla. I ask you, Allah, for forgiveness. I ask you, Allah, for forgiveness. I ask you, Allah, for forgiveness. Please forgive me for the sins that I'm about to commit.

Santana knew the big man upstairs was frowning down upon him, but as he was taught day in and day out—Allah was the Most Merciful, Most Forgiving. Santana was sure that God saw the purity of his words. His actions . . . now that was a whole other conversation in itself.

He was the cause of all the drama, tragedy, heartbreak, and loss. He was responsible for it all, and he knew that in due time, his karma would eventually catch up to him and serve him a cold dish. Santana was prepared—or so he thought, anyway. At the moment, he mattered none. It was all about Darla.

He couldn't stop thinking about how close Darla came to losing her life behind his bullshit. He was elated at the fact of her survival. She deserved to live. He was the one that deserved death.

***

When Doctor Patterson delivered the news that Darla had successfully made it out of surgery, the waiting room soon began to dwindle in size. The news of Darla's survival was all that most people needed to know.

Santana, on the other hand, stayed in place until the time came that he helped Melquan work on his ABCs and 123s. Santana wanted to distract Melquan's mind as much as humanly possible so that the reality of what took place earlier that day could eventually become just a clouded thought of his past.

Though Santana doubted it, it was worth a shot in the dark. It just wasn't healthy for a child to experience that kind of trauma.

Before Santana walked to the back to sit with Darla, he reassured both Momma Collins and Sofiya that it would most likely be wiser to go home, get proper sleep, shower, and eat—so when morning came, they could be mobile and alert.

Reluctantly, they agreed, taking Melquan with them for the night.

Santana just sat a few feet away from his love, pondering his thoughts. He tried hard, but couldn't concentrate on nothing but the tubes and machines. There was no way that the love of his life was supposed to feel this kind of pain. It was no fucking way.

The whole ordeal was fucking with his head. First it was Haseem. Now Darla. Who was going to be the next victim? And what would their tragedy look like? The thought alone made Santana cringe. He had a lot weighing on him all at once. He sighed deeply, trying to calm his nerves. Santana was ready to free the weight from his soul.

He scooted his chair closer to Darla's bed so he could caress her hands as he waited on her to wake. He rubbed the backs of her hands gently, back and forth, until tears began to well up in the corners of his eyes.

He didn't even attempt to stop what he knew was coming—his breakdown. It was long overdue. The skeletons in his closet were stockpiling. At this point, the only way to soothe his heart was to get the pain from within. He needed to speak the hurt away, whatever that meant.

Ironically, Darla had taught him a way to calm himself and not overthink situations. The exercise was designed to peel away the layers of stress and heartache in hopes of clearing the soul. Santana had never really taken the exercise seriously . . . until now.

He wasn't only going to try it—he was actually counting on it to work. Santana swiped his hands across his face, wiping the tears away. He began to cleanse his soul the best way he knew how.

"I don't know what I'm doing, so I'm just going to talk to you, La. Look, Ma, I can't express how sorry I am for lacking on protecting you and Quannie. This weak-ass beef is the product of my bullshit. Even if I try my hardest to steer clear of trouble, it finds me.

Look at the beginning of FB's ill—but understandable—hatred for me. Breeze, I had to kill him. I had no choice. At that moment, it was simply kill or be killed. Even before that, I've been the cause of so much hate, death, tears, and agony . . . that this shit can't be real.

Like for real, La—how could all this pain be attributed to one person? A nigga just wants it to stop. When will the madness stop, La? Maybe when I'm dead and gone. When someone cries the tears that only the reaper can bring.

How hard can it be to live under normal circumstances? Is that too much to ask for?"

Santana cried a deep cry. He was wounded emotionally. He used his shirt to dry his face the best he could. He took a deep breath and sighed loudly. Santana rubbed Darla's fingers. He cleared his throat before pulling away more of his layers.

"Why the fuck am I either forced to flee or kill in order to live? That's a foul life. But you—you and Melquan balance my evil. I'm only sixteen years old, ma, and look at the shit a nigga had to endure just to still be here. Some by choice, but most by obligation."

Santana couldn't help himself. He laughed and cried—because he knew his life was some bullshit.

"All the souls that I have taken . . . all the souls that have been taken from me. When will the score be even? Is that what it must take to live normally?" Santana laid his forehead on Darla's hand. He cried. He cried for the souls he lost inadvertently to his actions. He cried for the souls that he took in the name of seeking peace and revenge.

Santana just closed his eyes tightly and wept. He just wanted to be happy, and it was so hard. Either God or the devil was making it impossible to achieve.

Darla stirred, squeezing his hand slightly. Santana lifted his head and tried to wipe at the tears rolling down his face before Darla could see him weak and lost. Darla held on to his hands and shook her head, from one side to the other. No, she tried to say, but couldn't. She didn't want him to feel the need to keep hiding himself from her.

What is he hiding from? she asked herself.

Darla wanted to see the essence of his true self—away from the streets, away from the violence. Little did she know, the violence was the origin. It was all he knew.

Darla didn't understand where all his hurt stemmed from, because the person that she knew was calm, humble, loving, and generous. Those were the traits that she was accustomed to. This raw emotion was good. It was new. It was Santana fighting his demons—and she loved it. Not many people could deal with the person they really were. A vast majority lived solely off a façade they made up in their heads.

Darla was cool with Santana being reclusive to the rest of the world, but not with her. She had submitted to him in ways only they knew. Santana had the privilege of being a part of Darla's raw emotion too. The loss of her child's father almost captured her. She had almost lost herself behind the tragedy.

Santana had never really pushed the envelope on sharing her past, so she didn't. But Santana knew who Darla was inside and out—and it was beyond sexual. It was mental, emotional. Darla asked herself many nights how she was able to give herself to Santana so quickly, so easily. The only answer she ever came up with was: his aura. His aura screamed trust, and ironically, safety.

Darla was the truest definition of what you would call a ride-or-die chick. She had shown him she was all in—win, lose, or draw . . . life or death. All she asked in return was for

Santana to stop hiding behind the mask he held so close to his chest. Darla craved all of this man.

It was the tough situations that threatened their foundation—but like a new home, it remained sturdy and in place.

Santana looked up and searched her face for disappointment, anger, hate, or resentment. He was looking for the signs he knew should have been there. But, of course, to his surprise, his gaze was met and matched with nothing but love and warmth.

He wore a big Kool-Aid smile.

"I'm so sorry, Ma. I promised to protect you and Quannie, and a nigga lacked tremendously. Please forgive me. I just pray this doesn't hurt our child in the long run."

Fear instantly rose in Darla's eyes. She rubbed her stomach, hoping she was still with child.

Santana's phone rang. He pulled one of his hands away from Darla to see who the caller was. The caller ID displayed his mother's name and picture.

Without second thought, Santana sent her to voicemail. Before he had the chance to put his phone away, she called back. He was almost tempted to answer, but she had him in his bag with her current disappearing act. Santana sent his mother to voicemail again. This time, he powered off his phone, so he could be undisturbed while he had the chance to be alone with Darla.

He sighed, knowing when they did finally talk, Simfany was going to curse him the fuck out. But the solitude alone with his baby was worth it.

"Who was that? Everything okay?" Darla asked, concerned.

"It was my mom. She has the worst timing, man—I swear. I haven't heard from her in what feels like months. As a matter of fact, the last time we were all together was the last time I seen her. I talked to her briefly the night Haseem got killed, but other than that, we haven't had any contact whatsoever. At this point, the call can wait. I need my alone time with you. We have a lot that we need to discuss. And our babies are fine—both of them. When I leave, I don't want you staying up worrying about frivolous things. You make sure—"

Darla cut his words short.

"Did you mean what you said a few minutes ago—when you thought I was sleep?" Darla asked, concern on her face.

"What you talking 'bout, La?" Santana asked, confused.

"About you wanting to live normally—without all the need to kill to survive. Did you mean that?" Darla looked at Santana with a worried gleam in her eyes.

"Of course. Who wouldn't want to live at peace? That's a dream of mine. The only niggas that want to chase bodies is the niggas that ain't caught one. Sometimes that shit weigh heavy, but of course I meant what I was saying.

To have the kind of peace I want comes with a price though, Darla."

"Do you regret any of them?"

Santana smiled and shook his head yes. He did regret killing Piru; that was his nigga. But after Piru pulled a gun on him, Santana knew he'd feel slighted. So the killer that lived in Piru had to be snuffed out. Otherwise, he would've been living another situation like the one he had with Jimdog's hoe-ass.

The only difference—Piru would've never closed his eyes until either he or his mother was among the dead.

"Yeah, there's one that I can say I wish I could take back. I miss my nigga. But what's done is done. Why you all of a sudden got so many questions?" Santana asked, wondering if trusting her with his skeletons was smart.

"Just curious about my husband. I want to know what kind of man I plan on spending my life with. Is that too much? Can I get a kiss? And by the way—I do forgive you. I was just making you sweat a little. Because you do know you were supposed to do a better job at protecting us."

Santana didn't say much. He just rose and kissed her lips.

He looked down at Darla's sexy-ass face and his heart waned. *How did I find not only one, but two amazing-ass women so early in life?*

Santana thought about Tijuana religiously. Her spark would always live in his heart—no matter who he called his girl. He had to live with the fact that he hadn't protected her either.

What Darla had just said sunk so deep in his heart that he just changed the subject altogether. But he knew her poking was only temporary. That was her. She poked until she was satisfied.

"Talking about Quannie . . . have you noticed that he's been calling me Daddy? And he's starting to say it more and more frequently. You should've seen your mom's face when he said it in the waiting room. I was dying."

Santana smiled, rubbing Darla's forehead, looking her in her eyes, trying to reach her soul.

Darla was so taken aback by what Santana had just said, her mind seemed to go into overdrive. She tried to think back to a time he spoke those words. She came up blank, because Melquan had never said them before. Not ever. So to hear that Melquan was calling Santana *Daddy* blew her mind.

Darla understood clearly—and she couldn't even blame her son, because she had also chosen Santana too. Santana and Simfany were the pieces missing from their family tree—or at least part of it. Melquan's acceptance was what really mattered. Him loving both Santana and Simfany was all she needed to see before they could take the next step.

Darla wanted to explain her past to Santana, but she decided against it and just went with a simpler version.

"Sounds to me like you've been chosen. So my question now is, do you step up or do you—owww!" Darla howled in pain. She had moved too far for comfort. Her shoulder throbbed. She was mad—but she knew she would live.

"You good, gangsta?" Santana joked, mocking how tough she had just acted.

"Yeah, I'm just fine, smart ass," Darla replied, frustrated with the limits now placed on her body.

"Answer my question. You know what I was about to ask you—don't play with me," Darla said, squinting her eyes, with attitude all in her tone.

"First off, Ms. Collins, fix ya muthafuckin' attitude. Your anger is misplaced—know that. Anyway, to answer your question, with your oh-so-evil self . . . of course I'm gonna step up to the plate. All I can say is that I'm honored."

"My question for you is . . . with Quannie being so young when his father passed, he may forget about his real father."

"I won't let that happen. I love you greatly, and you're fuckin' amazing—but I don't want my baby's father's memory to die just because you came in and filled his shoes. I wouldn't dare do that. So as our son grows, I will let him know who his real dad was, and you will show him daily who his father is *now*. That cool with you?"

Santana smiled.

"Facts, ma. I can definitely agree to that. There's no error there. I'm all in, you hear me? You already know the vibes. Ma, we forever."

Santana looked at Darla and just couldn't resist. He leaned down and kissed her passionately. Their tongues danced around each other until he was satisfied with tasting her lips. Darla's eyes remained closed.

"Ummmm, what was that for?" she said as she opened her eyes and licked her lips.

"To let you know that no matter what, my passion will forever run deep. I love you more than you could ever know," Santana replied passionately, removing a wild hair from her face.

"And it bet' not ever stop!" Darla said jokingly, in a matter-of-fact kind of tone.

Darla reached over and grabbed Santana, pulling him back in for another beautiful kiss.

"You're so amazing, La—I swear. You on ya Superwoman shit right now. You're my hero, that's for sure. And I'm pretty sure the lil' homie would be up on the list of admirers too."

Santana laid his head on her chest and listened to the rhythm of her breathing—to the thumping sound her heart made when she was nervous. He looked up, concerned.

"You good, Ma? You know I know the rhythm of your soul. What you nervous for? Something on ya mind, beauty? Talk to me—you know I'm a good listener."

"I promise, baby. I'm fine," Darla assured Santana.

Besides the bullets in her body, all was well.

***

Knock! Knock! Knock!

It was as if Darla felt the looming danger. She tapped Santana and whispered,

"Give me your gun. Hurry up! Stop playing." She lifted her covers.

"Nah, we good ma. No need—"

"Now!" Darla exclaimed, eyes squinting, jaw clenched.

"Santana! Hold on one minute!" she shouted toward the door.

Santana could see she was dead serious, and arguing with her wasn't worth the hassle. He took the Glock off his hip and handed it to her.

"Watch it, ma. No safeties come equipped on those."

Darla rolled her eyes as she hid the gun under her covers.

"Come in!"

The door opened. Detective Brian Williams of Charleston's Homicide Division walked in, smile radiant as ever.

"Good morning, Ms. Collins. Mr. Torres. Of course, I'm here to question you about what the hell happened in your home yesterday. We've met before, right Ms. Collins?"

Darla just looked at him, speechless. She didn't know what he wanted her to say in reply. Was she supposed to confirm or deny?

Detective Williams continued.

"If I'm not mistaken . . . it was the night of your cousin's murder—Nessy Garland. I'm not sure if you remember me, but my name is Detective Brian Williams of Charleston Homicide. I usually have my partner, Daniel Schooner, with me—but he's in the process of following other leads in the case. May I sit for a few minutes? I promise not to be long."

"Please. Babe, be kind and let Mr. Williams borrow your chair."

Darla gestured for Det. Williams to do what he wanted with the chair.

"Thank you." Det. Williams wiped the sweat from his brow and opened a red and black spiral notepad. Santana moved to Darla's bedside and held her hand for support. He could tell by her sweaty palms that she was frightened by the detective's presence.

Williams made a mental note. Santana also saw how nervous Darla was.

"It's gone be alright, momma. I'm here. At any time, we can ask for a lawyer if you feel shit is getting out of hand," Santana explained to her in a whisper. Though he felt Williams still heard him nonetheless, "You're good. I promise."

Santana looked over at her and smiled. Darla smiled back to the best of her ability.

"Well . . . sorry, I was going over some notes. I'm actually glad that I caught both of you together, because I also have some questions for you, Mr. Torres."

That made Santana stir slightly. He shifted in his stance—and that didn't go unnoticed.

"I'm not trying to stir the pot, I'm just trying to do my job and solve these murders. Which one of you would like to go first? And by the way, I must record any parties involved—you know, to leave out hearsay. You know, the 'he says, she says' problems. You catch my drift? Anyway, any takers?"

Neither Santana nor Darla volunteered to talk to the detective.

"Okay, well let me start from this side of the room. Mr. Torres, this is what I would call an unofficial interview—meaning, if I see no cause for further questioning, you most likely won't see me again regarding this matter. Is that understood?" Detective Williams asked, making sure all parties were clear on what he was saying.

Darla and Santana both nodded simultaneously.

"Also, once I begin recording, you have to make sure to answer audibly. I'm not here to be an ass. I know you've been going through a lot these past few weeks, so I plan to be quick, precise, and to the point. All I ask is that whatever questions I do ask, you be truthful . . . because if you lie, I promise I will eventually find out. I always stumble upon shit like that. I'm one of those lucky, talented detective-type niggas."

They all laughed at Williams' humor.

He continued.

"I'm from the hood too. I ain't always been a detective, so I may know a thing or two. Food for thought. Now let's get started. You ready?" He looked at Santana. The look Santana returned was one of uncertainty. It looked like it was about to be a long day.

"I'm gone be as ready as I'll ever be. Shoot ya best shot," Santana said confidently as he leaned against the wall.

Santana was nervous, that was for sure. He had never been questioned about a murder before. All he knew about this cycle of an investigation was from the A&E show *The First 48*. Santana had never been questioned in close quarters by a homicide detective before.

"Remember—be audible. Okay. On the night of May 17th, at approximately 11:30 p.m. through the early morning hours of May 18th—what were you doing and who were you with? Before you answer, if Ms. Collins is your alibi, I would like you to answer this next line of questioning in the hallway. It'll eliminate any bullshit, and I can check you off my suspect list. Not saying you are one . . . but you know what I mean. Sound good to you?"

Santana nodded in agreement, forgetting about the tape recorder.

"May I ask what this line of questioning is about?" Santana asked, already knowing the answer.

"Most certainly. This is pertaining to the murder of Shamir Stokes—also known in the streets as FB Sleeze."

Santana came off the wall and walked to where Darla lay. He leaned over and kissed her on the lips. Santana slid his hand under the sheet until he felt the cold metal of his Glock 17.

He looked Darla in her eyes and took a deep breath. Santana rose. Darla grabbed his hand. She pleaded with her eyes.

Santana had so much more to live for. Killing a police officer in a crowded hospital would surely mean his life was over. He took another deep breath—and let the grip he had on the gun go.

Chapter 4

We been too strong for too long / And I can't live without you baby / I'll be waiting up until you get home / 'Cause I can't sleep without you baby . . .

Simfany floated through her home in Baltimore County, singing to her heart's content. The vocals of Mary J. Blige carried her away to another place—a place that she missed so, so much. A place of love. A place of needing and wanting to be desired. She sang along, feeling accomplished, satisfied, and worthy.

Simfany was on cloud nine. She had just hung up with Recovery Point Rehabilitation Center in California, confirming Lonnie's safe arrival into their care. Simfany was excited for Lonnie; she needed her sister back, that was for sure. So when she reached out to Lonnie for the umpteenth time and offered assistance—and Lonnie agreed—Simfany was elated. She was so happy, she had cried for days. She had asked God for that moment time after time. Finally, it had arrived. And getting off the phone with the California Rehabilitation Center brought the emotion full circle.

The rehab Simfany sent Lonnie to was highly recommended, the program was designed to counsel, rebuild, and test the laws of desire and abstinence. Simfany just had to call and tell him the good news. She had to. She was proud of her sister. Dancing her way into the kitchen, Simfany picked up the house phone from its cradle and dialed Santana's number from memory. It rang twice before going to voicemail.

Little fucker.

Simfany laughed as she called him back. *Surely he will answer, especially when he realizes I'm the person calling*, she thought. But to her surprise, she was sent to Santana's voicemail again.

"Whatever," Simfany said out loud before placing the phone back into its cradle on the wall. *Someone has to have his phone or that nigga would've answered*, she thought, walking back into the living room to change the song. Simfany loved Mary J., but she wasn't that much of a crazed fan to loop her song on repeat and listen to it back-to-back.

So far, the day had proven to be a good one. The sun was out, and though it wasn't quite summer yet, it was creeping closer with each passing day. The clothing people wore and the cars they drove made it clear—summer was approaching fast.

Simfany looked at her Rolex. 11 :58 a.m. Two minutes before WSAC's 12 o'clock news. Simfany switched her Bose surround sound system from her stereo to her TV. She wasn't trying to miss the broadcast.

Over the past week or so, the city—and the counties around it—had turned deadly. Simfany didn't have the slightest clue why. One thing she knew for sure: something was up. Anytime the city's or county's murder rate spiked, there was usually a reason. This time, though? That was the main reason she watched the news religiously. Plus, she liked the news that WSAC reported. They kept the people of Maryland informed about who was getting it popping around the state.

Simfany turned the volume up as she walked away in search of her smoke box—a wooden box that Santana had made while locked up at Backbone Mountain School. Originally, it was for his mail. But when he was transferred back to Hickey pending placement for the riot he caused, he mailed it home to her. Simfany immediately put it to use. It's where she stored her pre-rolled blunts, weed, cigarettes, lighters, and a few other smoke essentials. One thing she did know, and hated about the box: she lost that muthafucka every single day. She never understood how something so big could disappear every time she set it down.

What the fuck! Simfany thought, annoyed as she searched high and low for the box. She hit the kitchen and checked all the usual spots she could've laid it. Then she looked up and sighed. There it was, sitting right on the dining table where she'd left it before turning on the stereo.

The news had just come on. Simfany turned the volume up on her TV so that no matter what room she was in, she could hear the segment.

"In recent weeks, violence has spiked in Baltimore City, Dundalk, Essex, and Harford Counties—leaving the state in a state of fear and disarray. Police Chief Marshal Wakings gave an official statement this morning after a meeting with the Attorney General's office and other agencies—"

"Damn," Simfany said out loud, surprised, as she pulled a pre-rolled joint from the wooden box in front of her. She put the blunt to her lips and lit it. The exotic taste of weed and blueberries filled her lungs.

Dang, she thought, as the weed instantly hit and calmed her soul.

She outstretched the blunt and looked at it for a second, shaking her head with a smile. Then she took another strong pull, inhaling the ganja and releasing the smoke from her nose casually.

On the screen, the city's police chief stepped up to the podium to address the public. The "Breaking News" banner popped up almost instantly after Chief Wakings started talking.

"Good afternoon. As many of you may or may not know, in the last several weeks there's been a spike in violence across the region. The violence has increased in Baltimore

City, Baltimore County, and Harford County—mainly Dundalk, Essex, Edgewood, and Havre de Grace. The murder rate has risen alarmingly.

On the morning of May 8th, the body of Gloria Rayne Rivera, 21, was found near her home with multiple gunshot wounds to her neck, face, and torso."

A picture of Gloria—either her high school photo or driver's license—flashed across the screen. Simfany recognized her instantly.

"That's why you wasn't there that night," she muttered out loud, like Gloria could hear her.

She hit the blunt again, sucking the smoke into her lungs greedily. She shook her head slowly from side to side. A pang of guilt crept over her while looking at Gloria's face.

It was sad, but low-key, Simfany was relieved she wasn't the one who had to pull the trigger. Because if Gloria had shown up with Kevin Brooks that night, she would've been the one to take her life instead. The circumstances would've been different, but the outcome? Still the same.

Her fate had been written. Gloria had been called home.

Something had felt off about her from the jump. Simfany couldn't explain it, but something wasn't right. Her gut had told her to watch that girl close. Maybe it was the way she was coming for revenge on her ex, or maybe just how pressed she was about the whole situation—but her inexperience threw everything off.

Simfany had wanted the Brooks brothers bad enough that she went against her gut and kept it moving anyway.

Oh well, she thought, shrugging. She took another hit from the blueberry kush and inhaled deeply.

"This one for you, lor momma," she said before exhaling and growing lightheaded. The news segment seemed to slow down.

"Gloria Rayne Rivera, 21, was the daughter of Baltimore's infamous 'alleged' drug kingpin Carlos Ramon

Rivera . . . information gathered surrounding this has been passed—"

The words turned to haze.

There was no way what she'd just heard was right. She laughed nervously.

Yeah, yeah, I'm high as fuck. She laughed again. *No weed ever had me trippin' like this before.*

But when Gloria's and Carlos's pictures popped up side by side on screen, Simfany knew she wasn't imagining shit. Their connection was real.

Her jaw dropped open.

No, no, no, no, no . . . how could this be? Simfany thought, getting up from the couch and running her fingers through her hair.

"What the fuck!" she screamed. "You dumb ass bitch!" Tears threatened to fall from the corners of her beautiful, slanted eyes.

Reality hit.

She was a dead woman walking.

Her head started to throb, and she had to sit down.

"I didn't kill the bitch," she told herself, trying to self-soothe. "Fuck . . . fuck . . . fuckkkkkk!" she yelled, slamming the blunt box into the loveseat beside her.

Its contents flew everywhere.

Simfany froze in thought.

What the fuck do I do? What the fuck do I do?

She patted her body down, checking for her phone. But she knew she didn't have it—she'd just used the house phone to call Santana.

She moved through her two-bedroom spot, searching for her T-Mobile Sidekick 3. After minutes of coming up empty, she headed back to the kitchen and grabbed the landline again.

She dialed Drew.

"Come on . . . come on . . ." Simfany muttered impatiently, waiting on Drew to answer. He picked up on the last ring.

"Yo? Who this?" Drew answered, his words slurred.

Damn, Simfany thought. *It's only midday and Drew frosted already.* She made a mental note to address that later. Now wasn't the time.

"It's me, baby boy," she replied, irritated.

"Oh, what's up, momma? What you doin' callin' me from this weird-ass number?" Drew asked, his tone suddenly different—clear and alert. Like he hadn't been high at all.

Simfany smirked. *Damn, he good. Got me and everything.*

"What's up? Boy, you good? I was just 'bout to get in that ass about ya lil' slurring and shit. You too damn smart for your own good, yo. I swear—I can only imagine what you and my bad-ass son used to cook up." She laughed loud. Simfany needed that laugh.

"But anyway, I don't know where the fuck my phone at, and I need P's number. Like ASAP. I can't remember nobody's number—that's why they in my phone. I know, I know . . . I should know it, but ya Ma Dukes is baked right now. Don't judge me."

Drew laughed. It was facts. Simfany was a certified weed head—she stayed high.

"What's new? Talkin' bout somebody slippin'," Drew teased.

"Shut up, boy, and give me the damn number," she said, sucking her teeth loud.

"You got a pen?" Drew asked. "I bet that ass too sparked to even know where one at, huh shorty?"

He loved talking shit to Simfany. Since the day she stepped back into Maryland, their bond had grown stronger every day.

Drew had gotten out of the hospital 10 days after being rushed in with multiple gunshot wounds. Right now,

Simfany knew he was holed up in Towson with a fine older woman named Isis Taylor. She was cool with it. Her second son was safe—and that's all that mattered.

"Oh, so now niggas got jokes," she said. "I got one better—just heard it a few minutes ago. One of the illest ever muthafuckin' heard. You wanna hear it, or you gonna be a sour butt?"

Simfany shook her head and smiled. When she looked up, she spotted her phone sitting on the microwave, still plugged in. She felt dumb as hell. Just shook her head.

"Why a nigga always gotta be names, yo?" Drew cracked up. They were always goofy like this.

"And what's the weak-ass joke you got? 'Cause ma, I love you and all, but yo jokes ain't neva funny. Except that time you told shorty she looked like Darkwing Duck. You was hella wrong for that, but on dead homies, you was spot on. So let me hear it. And—did you grab the pen yet?"

"Nah, I ain't have to. Soon as I looked up—bam! My phone was sittin' there plugged into the wall, talkin' shit. You ready?"

"Yup."

"Knock knock."

"Nigga, what?" Drew laughed hard as hell on the other end.

"Why you laughin'? I ain't even said shit yet. You slow . . . anyway. Knock knock."

"Who's there?"

"Carlos."

That name made Drew pause. Still, he played along. "Carlos who?"

"Carlos is Gloria's father!" Simfany yelled, laughing obnoxiously like the shit was funny.

And maybe it was.

It was a real fuckin' tragedy—for everybody involved in Gloria's death.

Silence hit the other end. And it was eerie.

All Simfany could hear was Drew breathing through the line.

"You still there, baby boy? I'm guessin' you ain't find my joke too funny. Hmph . . . believe it or not, me fuck neither. But now my question is—"

"Call me back on your cell. I need to confirm this real quick. Love you. Hit me straight back. I mean it."

"Love you too."

Simfany hung up and walked into the kitchen. She unplugged her phone, dialed Drew's number—and then hung up. She didn't call.

Instead, she scrolled through her contacts until she found Santana's name.

She opened a new message thread and finally replied to him.

No wonder he mad at me, she thought, staring at all the unread messages from Santana—her favorite person in the whole damn world.

I'm sorry I haven't reached out like I promised many times. I have no excuses. I love you and I hope you can and will forgive me. We have a lot that needs to be discussed . . . A LOT! Call me when you get the chance. I will make myself available. Also, congrats. Damn, I see you wasn't going to tell me that I was about to be a granny. That's another topic though. (Sticking my tongue out) I'm sorry, Tana, please don't be too mad that we can't talk about it. You know the hours we put in at times overlap one another, but I promise my silence isn't intentional. Again, I love you. I'm sorry. Call me ASAP! Be safe, my love.

Simfany re-read the text message once more before she sent it. Simfany searched through her contact list again in search of Peedi's information and froze at the sight of Paris's name. Simfany closed her eyes and silently said a prayer for the lost soul. Stupid ass broad, man. She couldn't help but think about Paris in that moment. Simfany had really grown to love Paris. She felt bad every time she thought of the day she ended Paris's life. She thought she knew who she was dealing with, but Simfany was sadly mistaken. God had taught her a valuable lesson with dealing with outsiders. Simfany clicked Paris's contact info and deleted it out of her phone—and out of her life—for good.

Simfany finally made it to Peedi's name; she opened up a message for him and began to type: *What's good, Baby Daddy?*

Simfany chuckled. She just knew that shit would get this attention. But the rest of the message would crush his heart; that was if they shared the same thought process, which she felt it would be close enough, if not spot on. She continued:

I bet that made your crazy ass smile. Anyway, good morning or afternoon, however you want to look at it. ldk if you're a news kind of guy, but the word on the web is Gloria ain 't fuckin' Carlos; that's his daughter. So whoever told you that rumor need to be flushed. But, anyway, to put a real smile on your face, I'm making dinner for two. I'm about to call Drew back. Hit me in about 20 min and I'll explain more about what ya favorite dishes should be and why. Love you, handsome. 20 minutes. No sooner. No later. Be good, cuz . . . Lol.

Simfany backed out until she returned to the main screen. Her heart fluttered. Her screen saver was a picture of Tijuana and Santana kissing outside of her studio apartment in Baltimore County. Simfany loved the picture, this one in particular. It showed a time when the future was so unforeseen, but yet captured a moment so real and magical. It also reminds her of the twins that would never be. The ones that died inside Tijuana that fateful day outside in Washington Park. A lot of emotions ran through Simfany as she stared at that picture. The tear that hit her screen told her that she was crying. Simfany sniffled, and cleared her nasal cavity. She missed Tijuana tremendously. Tijuana was pure; she had a good soul. At that moment, Simfany hoped that her friend was resting well and at peace.

Simfany wiped her face and dialed Drew's number by memory. She was probably about to be cussed out for taking so long to call back, but she really didn't give two fucks; these were her babies, not the other way around. Either way, Simfany knew Drew was gone talk shit regardless; it's just what he did.

"Yo, what's good, Ma Dukes? You took forever to call back. You fuckin' my groove up.

"My shorty was gon' surprise me with some lunchtime chewing, but you didn't call back. I wasn't sure if I was gon' have to put on my cleats or not. Anyway, did you find anything else out? Or was you doing everything but something productive? You know my lor nigga sniffin' all around ya lor panties and shit. That bitch thirsty. What you do to big bro?" Drew laughed. He was cracking up hard over the thought of Peedi chasing Simfany around. Simfany laughed right along with Drew. Drew hadn't had the slightest clue. The shit he was picturing, Simfany was already living. But she couldn't front—she liked the attention Peedi gave. Simfany hadn't felt desired in a minute.

"Lor boy, shut your young ass up. Worryin' about grown folks' business and shit. And you the one that told me to call back. But nah, seriously—I didn't mean to run the block party like that on you. That wasn't my aim, baby boy. I texted Peedi, I just wanted to put him on point about Carlos and Glo. Have you talked to him yet? He ain't never went this long without a reply. He probably in some pussy with his emotional ass. What did you look up, did you find anything different? Or did that sex talk run ya mind blank?" Simfany joked around.

"Nah, I got on Myspace to see if Glo ever mentioned anything about Los, or if she ever uploaded any pictures with him. I looked at her and her friends' comments. It was nothin' that would indicate she was the princess of cocaine. You know, like the demeanor that come with knowin' that you really it. It's hard to hide certain shit—to hide that you got money is one thing, but to know you hold a certain kind of power? Now that's a whole different demon all in itself. Her Myspace page scream teenager, not 21-year-old boss bitch. Excuse my French. She had a lot of pictures of her moms, and I think her uncle. He had gotten killed a few years back or so. A Dominican-lookin' nigga, could be either one of her parents' brothers. Shit, if you ask me, he favor Carlos—but you gotta take that with a grain of salt because of what I was searchin' for in the first place. Simfany, you know like I know—if that man come for us, we most likely dead. And the fact that his daughter was killed, possibly so is our families. Good thing with me, I don't got none. Literally. With that bein' said, why don't we just blitz the nigga while he in the dark about everything?"

"One, because it wasn't us who killed his daughter—unless it's some shit I'm not bein' told. And plus, I love that nigga. He done kept me alive the whole time I been in Maryland. He a good nigga that don't deserve to be killed by betrayal. I'm sorry, Drew. I understand the severity, and if it come down to him or us, I promise I'm choosin' us every time. You my son's best friend, so that make you mine, too. I love you like I birthed you, lor nigga. I won't ever let nothin' happen to you. Have faith in me and the decisions I make. I'll figure somethin' out soon. But I do promise you—if that nigga force my hand, I will kill him," Simfany said seriously.

"Listen, before I go, I want you to know that Gloria's ass wasn't innocent in her role either. Now I could be wrong, but outta all the muthafuckas in the Park, she picked the one nigga everybody know is a killer. Don't get it fucked up, Race not no bum ass nigga, but he not on no splurgin' shit either—'specially not for no females. She literally picked Race's ugly ass for a reason. That's what we gon' have to figure out. Gloria got secrets. We just gotta find out what they are. Don't stress about all this betrayal shit. End of the day, ma—we all we got! I love you, Simf. Stop stressin', yo. We gon' be good, shorty."

"Love you more, shorty," Simfany replied. What Drew said made sense, but what he didn't know—behind the killer, she was a bona fide worrier. Drew hung up, leavin' Simfany to her thoughts. They could be her worst enemies at times.

Simfany looked through her messages. No one had texted her back yet, which was surprising for Peedi—he usually hit back within minutes. Even Santana hadn't replied yet. Simfany scrolled down to Darla's contact info and placed the call. The call went straight to voicemail.

"Damn . . . don't nobody love me today."

Simfany got up and looked for a pen and a notepad. She needed to write down all the information Drew had given her about Gloria's Myspace page, his thoughts on Rocc, and what Gloria could possibly be hiding. Simfany wrote down everything she knew, seen, or heard.

Why was you so hell-bent on seeking revenge, chula? Simfany thought as she searched for something to write down all the facts she had learned about Gloria. It was in that moment that Simfany realized—they never actually knew who Gloria Rivera was.

Simfany didn't understand. What had the Brooks brothers done to Gloria that made her seek help in killing them—Kevin in particular? How did they even know each other? Simfany was so thirsty for Kevin and Tez-Mo's blood that she let the essentials slip between the cracks. The whole time, Gloria could've been setting them up, just waitin' for the right time to strike. That was how bad Simfany ignored the signs of danger.

Simfany cussed herself for not listenin' to her gut feelin'. She knew something just didn't sit right with her about Gloria—and damn if she wasn't right. Simfany shook her head shamelessly. She just couldn't believe she was so reckless. She shook it off. It was nothing she could do about it now.

Simfany finally found a pen and a notepad in Santana's juvie tote. She wrote a few key points down and left the book sittin' at the dining table in hopes of puttin' more information in it sooner rather than later.

She sat down and picked her phone up, trying Peedi again. She didn't know why, but Simfany was starting to get jittery waitin' on his answer.

There was one thing about Peedi that did bother her though—and maybe amongst men it meant nothin'—but in the city she was born and raised, if a man "little bro" you or "little nigga" you, it means you beneath that person, in so many words. Simfany had heard Drew address Peedi as such on a few occasions now, and it light-weight confused her.

What Simfany had witnessed from Peedi since knowing him was a strong, loyal nigga that handled his business when needed.

"Why the fuck is that any of my concern anyway?" Simfany asked herself, thinkin' out loud.

Peedi's call went to voicemail. Simfany hung up and checked her messages again.

Nothing. From no one.

Simfany was beginnin' to get aggravated.

She sat and waited ten minutes before checkin' her messages yet again. She sighed in frustration. She just didn't understand—if she wanted to just talk shit and shoot the breeze, he would answer in a drop of a dime. But now that she needed him, he was nowhere to be found.

Simfany swallowed her pride and called Peedi again. Peedi's phone just rang and rang. Simfany hung up disappointingly before the voicemail had the chance to pick up.

Fed up, Simfany went and laid down, baffled at the whole ordeal.

***

It was crazy how small the world was—Simfany just couldn't get her dear friend Carlos out of her head. She was stressed out. It was literally gonna be the death of her.

Simfany had become obsessed with finding the truth. She had even went as far as to scan Gloria's Myspace page herself. And at first glance, Drew was right—Gloria looked like a regular teenage girl in love. Gorgeous, radiant, full of life.

But what Drew missed that *she* wouldn't, was Rafael "Big Cito" Rivera.

Muthafucka, Simfany cussed. That was the connection. Big muthafuckin' Cito.

Simfany just couldn't believe it. She had forgotten all about Carlos's younger sibling.

She could vividly remember her first—and last—time ever meeting Big Cito. It was when Simfany first came to Baltimore, before all the bullshit began. It was around a time when things were still fun and peaceful.

Her and Byrd had been out for a night on the town. Simfany smiled at the memory.

Damn, how she missed the time she spent with Byrd.

They were at the infamous club ***Hammerjacks***—*Baltimore's livest, but deadliest, club at the time. When Big Cito entered the building, the loved he received from the city was epic. The lights were dim to a low. So seeing folks was hard, but the love in the room was loud. Byrd? Not so much. What Cito ain't know was, Byrd was the first one he pulled up on to show love. Simfany watched from a distance, babyin' the Henny in her cup. She peeped Byrd playing cordial. Later that night, Byrd brought Big Cito over and introduced him as Carlos's baby brother. Simfany quickly caught on to the snide looks from Byrd and played her position.*

Fortunately, Simfany and Byrd made it back to her West Baltimore home without incident. After that night, Simfany had never heard or seen Big Cito ever again until now, on

Gloria's Myspace page. Simfany looked around a little more before logging out of Myspace.

Simfany scrolled through her contacts, heart thumping as the cursor landed on Carlos's name. She ain't even know why she was on it to begin with, or why he even still scared her the way he did. Carlos had already proven to her many times that he was there for her. Yet that still didn't stop her heart from feeling like it was about to explode from fear. Maybe it was the fact that she felt like she betrayed him in an ultimate way. Because Simfany knew that if she was an innocent party in all of this, the first thing she would have done was call to make sure her friend was good mentally. And though she wasn't totally innocent, her heart still broke for Carlos. She couldn't imagine losing Santana. The only solution that could make shit right was her honesty. *Telling the truth couldn't be that bad*, she thought. End of the day, it was Gloria who brought the whole revenge idea to them. No one knew that she was once Kevin Brooks' first and only love. Gloria hadn't volunteered that information; not only that, but Gloria hadn't died to no one involved in the plot.

Simfany still had no clue who killed Gloria and why. *What the fuck you had going on, mamita?* Simfany wondered, wiping the lone tear racing down her face. If the situation came down to the inevitable, she prayed the saying was right: the truth shall set you free. Her only explanation to the madness was the truth. Simfany's breathing quickened as she chose to send her dear friend a message. Simfany wrote from her heart, hoping that it was just enough to soothe his.

Chapter 5

Zach was oblivious to the stress of the world. He had purposely left his phone at home on its charger. He was for sure getting tired of all the bullshit that came with having one. So when he received the call from his childhood best friend, Ja'Shawn "Stoney" Claytor, to make the 3½-hour drive to Charlotte, North Carolina, he plugged his phone in and left.

Just like that—he left.

The only person in the world who knew where he was, was Santana. And that was only because Zach knew if his friend thought he had met an ill fate, he would have painted the city of Charleston red in search of answers. And though the streets needed cleaning up from fuck niggas, that was blood he didn't want on his hands. So he did the next best thing—he gave Santana a heads-up.

The drive to Charlotte was well needed. Zach had finally gotten his chance at peace—to be one with himself. He was able to get the therapy he needed from that three-hour ride. Stoney had called that same morning before he went to school, trying to explain a letter he'd received from Rodney just days prior. All Zach got from Stoney's rambling was that Rodney wasn't feeling him for hanging with Santana, and that he was going to kill him for what happened to Haseem.

Though Zach wasn't the tough-guy type, he also wasn't the type to take threats lightly—and he damn sure wasn't one to joke about shit like that. Don't get it fucked up though: before all the bullshit, Zach would've laughed it off and wouldn't have paid Rodney any mind. Seeing young people get killed was shit you saw on the news somewhere else in America—not Charleston. Niggas got killed, sure—that wasn't unheard of—but teenagers and innocent people? That was rare in Charleston, West Virginia.

To Zach, it would've just been another shallow threat, especially coming from Rodney. Niggas were running around Charleston using Rodney as target practice. In the months before he got locked up, Rodney got shot in the stomach and in the hand. He talked tough, but both situations went without consequence. So worrying about Rodney wasn't something Zach was trying to focus on.

That was then. But now—since the death of Haseem—he took everything literally and seriously. He wasn't taking any threats lightly. And to make sure what Stoney said was facts, he hopped in a rental and sped to North Carolina. Zach wanted to be there before school let out.

He pulled up just past noon, hair wild and unbraided. The silence in the Claytor home was awkward. The vibe was off. The only person there when he arrived was Jamesa "Meme" Claytor—Stoney's older sister. Growing up, Zach had the craziest crush on her. But if you were a man with a set of eyes, you'd understand. Meme was beautiful. Stood 5'8", caramel-complected, hazel eyes, full lips, and beautiful silky black hair. Back in the day, Meme played sports—so she was built like a stallion. Literally.

The silence deepened as Zach sat between her thighs, getting his hair braided. The crazy thing was, neither of them even realized how quiet it was. They were so caught up in their own issues, the awkward silence didn't even register.

After braiding half of Zach's hair without a word, it finally clicked in her head that something wasn't right. It took her a little while to notice, but she did. Naturally, both her and Zach were silly as hell, and though she had her reclusive moments, she didn't think she had ever seen Zach that distant.

Jamesa wasn't trying to pry, but she loved the annoying little nigga, and seeing him so lost in thought bothered her. She had to know what was going on—it was the Meme way.

"What's on your mind, Zachariah? You've been pretty quiet down there. You good? Talk to me—you know I talk back, babes," Meme asked, sincerely wanting to know what was going on with him.

Zach laughed, because he already knew he was probably looking crazy to her. He couldn't help it though. He had serious shit racing through his brain and no way of releasing it. No one to talk to whatsoever. Either it was someone he couldn't trust with his demons—or it was Santana. And if the release was Santana, it usually didn't help. That nigga was just too real to sugarcoat the truth.

And how he was feeling? He needed somebody to lie to him, just once. Tell him everything was going to be alright.

Meme was literally family, but he didn't know if trusting her with his demons was smart. He needed a release so badly, though, he didn't even care anymore.

"Man, I don't even know where to start, Mia," Zach said quietly.

"Damn, I haven't heard that name in so long. You can talk to me. I won't judge you, I won't repeat shit you tell me. I just ain't seen you so somber. Seeing you like that is bothering me, baby," Meme said as she hugged him around his neck.

"Thank you. A nigga real live needed that. Ever since Haseem died, shit been crazy. Niggas want me dead for real, and thinking 'bout that shit every waking moment is fucking my head up. I'm trying to bounce back, and most of the time I feel like I do, but it's the times I feel safe that I think about this dumb shit. Don't even make sense, does it? I know, tell me about it." Zach laughed anxiously. "They got a nigga playing with guns now, murders getting closer and closer to the crib. It's sad to say, but if something doesn't change soon,

I may not see my 17th birthday. That shit sound crazy to even say. It's a hard pill to swallow, that's for sure."

Zach had to stop thinking and talking about dying, but damn, it was hard. It was his reality. The thought of dying before actually getting the chance to live broke his heart.

Meme stopped braiding his hair and turned his head slightly toward hers so she could look him in his eyes as he answered her next question.

"Soooo . . . let me ask this: why don't you just stay down here with us in Charlotte? You know the fam would love that—especially Stoney! You ain't missing shit in Charleston. Zach, stop ya bullshit. You wanna live, you know how. What's keeping you so attached to Charleston anyway? Tell me, I'll wait. And fo' God be my witness, you bet not say no pussy. I might punch you." Meme balled up her fist and cocked it back like she was about to hit him.

They laughed in unison, but he knew she was dead serious.

Zach was loved dearly around the Claytor household. He had a role there—he was their brother, son, and uncle. For every member of that household, he meant something. This literally was Zach's second family. Meme was just so used to Zach getting on her damn nerves, feeling his damn self on his light skin shit, being loud, or trying to steal feels of her ass. You know, just being him.

She had never seen this nigga that sat in front of her before.

What the fuck is going on in Charleston? Meme thought to herself as she braided another row into Zach's head.

"Aye!" Meme exclaimed, popping him in the head with her comb.

Zach jumped, startled. "Yoooo! What the fuck?" he yelled at Meme, rubbing his head where it hurt.

"Don't nobody care about ya attitude, nigga. Answer my muthafuckin' question. Give me a valid reason why you aren't willing to leave Charleston. Because we both know it won't take no effort if you decide to stay. You need to get as far away from them FB niggas as you can. I'm fucking serious, Zachariah. Damn!"

Meme couldn't stop the tears from falling down her pretty face. Zach could see that Jamesa was hurt—but over what? Zach didn't understand.

Meme wiped her tears away and started braiding his hair again.

The awkward silence returned. Meme broke it with another playful slap to the back of Zach's head.

"I'm . . . gone . . . fuck . . . you up," Zach said, trying to get up off the floor. But he couldn't, because Meme tightened the grip around him with her thighs. She was laughing so hard she couldn't breathe.

"I'm glad you find smacking the back of my head to be amusing. I'm fucking you up, I hope you know that. These thick ass thighs will eventually get tired. You know what . . ." Zach laughed before turning his head and playfully biting Meme's inner thigh.

"Owwww . . . Zaaaaccchhhhh . . . that hurt. You being mean." Meme laughed, rubbing the inside of her thigh. "Then tell me—what cat got ya tongue?" she teased, scrunching her face up and sticking out her tongue.

"Not yet," Zach said seductively, trying to turn his head into her crotch.

Meme screamed and giggled, locking her thighs around his head again—but this time, it was for dear life.

Zach cracked up.

"You so damn nasty," Meme giggled, loosening the grip she had around his body. There go my baby, Meme thought, glad that Zach had snapped out of his current rut.

"But for real, can you please help me understand why you don't want to leave Charleston and come down here with us?" Meme asked solemnly.

"Okay, let me ask you this first—why are you so interested in how I'm living my life? Don't get me wrong, it'd be a lie if I told you I wasn't scared outta my mind. But why, Mia . . . why is it important to you how I live my life and where I live my life? Why don't I want to leave Charleston? Another why-does-it-matter question. All these questions fall under the girlfriend and mother category. And the last time I checked, you didn't qualify for either. So if I answer your million-dollar question, will you answer mine?"

Meme didn't answer immediately. He just felt the braid getting tighter as she finished the last of his cornrows.

"Unhuh," Meme said, trying to get up from the sofa, rubbing her pussy all on the back of Zach's neck. Meme was forced back down into a sitting position—she was just too thick to stand up with Zach's head in between her legs. When Zach's perverted ass didn't move, Meme busted out laughing.

"Move, boy, with ya nasty ass." Meme mushed Zach's head playfully from between her thighs and stood up. Zach looked at Meme innocently, as if he didn't know what she was talking about.

"What?" Meme looked at him and rolled her eyes flirtatiously.

"For real though, sit down. All jokes aside, I'm not leaving Charleston for multiple reasons. One being the most obvious—I'm not about to let these muthafuckas run me out my own home. I'll be damned if I let a nigga run me outta my state. I rather die on my soil. As stupid as it sounds, I'm dead serious. And secondly, I can't leave bruh out there to fend by his lonely. He ain't do me and Heem like that, I'm not doing bruh like that neither. I love my nigga too much to just abandon ship like that. But if it helps, I will consider what you talking about, 'cause it definitely makes sense. And two, ya sexy ass'll be here. I answered ya question—now ya turn. Why are you so concerned, love?"

Zach looked up at Meme for an answer. A jar of Blue Magic grease sat on the table in front of him. He opened it and applied grease into the middle of each braid until his hair was properly greased. Zach turned and saw Meme just staring at him.

"Are you not gonna speak on it? What's running through ya mind?"

"No bullshit, I just want you to get the fuck outta Charleston, bruh, because it's not safe for you or your tough-ass friend. Hanging around with that OT nigga done got you in all types of bullshit. Un unh, un unh."

"Well, for the record, that OT nigga you speaking of actually didn't get us into nothing—Haseem's hot ass did. His idea. But we all went along, so we all gotta deal with the consequences bestowed upon us. Meme, a nigga real live frightened, bruh. I can't hide it. You can see it on my face. But know this—the same fear is what motivates me to extinguish that light behind Fatty Man's eyes. And that go for any nigga rocking with them soft-ass niggas.

I love this family. And kicking it with you guys daily would be love. But being a man and holding shit down is what made you guys love me in the first place. Had I been a coward, your family would've never taken a liking to me. Right or wrong?"

Meme bit her bottom lip and shrugged. It was a valid point Zach was making, but she just couldn't let him escape like that. Meme outstretched her hands to help Zach off the floor. Having a conversation of this magnitude wasn't supposed to be held like this. She needed Zach on his feet and in her space. Zach dusted himself off as he rose and sat down on the loveseat across from Meme.

"You're right. But baby, this is totally different. This is some death-before-dishonor kind of bullshit you screaming. My nigga, these men aren't living like that. And you'd be in the small percentile if you do. That's my advice. You can take heed or not, I don't know. But I've shed what all tears I'm gonna shed about this situation. You grown, and by all means, do you, boo. But know what you doing, because this shit here ain't a game you playing. This a game amongst killers, demons, and reapers. You must be one to survive.

With that being said, I'm finna go wash my ass before my daughter gets off the school bus. Think about this game you and this OT nigga playing."

Meme got up from her seat and walked off, headed to the staircase. Meme momentarily stopped in her tracks before ascending the stairs. She turned and asked Zach the most pivotal question yet.

"Which one could you trust that OT nigga to be when it's reppin' time?"

Zach chuckled lightly because Meme just didn't know the half.

"The truth?" Zach asked, rising from the loveseat, making his way closer to where she stood. He wanted her to see the sincerity in his eyes when he answered her question.

"Why of course. Your secret is safe with me, if you wondering anything along them lines. This conversation I know will be what haunts me when you gone. But I'm serious—which one, if any, could you count on dude to be for you and himself?"

"Mia, bruh—the reaper! On Heem, bruh the epitome of what the reaper is. Tana 'bout that action. When I said niggas had me playing with guns . . ." Zach smirked. "I wasn't talking 'bout the opposition."

Meme just stared at Zach momentarily. His words not only sent a chill of goosebumps up her arm, but it made her pussy soaking wet. Meme could slightly understand now why leaving Charleston wasn't an option. Zach was running around with a killer on his team—and though the thought lingered of him being killed, so did his survival.

Meme shook her head, snapping out of her reverie, and ascended the steps in silence. She looked down at Zach one last time before shutting the door behind her.

Zach sat back down on the couch and turned on ESPN. He pulled a Dutch Master and a glass of *loud* from his pocket. He looked at his G-Shock—it was 1:30 in the afternoon. He knew Stoney would be home shortly. Zach rolled his blunt with perfection and thought about the reason he was even in North Carolina.

"*Over a muthafuckin' letter, son.*"

Zach could hear Santana clearly as if he was sitting right beside him, still pissed off. Though his friend made perfect sense, it wasn't about the letter, the trip was about the sender and its intent. Zach drove three and a half hours for one thing and one thing only . . . clarity.

Chapter 6

Simfany sat at the dining table, feet tucked underneath her as she scrolled through her phone patiently waiting for Peedi to return her call. She had figured the message she sent him earlier in the day would have warranted an immediate response, but as the hours crept along, she realized how wrong she truly was. Not only had Peedi not called, but he hadn't responded at all. Period.

Simfany sat at her kitchen table, vexed, twirling her finger around in a glass of Hennessey she had poured 30 minutes prior. Peedi wasn't the only that hadn't responded to her messages; Santana or Carlos hadn't either. Her feelings were hurt, especially by Carlos. Peedi? Now that was a whole other story altogether. Simfany felt like she was the only one truly worried about the potential consequences surrounding the betrayal of Baltimore's most dangerous man. She was lost.

How can this nigga not see the importance of my fucking message? What the fuck! she thought venomously, snatching the glass from the countertop aggressively, spilling liquor everywhere before taking a big gulp. The alcohol took her breath, burning her chest all the way to her stomach. Simfany closed her eyes and let the warmth overcome her body. She picked the liquor back up and refilled her glass to the brim. She was about to drink until she felt numb. What she was feeling she never wanted to feel again. Rejection. Damn, even by her flesh and blood. Her favorite person in the world wasn't even fucking with her. Simfany knew she couldn't blame no one but herself.

Simfany picked her phone back up and scrolled through her messages for the millionth time to make sure that the messages were sent on her end. And just like the last time she checked, they were. Simfany rolled her eyes and tapped her leg up and down in frustration.

"FUCK!" Simfany yelled, tossing her phone across the dining table. She picked up the double shot glass and downed it in one gulp. Simfany gagged as the liquor torched her chest, threatening to come back up. She clenched her fists as tightly as she could—so tight her fingers lost color momentarily. She just sat there for a second, trying to regain her composure.

That was insane, she thought, rubbing the warmth out of her chest cavity. Simfany got up—she needed to occupy her mind. She needed to take her mind off the reality of life for the moment. It wasn't really much she could do, so she aimlessly walked through her townhouse, looking for anything to do at this point. Anything to get her mind off the bullshit going on.

The bag of Blueberry Kush sat on her dresser. She disregarded it. She was tired of smoking. It wasn't helping. Plus, she'd already smoked four blunts and drank five double shots of Hennessy. Her mind was already numb. Getting any higher was pointless—the drugs were just gonna intensify her paranoia.

"Aaaaargh!" Simfany screamed to her lungs' capacity, picking up the first thing within arm's reach and throwing it against the wall with all her might. The shot glass put a nice-sized hole in the dining room wall before hitting the floor and shattering into a million jagged pieces.

"I fucking hate you! I fucking hate you!" she yelled over and over, tears falling rapidly down her face as she broke down.

"I fuckin'—" she sniffled, trying to hold herself together. "I fucking hate you!" Simfany screamed uncontrollably, melting to the floor helplessly.

She was losing it. Simfany should've been celebrating the beginning of Lonnie's journey to sobriety, but instead her marble floor was where she laid—distraught, holding on to herself for dear life. Her body shook violently with each tear that rolled down her face.

Zzzz . . . Zzzzz . . . Zzzzzzz . . . Simfany's phone vibrated against the wooden tabletop, causing it to spin in small half circles. The noise of the phone broke her from the mental attack she was having. She looked around suspiciously, knowing she had just heard something buzzing. Simfany sniffled back tears, cleared her nose, and wiped her eyes.

I'm losing my muthafuckin' mi—

Zzzz . . . Zzzzz . . . Zzzzzzz . . .

There it was again. This time she recognized the sound.

My phone, Simfany thought as she stood up and grew lightheaded. She stumbled, almost losing her balance. She tried to hold herself against the wall for support but lost her footing and fell hard on her ass. She was too drunk to even complain about pain.

The only thing running through her mind was to answer the phone—and even that was proving to be an impossible task at the moment. She finally got off the ground and dropped into one of her dining chairs, slouching lazily as her head spun viciously. She felt like she would throw up any minute.

Simfany sat there for a while with her eyes closed, hoping the spinning would stop. She was way too intoxicated for comfort, yet she still fought through the nausea, dizziness, and loathing.

What the fuck. I'm done with that drinking shit, Simfany promised herself, rubbing her temple gently in hopes of releasing some of the pressure.

After a few minutes, her body and mind finally began to gather themselves. She picked up her phone and saw that she had a missed call and a new message. She logged into her messages. The name that lit up damn near sobered her up instantly.

Carlos—Baltimore's most feared had finally responded to her message.

Her heart skipped a beat as she opened the message from her dear friend:

Are you okay, chula? After reading your message, it alarmed me—all the while replacing worry with a smile. Does that even make sense? But I can also sense that something has your mind unsure and unsettled.

But why? I would love to see your face. It's been a long time. How about tomorrow? Again, mama, thank you for making a real effort and checking in on me. It's greatly appreciated.

Send me your address and a time to show. I'm not taking no for an answer.

Love you, mami. I look forward to seeing you tomorrow.

Simfany exhaled loudly, not realizing that while she read Carlos's message, she had held her breath in anticipation. With the biggest problem now neutralized, it seemed like she could finally breathe a sigh of relief since seeing the segment about Gloria. Simfany was safe—for the time being at least.

She was still very much intoxicated, so before she forgot, she picked her phone back up and sent Carlos a reply. Simfany sent him the address to her home, a grocery list, and the time she would be available for him to show up on her doorstep.

Before she could even finish the text, her phone began to ring. The default ringtone told her whoever was calling wasn't saved in her contacts. But with everything going on, she wasn't tryna miss no calls, so she answered—hoping it was something of importance.

"Hey?" Simfany's words slurred slightly, the liquor still lingering heavy through her body.

"Simf, you good? You been drinking?" Peedi's voice came through the line. Simfany rolled her eyes the second she heard him. She got pissed off all over again.

"Nigga, what the fuck do you want? I no longer have any use for your call. You young niggas, I swear." Simfany barked, grilling Peedi for his absence.

"Huh? Man, what the fuck is you talkin' about shorty? I'm lost as fuck, yo." Peedi replied, genuinely confused.

"Fuck you mean? I'm not about to play this game with you, Darius. I'm busy tonight. Off my line!" Simfany snapped, still drunk, and hung up on him.

Peedi wasted no time and called directly back. Simfany reluctantly answered.

"Yes, Peedi?" she sighed loud enough for him to hear the frustration dripping from her tone.

"Shorty, look, I don't know what the fuck your problem is with me, but on my gang, you better curve that shit or we gone have a muthafuckin' issue. Now tell me what the fuck is goin' on. Please."

Simfany sat silent, holding her head in her palms as the world spun behind her eyelids. It was just too much goin' on at once.

"We good. Just holla at me in the a.m." she finally muttered.

"Man, where are you?" Peedi asked, ignoring her brush-off.

"Home," she said, barely getting the word out.

"Where is home?" he pressed.

Without hesitation, Simfany gave him her address.

"I'm coming now!" Peedi assured.

"Why?"

"Because, one—I want to. And two—it sound like you need to bounce back. I ain't never seen you like this before.

It's cool though. Everybody got they moments, lor momma. Plus, sound like ya sexy ass might need me."

True, Simfany admitted mentally—but not out loud. "I'm not talkin' 'bout that. I'm talkin' 'bout why come now? I asked for you hours ago. I wanted to discuss some serious shit with you, and you left me on stuck. Why come now? I . . . Don't . . . Need . . . You . . . Any . . . More!" Simfany said, emphasizing every word.

"Ohhhh, now it makes sense. My baby mother had my cell phone all afternoon. I dropped my daughter off earlier, and she had my phone playing games on it while I drove back into town. That's why my baby momma was tripping earlier. I was wondering what the fuck she was on. She just got to trippin' out the blue, askin' me about havin' other kids and shit. I didn't have no clue what the fuck she was talkin' about. Whatever message you sent me made her refuse to give me my shit back. So I bounced on her goofy ass. Had to go buy another phone on some meantime shit. You thought I was ignorin' you? That's why you actin' like you got this cut lor attitude? Sound like ya gangsta ass was finally missin' somebody else besides ya muthafuckin' self." Peedi teased.

"Nigga, what?" Simfany shot back, agitated as fuck.

She was so drunk, his words didn't even register. They went in one ear and out the other. Her throbbing headache was the only thing that had her attention. She needed relief—Tylenol, aspirin, something. Her head just wouldn't stop spinning.

This why I don't fucking drink. This fuckin' reason right here, she thought, rubbing her temple in slow circular motions, hoping to rub the pain away.

"I'm just askin' a simple Q&A, shorty. Wasn't nobody tryna ignore you, not purposely anyway. What would be my reason for lyin' to you—or even ignorin' you, for that matter? I didn't know anything was goin' on. I'm on my way over. Anything you want me to bring in particular?"

"Aspirin. Tylenol—lots and lots of Tylenol. Blunts. And food. I feel crazy. I have to lay down. I drank too much."

"Say less. Get yourself together. I'll be there soon, baby."

"Drive safely, lor nigga," Simfany replied, testing him.

He took her slight in stride—and ignored her.

"I'll be—"

"If you don't shut up and hurry ya ass up. My brain feel like it's 'bout to explode any minute. Please hurry the fuck up." Simfany hung the phone up and walked back into the kitchen, placing her phone back on the charger above the microwave—making sure it was in plain sight this time around. But knowing Simfany, she'd probably forget again and end up searching high and low for it. She definitely needed to get her shit together—mentally, physically, and emotionally.

Simfany walked into her master bathroom and ran the water. She needed to relax, and she knew just what she needed—a bath. The drive was only 45 minutes from Washington Park to her Baltimore County home. Simfany knew Peedi could make it in 30 if he used the interstate. She was cool with him taking his time; she needed a minute to bounce back anyway. But she had to be honest with herself—just the thought of Peedi racing up the interstate for her put a smile on her face. Simfany couldn't front—Peedi was cool as fuck and about his action. Plus, the little nigga was sexy as hell. Simfany always kept her composure, but damn, it was hard not to notice him shine.

Trying to brush the thoughts of Peedi out her head, Simfany walked into the master bedroom. Still slightly drunk, she stumbled over the placemat, barely catching her balance. Her heart raced a mile a minute—she had almost taken a nasty spill. Thankfully, she was able to grip the edge of the tub.

Simfany sat down, reached for the cold water, and turned the knob until it couldn't go no more. She kept her hand under the stream until it reached freezing. She needed to sober up, and this was the only way to do it. After she was satisfied with the temperature, she leaned into the tub and splashed water on her face repeatedly. The cold felt good. Simfany cupped both hands under the faucet and splashed water on her face a few more times before finally turning it off.

Damn, she thought, as the water momentarily numbed both her hands and face. Simfany grabbed a face towel that hung against the wall on the towel rack—a new fixture she'd just installed weeks before.

She wiped her face dry and laid the towel across the edge of the tub. Then she adjusted the water again, but this time to her liking so she could take a much-needed bath. She began to undress, trying hard not to think about the situation she was currently facing. But how could she not think about it?

The one person besides Santana that she trusted, she'd now—ironically—secretly betrayed. And that shit wasn't sitting lightly on her soul.

Granted, she was terrified to death of what the consequences could be. But that wasn't what consumed her. It was the feeling of betrayal. She felt like she had betrayed Carlos to the core, and lying to him—acting like she knew nothing—was taking its toll. But damn, what was she supposed to do? It was nothing she could do. Simfany understood that if Carlos found out about the plan they came up with, he would for sure kill her and every soul involved—regardless of how big or small the role.

Simfany snapped out of her momentary daze and walked into the hallway in search of her favorite bubble bath soap (Lilac and Shea Butter). It was a Christmas gift from Darla. The bubbles damn near created an atmosphere of their own. As soon as Simfany poured the crystal beads into the water, the aroma traveled through her home. It was one of the reasons she loved the beads so much more than liquid soaps.

She inched her toes into the water, adjusting her body to the temperature. Simfany moaned. It was perfect. Without further hesitation, she popped off her bra and inched out of her panties. Simfany cautiously slid into the bubbles and closed her eyes, letting the warmth of the water and the scent in the air take her frustrations away.

She relaxed for the first time since seeing the newscast earlier that day. She knew this comfort was only temporary, so she tried her best to enjoy what peace still remained.

***

"Mr. Torres . . . Helllloooo . . . Mr. Torres, can I please have a word with you outside in the hallway? I would like to get this done as quickly as possible, if you don't mind," Detective Williams said as he opened the door, waiting for Santana. Santana sat at Darla's bedside, indecisive as hell. He looked at Darla, then looked at the detective. Santana felt the metal under his fingertips.

"Go, baby, please. I'm gone be alright. I promise," Darla assured Santana, laying her hand over top of his tenderly. Her gesture alone was enough to make Santana release the grip he had on the gun.

Santana could tell the detective was growing impatient—his mannerisms said so. But Santana didn't care. Nigga you can't be like that. He let you take Melquan from a damn murder scene knowing you not his muthafuckin' father. Santana was having an inner jihad with himself. But his conscience was right—the detective did some stand-up shit for them. Melquan could've been going through the motions of who knows what to get back.

"Please, Mr. Torres, today, sir." Santana understood his frustration. He followed the detective into the hallway.

"What's good?" Santana asked nonchalantly. He knew if Williams was asking questions, they most likely had nothing. That's what he learned from TV, at least. Plus, if they had anything worth shit, he'd for sure be in handcuffs on his way to jail. And usually, that would be true—but not in this case. There was a whole lot of shit in play behind the scenes.

Just the thought alone of him losing Kat over arresting Santana made Detective Williams sick to his stomach. He literally knew—in order to have one, he had to let the other go. So he did the bare minimum, ironically in a case he re-opened and wouldn't let go. Williams knew eventually he'd come to a cross in the road where it would have to be his career and the lives of his community—or Kat's fire ass pussy and head.

But how can I not investigate this little nigga? Williams thought to himself. Since his arrival, bodies had been dropping left and right. Not saying Santana was the person responsible—but facts were facts. Since Santana's feet hit the streets of Charleston, people had been dying. Not only were street figures being killed—women and children were also among the slain. And they were all Black, his people, from his community. He needed to find out what was going on at the least. This was his city. He felt justified in his endeavors.

Unfortunately, that was all in the beginning of his investigation, before he fell in love with Katherine Torres—the aunt of his primary suspect.

As Williams stood in the hallway and looked at Santana, he asked himself if the young man leaning against the wall biting his fingernails could really be capable of murder. *And if he was, how would I get him off the streets without losing Kat in the process?* Det. Williams knew he had no future with Kat if Santana ever got locked up due to his investigations—or so he assumed, at least.

Detective Williams knew more than he was given credit for. He contemplated and thought about what he wanted to do with the information he withheld. Det. Williams bit his tongue and spoke.

"What's your issue with me, Mr. Vasquez?" Detective Williams asked in a low baritone only they could hear. Santana looked at the detective suspiciously. There was no one in the hallway, coming or going. The white hallways were immaculately clean and empty—besides the occasional nurse making rounds. The corridor was long, empty, and cold.

The detective watched as Santana began to fret at the mention of his government name. Got ya ass! Detective Williams thought excitedly.

"Man, who the fuck is that? No disrespect, but please don't confuse me with other people. You buggin'. I really don't have an issue—you the one on my ass. You literally pop up any place I'm at. You a homicide detective, but you still show up to question me and my girl about some air shots. What do you really want? Like for real, son—because I'm not telling you nothing, I know nothing, but I sense you know that already and yet you still on my ass. What the fuck am I doing that makes you want me off the streets so bad?" Santana asked sincerely as he leaned back against the wall, biting his nails and looking down the hall trying to avoid eye contact. Detective Williams walked closer.

"I know who you are, Santana. But the only reason you're still walking these streets is because of Katherine's love for you. Her love runs extremely deep for you, and my love for her runs even deeper. Count ya blessings because—"

Santana waved his hand furiously, interrupting.

"Listen, man, I have no clue what you talking about at this point. I want a lawyer."

Santana tried to further convince the detective that he had his information all wrong. Williams' face scrunched up as he flared his nose at Santana angrily. Detective Williams searched his thoughts for the right reply—because he was treading on a fine line. He stepped closer until he was only inches away from Santana. He looked around once more, then spoke—making sure he chose his words wisely.

"Look, little nigga, I'm trying to look the other way best as I possibly can—without breaking the muthafuckin' law myself. All because I'm fuckin' with ya aunt. Chill the fuck out with that hot ass shit you doing. That shit you pulled on that Westside yesterday—never again, my nigga. That shit can't ever happen again. That boy's mother is screaming for your head. What the fuck is wrong with you? Sit ya pretty ass down, bruh. For real! You can think I'm bluffing—try me. My heart goes out to you. You just lost a close friend and your girlfriend just, you know . . ."

"That shit can make a nigga wicked, so I understand. I understand more than you give me credit for. Express your pain differently—it's only so much I can ignore. Get ya shit together."

Detective Williams reached his right hand out. Santana stared at him, confused. He didn't know what to say in reply, so he didn't say nothing. Santana sighed as he swallowed his pride and reached his right hand out in return, giving the detective a firm handshake. He wasn't worried about the Hallmark speech—it was cute, almost had him for a second—but he didn't care. He could care less.

Santana was only concerned with one thing and one thing only, and it had nothing to do with the streets of West Virginia. He needed to know the extent of the detective's knowledge on who Santana Vasquez was. Nothing else mattered.

The handshake confirmed their understanding. Santana walked back into the room, Detective Williams in stride right behind him. Darla stirred when the men re-entered the room. Her eyes said she was scared, uncomfortable, and confused. Her gaze searched his for answers.

"No disrespect, Detective, but I have asked Darla multiple times to retract her memory for me, and I think it's just too early. Is there any way you can come back another time, give her some time to heal? She was just shot, plus the meds—"

Williams put his hands up in surrender.

"I have no issue with that, Ms. Collins. But I will be back first thing in the morning to follow up on a few things. Please get some rest, and I pray you feel better, Ms. Collins," Detective Williams stated sincerely.

"I'm okay. I just want to get this over with. Every time I even think about it, it just—" Darla shivered as the memory vividly replayed in her mind over and over. She needed to get that shit off her chest, sooner rather than later.

Detective Williams looked over at Santana for confirmation to continue. Santana shrugged. He was leaving that decision up to Darla.

"She's grown, bro," Santana said plainly.

Detective Williams grew excited, taking his notepad back out and putting up the recorder. Everything he learned at the hospital he was taking in greedily. He wasted no time pulling a chair up to begin his line of questioning.

"Do you know who shot you, Ms. Collins?" the detective asked Darla, but kept his eyes on Santana for any telltale signs of recognition. Santana didn't flinch or seem to waver.

"No, I do not, sir," Darla responded immediately. Santana gripped her hand lovingly.

Williams continued.

"Do you have any clue why you were targeted? Anyone new that you've been around who could have caused this?"

"People like who?" Darla asked, clearly irritated by his line of questioning. She felt like he was focused solely on Santana, and she wasn't about to partake in that.

"Please don't beat around the bush, Ms. Collins. Do you think you were targeted because of the relationship you have with Mr. Torres? Because it is no secret that he is a heavily sought man in this city. I just—"

Darla put her free hand up to stop the detective in his tracks.

"Look, let me explain something to you. That man over there has kept me and my child safe. He has fed and clothed me and my child. Please stop asking me questions about him, because I will not answer any of them. Your line of questioning is foul and out of pocket. I was shot by a random act of violence. I don't know what they wanted or what they came for. I have no recollection of that day, so please."

Darla teared up thinking about the ordeal. At this point, all she wanted was for the detective to leave.

"Okay, okay. I apologize. Can I ask one more question, please?"

Darla sighed but reluctantly agreed.

"Why did the person who shot you get killed and left for dead in your home?"

Detective Williams knew that was gone throw some salt into the game.

"What!" Darla exclaimed in total shock. *How does this nigga know all of this information? He has to be guessing*, she thought. Darla looked up and locked eyes with Santana. The look on his face told her he also wanted to know the answer to that question.

"You heard me, Ms. Collins. Why was there a dead gang member in your home?"

"I don't even know what the fuck you're talking about, sir." Darla began to get irate.

"I was shot trying to protect my son. I don't know anything about anyone, going beefs, or why a known gang member was gunned down in my home. I was in the midst of fighting for me and my son's life. I'm sorry if I'm not the witness that you are looking for. That shit happened too fast, thank God. I'm sorry, Detective."

"No, thank you, Ms. Collins. Mr. Torres." He nodded.

"If I have any more questions, I'll be in contact. If you remember anything—if anything arises—here's my card. Call me."

Detective Williams sat two cards on the countertop closest to her bed so they would be within arm's reach.

"Again, thank you. I will be in touch," Williams said one last time before departing. He closed the door behind him, leaving the pair with the conversation at hand.

The silence in the hospital room was awkward. Santana held his tongue, because the one thing he couldn't do was act like he was mad—because at the end of the day, he was the cause of all the madness. But he still wanted to understand what the fuck was going on. What the detective had said sounded crazy—he had to admit.

As Santana's mind raced, he glared out the large glass windows. So many questions were running through his head at the moment. He went through every possible scenario in his head that could end with that outcome, and time after time, he came up blank. He just couldn't fathom why it was a dead PB nigga in Darla's living room. It just made no sense. He was missing something. Santana wasn't talking shit or being an ass—the fact that he was being so quiet spoke volumes, louder than any octane possibly could.

"So, are you going to ask me what's going on, or are you going to draw a conclusion on your own?" Darla asked coldly, snatching her hand from his grasp. Darla was pretty upset. Santana knew she was pissed at him.

How dare he question my loyalty only a fucking day after being shot over his actions. How fucking dare he? Darla pouted.

Santana's face softened. He was tripping, and he knew it.

"I don't even care, Ma. I haven't drawn any conclusions. I'm just clueless and confused, that's all, love. If you would like to elaborate, that would be amazing, but no pressure. I love and trust you wholeheartedly, so for real, it doesn't matter. I almost let my mind get the best of me, I must admit. But I promise you, beautiful, I'm good. We good."

Santana smiled, taking Darla's frail hands back into his, kissing them with passion and care. Santana really adored Darla—anybody could see it. It showed in his every action regarding her.

"I love you, Ma," Santana said, looking Darla deeply in her eyes.

"I love you too, papi," Darla replied, as a tear formed in the corner of her eye. Santana wiped it away and kissed Darla's moist lips passionately.

"Seriously, Ma, I'm so very sorry. A nigga didn't mean to blatantly question your loyalty, not one bit. I'm sorry, momma."

Santana felt like he couldn't apologize enough. He had kissed and wiped away her tears, yet they still poured uncontrollably. He had hurt Darla severely. Darla calmed herself to the best of her ability before she spoke.

"I love you, baby. I forgive you; I know you meant no harm. You are an amazing soul. I will go through whatever for you and our son any day, without hesitation. I mean every word of that."

Darla explained truthfully. She felt so safe and so loved. The feeling Santana gave her was just so surreal.

"I know, momma, I know. Thank you for forgiving me. Seriously, that shit means a lot, because just the thought of you being hurt on my account has been eating a nigga alive. It's crazy how you know my mind and heart so well."

"I don't ever want you to think twice about ever trusting me. Nigga, I will die for you and with you. The little nigga Gleek got killed because he was the one aiming his gun at Quannie as he rounded the corner. The ironic thing about it all—Fatty was about to leave until Quannie woke up."

Santana seen the look on Darla's face change as she recollected what happened leading up to the moment she was shot. Darla continued.

"Quannie had woke up from his nap and opened the door. You know Quannie's door makes that stupid-ass noise when it opens. Anyway, they heard the door open and that put them on alert. I had just told them that Melquan was out with Sofiya at the movies. When I realized that shit was going left, I began yelling and telling them that our son was the person coming around the corner. The Gleek nigga never tried to put his gun up—he kept it aimed at the entrance. Without thinking, I ran and covered him up, getting shot in the process. That bitch-ass nigga shot me intentionally. Before I passed out, I heard more shots and Fatty Man running his mouth."

Santana still looked confused as to why Fatty Man would kill one of his own soldiers for the opposition's girlfriend. It was something that Santana was missing—that was for sure.

"It has to be a reason though, Ma. Do y'all have some kind of history with each other? I know Charleston only but so big, so I know at one point or another y'all were either friends or lovers. I pray the former than the latter, but some kind of history has to be there if he is smoking niggas over you. Because I could never do no shit like that to my niggas. Yeah, I would be pissed if my nigga killed a female or a child, but I'm not ending their life about it. So what—"

Darla poked her lips out and rolled her eyes, interrupting Santana.

"If you would stop cutting me off, sir, I would be able to speak my piece. May I please continue?"

Santana laughed, putting his fingers to his lips and imaginarily zipping them shut, giving Darla the floor.

"Okay look . . . all I can do is shed a little light on what I do know. I don't know why Fatty shot his homie, that's the truth. I was going out by the time the second shot hit me. I was falling in and out of consciousness. I have nothing to hide, love. I hope you understand that. Okay, moving on . . . I was young when I got pregnant with Melquan. My baby daddy's name was Raymond Mills, but everybody called him Rayo. Fatty and Breeze was both my baby dad's best friends since their sandbox days. Don't get me to lying, but I think Fatty may even be his real cousin somewhere down the line—I don't know. But I do know that he was raised with all them lame-ass niggas: Von, Breeze, Fatty, the nigga Remy, and Sleeze. Crazy shit about that—Haseem ran up under them also. Haseem has a few family members in that FB shit."

"Anyway, all of them was raised by Ms. Rhonda at one point or another. Ms. Rhonda is the mother of Von and Breeze. They all had grew up basically as brothers. Rayo hung with them daily until he found out that I was pregnant and he was about to become a father. I became his main priority then—a lot changed. Oh, and before I forget, Raymond was not a member of Full Blooded. To be honest, I'm not even sure that was even a thing back then. It may very well have been, but I'm not sure. That kind of shit don't turn me on, no pun intended, my love." Darla said, sticking her tongue out.

"None taken, beauty. Keep going, shit is getting good." Santana joked back, looking at her with amusement.

Got that ass back, he laughed to himself. Darla raised her hand and flicked him off. She smiled and continued.

"Raymond was the soft get-money kind of nigga. Him and Zach damn near the same kind of person."

Darla snickered because of the look on Santana's face. He didn't like the shot she had taken at his homie. Santana smirked but said nothing. He didn't want to interrupt her.

"He was the get-money type. He wasn't no bitch or no shit like that, but he wasn't no tough nigga either. When it came to playing with guns, he left that to Fatty and them. The ironic shit about it—you and him . . . whoa, night and day. But y'all hearts? Very similar in many ways.

"Anyway, one night Melquan needed diapers, so Rayo walked to The Shop-N-Go. On the way back, a car shot the block up, hitting him ten times and ending my baby's life."

The tears that began to run down Darla's face hurt him—but only for a second. A small amount of jealousy ran through him. He couldn't explain why; it just temporarily ran through him. Santana knew that her kind of love, a person only found once—*that's if you were lucky*. So sharing Darla's love with anyone, even a person that no longer existed in this world, was tough for him.

Santana wiped her tears away with his thumb and planted the gentlest kiss to her forehead. He wanted her to know that he was there, no matter what. Darla could feel the love. She smiled a bright smile and grabbed ahold of Santana's hand, kissing the middle of his palm. She rubbed his palm along her face as she closed her eyes. Santana looked confused, but he still sat in support. Darla wanted to make sure that Santana was real and not just a dream. She opened her eyes without further word and continued, hand in hand.

"I'm sorry. It was a big thing, but not huge. To be friends with some of the most menacing people of this state, and nothing happens after you're killed? It raised a lot of red flags for me. That's why you see I don't fuck with no one unless we carry the same blood—and even some of them, I stay away from. If it's not Sofiya or my mother, I try to steer clear of it. And me and my mother been on rocky terms. Rayo's murder opened my eyes to the true definition of betrayal and phony. Like, serious, love—no one was shot, stabbed, beat up, or even blamed for what happened to my baby father. You might've seen a message posted on Myspace around the anniversary or somethin', but they did my baby wrong. Every time Breeze would see me, he would make sure I was good—mentally and financially—and he would strangely apologize repeatedly about what happened. But that was in the beginning. One thing I can say though, Raymond's death fucked Bre'Shawn up. Breeze was never the same. That shit made him into the violent person everybody knew before he was killed. Rayo's death changed a lot of people, including me. It made Fatty quiet and distant. Where this vocal nigga came from that we see now . . . I have no idea. Well, hold on, don't get me wrong, that man has always been extremely violent, just not as loud and boisterous. I think him killing Von and Remy did that. But I just feel—"

"Whoa, wait, what? What makes you say that Fatty killed Von and Remy?" Santana asked astoundingly. That was the first time he had ever heard that one. Surprisingly, it made more sense than any other rumors he had heard regarding Von's death at least.

"No one said it, but it's obvious. Nessy was my cousin, and though sometimes she would say bullshit about things she knew, majority of the time she was dead on point with her information. Nessy ran her mouth to Remy about that day outside of Shop-N-Go—you know, the day you got shot. She had exposed Fatty as a bitch for running away on Breeze after you killed him. Nessy told me what happened to Fatty one day at one of their meetings. Basically, Remy told her that Von pulled his gun on Fatty and told him to leave the Chuck or die. He left for a few hours, a day, man I don't know which one—but when he finally popped back up, Nessy, Remy, and Von was all found dead. And in that same order. He came back, claiming his throne, and now it seems like he the most feared man in the city. That has to be public knowledge, because niggas had love for Fatty Man, don't get me wrong—but this dick-eating shit they doing right now is new. People may not like know-know, but they got an idea. Fatty is feared now—I seen it that day in my home. And no, no one told me none of this. It's just what I came up with, because it's the most logical. Serious, babe—three people from the same social group gets killed, and just so happened they all got into it with one of Charleston's known shooters? That shit don't take rocket science. These lame muthafuckas just don't wanna see that fat-ass elephant sittin' in the room. It's none of my business or yours, so why care? But you see where I'm coming from?"

Santana nodded in bewilderment.

Okay, so Darla did pay attention—more than he had ever given her credit for. Touché, Santana thought, raising his hands in surrender.

"Damn," was all he could muster in reply.

"Damn it is. I received a phone call like ten months after Raymond passed away. The caller tells me that Breeze and Fatty Man were the drivers of the car that killed Raymond that night, and supposedly Raymond was killed by mistake. They thought he was someone else they were beefing with. Shortly after that call, I began getting envelopes placed in my mailbox with Melquan's name written on it. But that stopped recently. After Von got killed it started again—but it stopped for good once me and you took our relationship to Myspace. Which of course I'm totally fine with—I don't know, it is what it is. Breeze is gone now, so I'd never know. And Fatty—he's so used to killing his friends I wouldn't put it past him. I figured him killing Gleek before he got the chance to kill me was his way of making things right. But please know, other than Rayo being their friend, I've never fucked, conversed, or been friends with any other men. Breeze was the closest thing that I can say I had to a friend with them—and that was solely because of the shit he was doing for Quannie after Rayo was gone. But I think the guilt pushed him away. You know what, let me take that back. Now that I'm explaining this to you in detail, I realize Breeze was the only friend that I actually had at that time. He paid for the homegoing, he helped feed and clothe his best friend's child. He did many things for us. Even then I still never chilled with him. I never once ever been alone with him for any amount of time. It was always hi and bye kind of shit. But as I said, after that phone call came through, my hatred for them—especially him—grew. I hate them niggas to my core. And before you ask why I hated him more when they held the same responsibility—it was because he was the one that played the hurt brother. He played the role knowing he was responsible for the demise of my baby father."

Darla wiped the lone tear that slid down her face. She took a deep breath and exhaled.

"I hate talkin' 'bout this shit, Santana. So I pray after this, you'll trust me enough so I'll never have to talk about it again. I'm not hiding anything from you. I love you. I'm begging for your trust, baby. Our newborn needs you to trust—"

"Not to change the topic, but talkin' about the baby . . . what if I still have to go and do forever over that bogus-ass murder charge in Baltimore? Then what?" Santana asked, almost forgetting about it completely. Talking to Detective Williams brought it all back into perspective. He had been living in Charleston freely, doing any and everything he wanted. So much that mentally, he had sidelined the most important thing he had going on in his life.

"Then what? What the fuck does that even mean? Then what?" Darla laughed Santana's question off. She was starting to become annoyed by his line of questioning. He had questioned her love and loyalty too many times that day.

"If they give me twenty, thirty years or even life—I don't know—but what if they give me some unreasonable shit, then what are we gonna do? Where will we stand? I should beat it—I wasn't in the city that morning, but I got no way of proving it."

Darla squeezed his hands as she looked into his dark brown eyes.

"Well, Santana, you should've thought about all of this before you shot your sperm inside of me. Secondly, if your fate is for you to do twenty or thirty years, then I guess it's mine too. I'll move to Baltimore one, become your wife, and hold you the fuck down. Why is that so hard for you to believe, Santana?"

Darla squinted her eyes into icy slits. He could tell that he was pissing her off—yet again.

"Man, I'm just asking. Women say they'll be there all the time and leave before sentencing," Santana replied in a matter-of-fact kind of tone.

Darla let Santana's hand go.

"And how the fuck would you know, Santana? You've only been in juvey once. You don't know shit, and furthermore you ain't never had a queen like me. If I didn't want to or wasn't going to hold you down, nigga, I would just say that. Baby or no baby. A baby don't keep me—the man and the way he treats me is what keeps me. So rethink these conversations you keep bringing up, because you borderline gettin' disrespectful. That's twice today! Do it again, I double dog fuckin' dare you!" Darla said sternly before she coughed. She closed her eyes and grabbed her chest in pain.

Santana tried to grab her to make sure she was okay, but Darla pulled out of his grip fast and strong.

"Don't touch me, nigga!" Darla said venomously.

"Come on, Ma. I'm not tryin' to be disrespectful. But I want you to know, holdin' a nigga down in prison for that long can be strenuous—on both you and me. I know you're serious, you look serious, and may even feel it wholeheartedly—but as the years pass, we may begin to change and want different things. Mainly you. No pun intended. I'm just asking to make sure this is what you want, ma. That's all!" Santana stated sincerely, truly meaning nothing by the questions he was asking. It was obvious that Darla was past talking about the whole ordeal. She was pissed, and he could see that.

"Whatever. Why wait until then to want something different? We can end this lame-ass shit right now and don't worry about all that extra shit in the future. How about that? These bullets hurt anyway. I shouldn't be getting shot about shit that don't—"

Santana busted out laughing. It was all he could do at that moment. He was getting so angry, he could literally feel his face growing hotter and hotter by the second.

"I'm gone let that slide because I know you in your feelings and you don't mean that shit. But you must understand that I've heard it all before. You ain't no different from the first female who told me those same muthafuckin' words."

Darla looked at Santana in total shock, her mouth gaped open. She was so disappointed and hurt by his words that she instantly started to cry.

"You bitch-ass nigga! I almost died because of you. My son almost was shot because of you. My son was close to death, Santana." Darla used her thumb and forefinger to show him just how close they had both come to being a casualty in his weak-ass war.

She continued.

"I told you to handle that shit because I knew you were hurting over Haseem. I didn't tell you to taunt niggas until they came and tried to capture and kill the closest thing to your heart. You out here doing stupid shit, nigga—knowing that I'm out here alone with your son unguarded. Who the fuck does that? Yet I have forgiven you for what you put us through. You pullin' guns on niggas' mothers and siblings? Kickin' candles at memorials? What kind of reaction did you think you were gonna get? Huh, Santana? But yet Darla—me—is still laid in a hospital bed with bullet wounds in my body, beggin' to ride a life sentence out with you, and you spit in my face and tell me, 'No, you've *heard it all before*'? Nigga, leave! Get . . . the . . . fuck . . . out! You's a stupid-ass muthafucka. I said get out!"

Darla screamed. She covered her face and cried uncontrollably into her palms.

Santana knew what Darla was saying held hella weight, but he also knew that the right words could woo and sway anybody. He wasn't one of those people. He believed in actions.

Santana knew that when words were spoken, they held great value—and usually, the person speaking meant well at that time. But in time, the actions didn't align with the words. And no matter what anyone said, no one could make him feel different. Because seriously, who in their right mind would sign up to do life in prison with someone—no matter if it was a family member or a significant other?

The thought alone sounded stupid to him.

Santana knew that Darla wanted to be comforted, just not at that moment. Darla would eventually get over the conversation—that he knew. He could clearly see she was upset and fed up with his bullshit, and he couldn't blame her. He understood totally. If he was her, he'd be acting the same way.

Santana had other shit that held precedence over her feelings right now.

Santana looked at Darla, and the tears streaking down her angry face truly broke his heart—because he had caused them—but he was done with all the mushy crybaby shit for the day. He had to get his mind right. It was time to tilt the scoreboard again. He was about to hit the city of Charleston and take muthafuckas' lack of peace.

Santana rose to leave. He sighed loudly as he stood—loud enough to let Darla know that he too was frustrated over the bullshit at hand. Santana leaned over to kiss her, but Darla moved her face, turning her head. He laughed at the gesture and kissed the side of her cheek anyway.

"I love you, Ma. You promised me forever. I expect and hope you stick to your word. You buggin' right now. Siempre?" Santana asked as he looked at Darla. She refused to look his way. When she didn't answer him, he turned for the door so he could leave.

When Santana reached the door and turned the knob, Darla finally spoke. "No matter what, right or wrong. And Santana . . ." he turned back around to face her.

"Make it count, because after this—no more. Unless it threatens our survival. Make them niggas feel me!" Darla stated coldly before turning back over in her bed, giving Santana her back.

"Oh, they gone feel you, that's for sure. That's on Heem. No more tears, Ma. We gone make it. I promise, you hear me? We good. We gone make it." Santana replied before he walked out of Darla's hospital room, shutting the door behind him.

Darla closed her swollen eyes tightly and said a silent prayer in hopes of protecting her true love from the harm only the devil could bring.

Chapter 7

Knock . . . Knock . . . Knock . . .

"Who is it?" Simfany yelled, making her way through the living room in long, sexy strides, in a hurry to answer the door. No one replied back.

"I said, who the fuck is it?" Simfany asked again, this time her tone filled with agitation. She looked down at her Rolex as she approached the door. It was 6:11 p.m.

This nigga should've been here—this better be him, I swear, Simfany thought, approaching her front door cautiously. She cocked the Glock in her hand, chambering a round. She had promised herself she would never be caught lacking again.

Simfany knew the gun probably wasn't needed—nobody knew where she stayed until a few hours ago—but taking the precaution was instinctive.

She looked out the peephole, and her body calmed immediately.

Peedi stood on the porch, bags in hand, looking handsome like always—fresh from head to toe.

With ya sexy ass, Simfany thought, fixing herself as best as she possibly could. It wouldn't help none, because regardless of the fact, she looked a hot mess in her Powerpuff Girl boy shorts and plain white tank top. Simfany shrugged. At the end of the day, she really didn't give a fuck.

She unlatched her fortress and opened the door, hand on hip with a whole attitude.

"Nigga, what the fuck! You was supposed to have been here over an hour ago. Yo, stop playin' me, for real," Simfany said, rolling her eyes irritably.

She stepped to the side to let Peedi through, but Peedi didn't move. He couldn't. He was stuck in a daze. He was at an extreme loss for words.

The boy shorts that hugged Simfany's thick frame was fuckin' him up. It looked like the Powerpuff Girls was painted on Simfany's body.

Peedi licked his lips succulently as he fantasized about what he'd do if given the chance. Anything they had to talk about regarding business had just gone out the window. All that consumed his mind now was sex. He wanted to fuck Simfany so bad, it was impossible to hide—literally. The erection poking through his jeans was a dead giveaway.

"You see somethin' you like, little boy?" Simfany laughed, removing her hand from her hip and shifting her stance, causing her boy shorts to rise tightly into her crotch, revealing the camel toe between her thighs.

"Man, you playing. And I mean absolutely no disrespect when I say this, but Simf . . . can I please get just one chance to make love to you? I just wanna suck on ya pussy, with no strings attached. You know what you doin' to a nigga wearing them small-ass shorts—I know you do. I just want one shot. I'd kill a whole muthafuckin' block for it," Peedi said in all seriousness.

Simfany smiled at his advances before turning into her home and walking away. Peedi walked in and closed the door behind him, securing all the locks into place.

He watched as Simfany made her way around the kitchen, grabbing plates and silverware, setting the table for two. Peedi tried—but he just couldn't take his eyes off Simfany's ass. The way it jiggled and bounced with each step she took fucked him up.

She so perfect, he thought, setting the Chinese food and groceries he brought on the dining table.

"Little boy, I promise you—you not ready for me. And I mean that in every aspect of the word. A lot comes with stickin' ya dick and tongue in this, believe that. If I'm making you uncomfortable, I can change. Matter fact, give me a second," Simfany said before disappearing into the room adjacent to the kitchen, leaving Peedi alone with his thoughts.

She re-emerged in the same attire—the only difference was the bra she threw on to cover her breasts poking through the white cotton top.

Peedi couldn't help but admire the raw beauty before him. He shook it off and kicked the thought of sex out his mind, finally shifting focus to the real topic at hand—Carlos and Gloria.

Peedi washed his hands and sat down at the table. He was hungry as hell. He hadn't sat down long enough in days to enjoy a hot meal. So he was about to take advantage of the leisure time that he had. Peedi took the Chinese food out the bag, then grabbed the Styrofoam cups and bottle of Hennessey.

"So shorty, tell me what's going on?" Peedi asked, picking up the bottle of Hennessey off the table and pouring himself a double shot. Peedi slid the bottle and a Styrofoam cup towards Simfany, Simfany raised one hand in decline. She could still feel the remnants of her earlier escapade; she was good.

Simfany explained what she saw earlier that day regarding the segment about Gloria.

Peedi listened intently without interrupting. Once Simfany was done, he spoke. "Look, Simf, even if what you're saying about Carlos and Glo is true, no one knows that we had shit to do with her and Kev linking up. That could've happened by chance on its own. The county ain't but so big and how you just explained it to me, you would be the last person that Carlos would expect to play a part in Gloria's death," Peedi explained.

"That's because of the history we share, but that doesn't mean I'm immune to that nigga's gun," Simfany replied.

"So, if you had to, could you lay him to rest?" Peedi asked seriously, watching Simfany's body movements to see if she was telling him the truth or not. Simfany chuckled.

"Are you serious? Is that a real question?" Simfany asked in disbelief. Low-key, she felt disrespected by that shit. The look on her face told Peedi he might have gone too far. *But how?* Peedi questioned himself. He knew Simfany could've taken the question disrespectful in a lot of ways. One, she could've seen it as a slight—by just asking her to harm somebody she held dear to her heart. He was confused; he really ain't know what to say, but he stuck to his guns and didn't let up. *Fuck it, we here already,* Peedi thought, as he answered Simfany's question.

"It is, and I'm serious, but it's not that serious if it makes sense." Simfany could tell that Peedi was nervous. He was tongue-tying himself.

"Listen, there isn't one person on this here earth that I wouldn't lay to rest if harm is involved. Flat out! And I mean no one, Santana included. And you know I love that lor nigga with all of my whole soul, but if he tried to harm me and made me have to protect myself, I'm sending him out of this bitch without hesitation." Peedi wiped the sweat from his brow. Simfany peeped the gesture but kept it to herself and stored it into her memory bank for a later date.

"I can feel that. When was the last time you spoke to Carlos?"

"Today, right before you popped up. I told that nigga to make sure he pulled up on me asap, that we needed to talk. So if I don't call you by tomorrow night, make sure you strap up and come looking for me." Peedi didn't know if he liked the fact that she was meeting Carlos alone. And if he was being honest with himself, it had nothing to do with her safety. It had everything to do with his. Peedi knew he was dead wrong for the larceny he held in his heart, because

Simfany had never given him reason not to trust her. But when life and liberty was on the line, he didn't trust anyone. Shit, he didn't trust his muthafuckin' self sometimes.

"I got you, you know that," Peedi responded sheepishly. Simfany caught the slight instantly.

"First off, what's up with that look and that weak-ass answer?" Simfany sat up and locked eyes with Peedi.

"What you talking 'bout, shorty? You trippin'," Peedi replied, trying to keep his cool. But his face grew flush, letting Simfany know he was feeling a way. The color in his face showed the telltale signs of irritation, but Peedi stuck to his guns.

"Yeah, a'ight, whatever." Simfany brushed Peedi's weak-ass response off and moved on. "But damn, why you ain't tell me 'bout this shit with Los till now? What you plan on talkin' to him about anyway—if you don't mind me askin'." Simfany gave Peedi her side eye.

So that's what this silly-ass nigga worried about. Simfany just shook her head at Peedi. She couldn't believe him—but there was also a part of her that couldn't really blame him. She had to admit, they were dealing with somebody very dangerous.

"First off, scared don't look good on ya fine ass, but the fact I can understand that Los is a different kind of threat—I'm gone let this one slide. But I'm not gone keep overlooking shit you doing, P. My baby father always taught me to believe who a person reveals themselves as the first time around, so stop! I'm in this field too, nigga. You either trust me or get the fuck away from me. Never ever test the waters. What does it matter what me and Carlos will be talking about? I know you not over there acting like you don't trust me now, because I swear it feel like you got my gangsta on trial right now—"

Before Simfany could continue, Peedi cut her sentence short.

"I would never. I was just asking you a simple question, my love. I do apologize if that's what it seemed like," Peedi said sincerely.

"Yeah, what-the-fuck-ever," Simfany replied, twisting her neck and rolling her eyes. She grabbed the 16 oz. Styrofoam and bottle of Hennessey that sat on the counter—she needed a drink badly. Peedi was stressing her to the max. The energy in the room had shifted from flirtatious to awkward.

Simfany didn't know if she was more furious about the fact that Peedi didn't trust her, or the fact that he had a valid reason not to. Either way, it made her mad—and made her think. Knowing what she knew right now regarding Gloria Rivera could get her killed or save her life. But in order to do that, names would have to be given, and lives would have to be taken. And at the end of it all, it could be back to square one: Simfany and Santana.

That thought alone broke her heart, because it was some people that she had grown to love through the journey. Hadn't she inadvertently harmed enough people already as is?

What was going to take place the next day with Carlos, Simfany hadn't had the slightest idea. She hadn't seen her friend in a long time. The meeting was long overdue, and she wasn't worried at all. Their war had nothing to do with her, and after her visit, it would remain like that.

If it was one thing that Simfany knew for a fact—it was a fact that Carlos would believe her over anybody and everybody. The only person that may have stood a chance to convince Carlos that Simfany had betrayed him in such a manner was already gone.

Simfany knew deep down inside she had no reason to sweat, but it wasn't her that she was worried about.

It was the man sitting across from her that she feared for.

***

Zach drifted in and out of unconsciousness. He felt too good from the weed he had been blowing on all day. He had lost track of time a while ago.

Man, where the fuck is this nigga? Zach thought, pissed, looking at the cable box that sat on top of the TV. The red numbers said the time was 7:24 p.m.

Zach sighed and reached into the ashtray. He blew the ashes off the blunt and lit it back up. The smoke gripped his insides tightly before he opened his mouth and exhaled.

Being in North Carolina was Zach's first real feeling of peace in a long time—a very long time. The war that had been going on was changing Zach's heart and soul. What he used to care about and yearn for no longer pegged his interest. All Zach wanted nowadays was to catch a body. It didn't matter if he killed one of Torrey's people or caught a member of the Fuck Boys. The bloodshed of the opposition was all he cared about.

After assisting Santana with killing Sleeze, he craved blood. But he wanted his own confirmed kills. The night they stood over Sleeze and watched him take his last breath had forever changed Zach. The spot in his heart that once held love, contempt, warmth, and care was now hollow and callous. He felt nothing. He was numb to all the death that surrounded him.

Zach knew he had to adapt to survive. Just the shit he was going through alone baffled him. He could only imagine how Santana looked at life through his own eyes.

What Zach had expressed to Meme earlier was his raw feelings. Being scared was a real thing—shit, it was actually an understatement—but he pushed on daily, knowing any day could be his last.

A conversation he had with Haseem one day was what helped push him forward, to stay focused and on point. He remembered the conversation as if it just happened days ago.

Zach remembered it clearly—it wasn't something he could ever forget.

It was about the facial expression of a FB member Haseem caught lacking. And Santana being Santana, he tried to explain his logic on the situation. But Haseem's hard-headed ass never wanted to listen to shit anybody else had to say. What Santana said went in one ear and out the other, like always. The memory of that very conversation would vividly stick with him until his dying date.

"Why didn't you send that nigga off, son? What the fuck?" Santana asked, confused and angry.

"Because that bitch-ass nigga ain't want no problems. Talkin' all that hot shit. He a bitch. That nigga was scared to death when he saw me hit that corner," Haseem boasted, the biggest smile plastered across his face.

Santana didn't find the gloating to be cool, funny, or cute. What he *did* find was Haseem to be one of the stupidest kind of niggas he had ever met—and he was just one of many. Santana tried to hold his tongue and let his friends live their own lives, but Haseem's ignorance just couldn't be ignored. So he spoke on what he felt.

"So let me get this straight—you let a nigga that would kill you live because his fear boosted your ego?"

Haseem got quiet.

The look of anger flashed across Haseem's face. *The changing of color in your face tells me I hit a nerve,* Santana thought. *"Listen, son,"* Santana continued, *"a wise man once told me: Dangerous minds hide behind unfocused eyes. That fuckin' means, a man who is taken as a joke because of the fear he portrays is never seen as a threat . . . until it's too late. You's a stupid muthafucka, son, I swear. I can bet my mother's life if that shit was the other way around, he'd be shopping while they fitting you for a casket, thinking to himself how easy that money was to collect off your goofy ass."*

That memory would stick with Zach until the day he was called upon by God. Because though Haseem was in his feelings, Santana's words, unfortunately, rang true. Not even two weeks later, the first time Haseem was spotted by the Fuck Boy clique, he was killed without hesitation.

Zach had asked himself many times: *Why? Why Haseem? Why not me? Why not Santana?*

And who the fuck thought like Santana did at times like that?

Zach looked at Santana's thought process as being unique, when in all reality, all Santana was—was a nigga that didn't want to die. He wanted to live, like everyone else. Zach had to admit now that the grief Santana gave them was for a reason. Santana moved accordingly to the situation at hand, whereas he and Haseem didn't—and Haseem losing his life was a product of that carelessness.

They figured niggas was just talking, running their mouths as usual. The only one out of the three who took the threat seriously was Santana.

Zach shook his head at his own foolishness and took another pull from the blunt in his hand. The smoke lingered, and he watched it swirl through the air until it disappeared. The loud smoke held in his lungs for a minute before he finally exhaled, letting out whatever didn't evaporate.

His mind had been on Haseem a lot lately. He just still couldn't believe that his best friend was dead—gone out of his life forever. Never having the chance to make a family, to be a father, a husband, or even a better son. A rash decision had cost Haseem his life.

Before this is all over . . . will that same decision cost me mine? Zach thought, afraid of knowing the real answer.

It was sad.

Zach just shook his head from side to side as thoughts and memories of him and Haseem flashed through his mind. He put the blunt back to his lips and pulled—it was out.

"Damn," Zach cussed when he realized the blunt had gone out yet again.

Zach sat at the edge of the loveseat and placed the blunt into the ashtray that sat in the middle of the living room table. He looked at the tail end of the blunt he was just smoking on and snarled his nose. Zach really didn't care too much for the habit for real, but it was his only way of coping with life at the moment. Plus, he knew he had to enjoy the pleasures of getting high while he had the chance, because back in Charleston, smoking was a no-no for him. After seeing how Sleeze got caught lacking, he vowed to never be a victim of those circumstances.

Fuck no! Zach thought to himself as he laid back on the couch.

The creaking in the floor snapped Zach back to reality. He stopped suddenly, feeling for the Glock on his waist. Zach's heart was pounding.

"Zachariah," Meme called from the top of the stairs, calming Zach's heart.

That's why I need to stop fucking smoking, man, Zach thought to himself. He was too high—he forgot that he was good, in a safe environment, surrounded by love.

Zach smiled at the thought of even being in North Carolina. He was happy he decided to make the trip because he hadn't seen his second family in a while. And at the rate he and Santana was going, it very well may be the last time he would see them.

Thinking about his extended family, Zach looked at his black and gold G-Shock. The watch read 7:40 p.m.

What the fuck? Where can this nigga be? Zach asked himself. He thought of everything but came up empty.

At that exact moment, he also realized that little Aaliyah wasn't running around everywhere and Momma Cat wasn't talking her shit like always. It could only mean they were together. Zach relaxed his mind and closed his eyes.

"Zachariah!"

Zach laughed when he heard Meme yell his name again, this time louder. He got up and made his way to the bottom of the staircase.

"Yooo!" Zach called back.

"Can you see if—" was all Zach heard before Meme's words drowned out.

Meme stood at the top of the stairs with nothing on but a red lace, matching bra and panty set by Victoria's Secret. Zach tried to be respectful and look away, but he just couldn't. He couldn't help but stare.

Meme's 5'8", 170-pound frame was almost God-like—complimented by her doe-shaped eyes, round ass, and thick thighs. Zach was mesmerized. He had never seen Meme in just her bra and panties before, so it fucked him up.

"Zach! Did you hear me?" Meme asked from the top of the landing, smiling from ear to ear.

She found it funny how a simple Victoria's Secret set could fuck a nigga up.

"Nah . . . nah . . . I ain't hear you, what you say?" Zach replied nervously.

Between being fried and nervous, he was all fucked up.

"I said can you see if my momma and them pulled up yet? Stoney and Liyah went shopping with her this afternoon."

"What time they supposed to be back?"

"Between eight, eight-thirty. Why?" Meme asked curiously.

"A'ight, bet. You got enough time then. It's seven-forty right now—well, seven-forty-three to be exact."

Meme shifted her stance, confusion written all over her face. She had no clue what Zach was talking about.

"Time for what? What the hell are you talking about?"

"To put some clothes on . . . or let me dig ya shit from the back. Either or, you got roughly 20 minutes."

Zach responded confidently. He was shocked at himself for the words he had just spoken, but how he felt—why not shoot his shot? All she could do was cuss him out and say no. Either way, he ain't have shit to lose.

"Little boy, you wouldn't be able to do shit with all of this, fuck is you talking about."

Meme smacked her ass and watched it jiggle.

Zach took the gun off his waist and sat it on the step nearest to him, then began unbuckling his belt.

Meme started laughing.

"Boy, what do you think you're doing?" Meme asked flirtatiously.

"I'm 'bout to show you ain't shit little on me but my muthafuckin' feet," Zach responded as he ascended the stairs.

"Little boy, if you don't go ahead—"

"What? You scared you gone be chasin' me afterwards? You keep talkin' all this hot shit. Let me show you. I'd never tell a soul," Zach said seriously, now standing directly in front of Meme.

Meme thought for a minute before she sighed deeply, mouthed fuck it, and reached for the button on Zach's True Religion jeans. Once Meme got past his jeans, she slid her hand into his pants and grabbed his penis.

Meme looked up in Zach's eyes and gasped in surprise. She instinctively bit her bottom lip in lust, before closing her eyes and yanking back and forth along his shaft, helping him grow harder and stronger by the second.

"Ummmm . . . damn, nigga," Meme moaned, just thinking about the possibilities.

Zach moved slightly closer, their bodies touched, and without a second longer, Zach leaned forward and kissed Meme passionately. They both were in pure bliss.

Their tongues found each other as they explored deliciously—it was as if their tongues were in a fight for position on top. Zach's hand roamed Meme's body until he felt the fabric of her laced bra. He cupped her one of her breasts in his hand—well, what could fit at least—and rubbed her lightly.

The moan that escaped her mouth made Zach's dick jump in her palm.

Zach's hand roamed along Meme's bra until he felt her nipple poking through the soft fabric. He pinched it lightly. Meme moaned on contact, turning Zach on to the max.

"Ummmmph." Zach was rock-hard in Meme's hand. She rubbed the head of his dick gently until pre-cum oozed from his penis. They locked eyes for a second. Meme took her hand from out of his boxers and licked the pre-cum from her palm, never breaking eye contact.

Zach shivered. He didn't know what just happened, but Meme had just shot a chill through his body—one that he had never felt before. *What the fuck!* Zach thought in bliss.

"Okay, little nigga, I see you got something you can do damage with. Now show me. Make me want this dick again. How much time we got left?"

"It don't even matter, we'll hear them pull up," Zach replied lustfully.

"I'm all yours then, daddy." Meme winked and waited on Zach's next move.

Zach knew he only had a short period of time, so he needed to figure out what he wanted to do—and fast. Whatever it was, it would have to be memorable. Zach knew he would have to leave his mark.

Zach grabbed Meme by the waist, turning her over. He let Meme position herself in any way that comforted her best. Once she got situated, Zach spat into the palm of his hand and rubbed his saliva along the head and shaft of his dick, making it easier to enter Meme's vagina.

God damn, Zach thought, taking a mental photo of Meme's wide hips and thick thighs. He couldn't wait any longer. He pulled Meme's panties to the side and rubbed the head of his dick along the wet lips of Meme's pussy. A moan escaped Meme's lips, hungry for Zach to enter her. She reached back and grabbed a hold of Zach's dick, guiding him slowly into her. Meme let go as Zach pushed, watching inch after inch disappear into her wound.

Zach pulled out after he got halfway in, then pushed back, starting the process over and over again—only this time digging deeper than the last.

Meme clawed at the wall and bit her bottom lip so she wouldn't holler. Zach began to pick his pace up once Meme got accustomed to the size of his dick, finding himself a rhythm. Meme's pussy was so tight and wet, he couldn't compare it to nothing he had ever felt in his life.

Meme tried to hold her composure, but her panting was getting louder and louder. Motivated, Zach picked his pace up another notch, hitting the pussy so hard that her ass and titties jiggled wildly with each thrust. Zach was crushing Meme deeply.

"Daddy . . . oooh . . . ummmmm . . . ummmm . . . shhi . . . daddy . . . fuck this pussy . . . plea . . . se . . . daddy . . . ooooohhh . . ." Meme cried out in pleasure.

Zach put both his hands on her right ass cheek and started hitting her harder and faster, angled sideways as he slammed into her pussy. That sent Meme over the top.

"Fuck! Ohh my . . . gawd . . . ummmm . . . ummmmmph . . . Za . . . ch . . . oh fuck. Owwww . . . owww . . . daddyyyyy!"

Meme began crying real tears, almost scaring Zach out the pussy, but her moans of pleasure kept his pace steady. Zach wanted to feel her in every way possible, so he slowed down and began to make love to Meme's pretty ass. He knew he very well may never get to make love to Meme again, so he had to savor every moment.

"Damn, daddy, you feel this? This pussy yours, huh?" When Zach didn't answer, she looked back at him and asked again. "Is it? You want this pussy to be yours, Zach? Ummmm . . . right there. Damn little nigga, what the fuck!"

Meme slowly began grinding into Zach, taking him deeper into her stomach.

"Is it? Tell me this pussy mine, Mia . . . tell me. Tell me I'll be able . . . fuck, this shit fire. Tell me I can have this pussy anytime I want . . . tell me and mean it." Zach said, pushing into Meme as far as his pelvis would allow. It was nowhere else for him to explore; he was hitting the bottom of her vagina.

"Daddy . . . I swear any . . . time . . . is wear . . . ooohh. Damn, Zach. Faster, you got a bitch . . . falling in love."

Zach picked his pace up slightly, but his pace was controlled—he was making love to her.

Meme started throwing her ass into him with rapid speed. Zach held on and matched her pace.

"Oh, shit, I'm 'bout to cum, Mia. What you . . . want me to do?" Zach asked, trying his hardest to hold back from exploding.

"Fuck!" Meme moaned, ignoring Zach's statement.

Zach turned slightly to the side without missing a beat. He entered Meme at various angles, sending her into a frenzy.

"Zach, I'm 'bout to—" Meme couldn't talk. The pain felt too good. She was in an ecstasy she hadn't experienced in a very long time. Meme threw her ass in circles as she exploded, damn near buckling from the pressure. Zach held onto her tightly and kept her on her feet.

Meme could feel Zach's dick beginning to swell before he warned her that he was also about to cum.

"Ma . . . fuck . . . I'm 'bout to cum . . . what you—"

Zach's words were washed out by the honking of a horn.

Honk! . . . Honk!

Fuck! Zach cussed to himself.

Meme, on the other hand, didn't pay it no mind. She turned around and dropped to her knees, taking Zach into her mouth. She knew she didn't have time to waste—she sucked him sloppy and fast.

Meme tickled the bottom of Zach's balls as she deep-throated him slowly, before picking up her pace.

"What the fuck, damn, Ma." Zach grabbed Meme's head as his toes curled and released his semen down her throat.

Meme sucked on Zach slowly, savoring every moment.

Honk! . . . Honk! . . . Honk!

"Ma, you trippin'," Zach said anxiously, looking down the stairs at the front door, hoping and praying that Ms. Kat or Stoney didn't walk through.

Meme ignored him and pulled his dick out her mouth. Zach laughed as he reached down and outstretched his hand in an attempt to help Meme to her feet.

"We gotta hurry up, Mia, before ya mother gets to showing her ass."

Meme shrugged nonchalantly, as if she didn't give a fuck.

"She'll be okay. But if you worried, take that ass downstairs and help them with them bags, playboy. My ass is about to get back in this shower," Meme replied, throwing Zach the peace sign. "Oh, and by the way, thank you for that fire ass dick. I can't believe your little ass is acting like that. You definitely got the keys to these panties if you act right. That's on Liyah. Just saying."

It was all Meme said before she disappeared into the bathroom.

Zach beamed with pride. Snapping out of his reverie, Zach fixed himself and descended the stairs. He took in a deep breath, retrieved his gun from the staircase, and opened the door smiling from ear to ear.

Chapter 8

Tez-Mo sat calmly across from his mother, his niece, and his younger brother. He was at a loss for words. Not only had his 10-year-old niece, Diamond, lost her mother, but she also just lost her father to the war that him and Kev had started. The red eyes that stared back at him crushed him to the core. The reason he even killed like he did in the first place was to make it home every night to these very people. The people he seems to bring endless pain to.

“So what’s your plan now, Teziar? Kevin? We are literally all that remains of the Brooks family. What are we doing, Teziar? Huh? You want to call the shots, make all the damn noise; what are we going to do now, Tez-Mo?” Ms. Brooks said sarcastically. Tez-Mo rubbed his head in frustration.

“Ma, please stop. I know you blame me for all this shit goin’ on—and I’ll eat that. But you not finna blame that thirsty ass nigga Reese on me. You heard the story as well as I did. That nigga saw a bad bitch that seemed to be having car issues at 3 a.m. and thought with his dick. It’s the only logical explanation — his dick the only thing he coulda been fuckin’ thinking with that night. Who the fuck falls for a bitch having car trouble that late at night? Not only that, but a bitch you ain’t never seen before, parked dead in the middle of your own hood?

Nah. I take blame for a lot, but no disrespect, lil’ momma — I ain’t takin' this one. And neither is Kev.” Tez-Mo shook his head side to side, emphasizing his seriousness.

He just couldn't let this blood fall on him—not this time. His hands already stained with too much.

Not this time, Tez-Mo thought to himself. He could admit when he was responsible for damage done, but to sit and take blame over a nigga's thirsty ways? Nah, fuck that.

Reese was supposed to be at home with his only daughter, promising her safety–comforting her in the most difficult time of her life. He should've been mourning the death of his other half, not out tryin' to get his dick wet only weeks later.

Tez-Mo held no sympathy for Reese bitch ass or his family. They could all suck his dick for that matter.

"But they came looking for—" Tez-Mo cut her off before she could even finish the sentence.

"Granted. But because me and lor bro been out there making muthafuckas feel our pain, we should have sent you and Momma off to a safe location. I been so consumed in painting this city red that I lacked attention here, and I'm sorry. I'm so very, very sorry. I don't know if I'll make it to see tomorrow. I only live to keep you two alive. So as long as I know that my favorite two women are safe, I'm good. You feel me?" Tez-Mo said, cutting Ms. Brooks' words short.

Tez-Mo knew what she wanted to say, and at this point, he was getting tired of being blamed for all the murder and mayhem going on around the city. He hadn't started the war—but if God so help him—he was gone end it, no matter how many bodies had to be dropped.

When Ms. Brooks just sat in silence, legs crossed, with no reply, Tez-Mo continued his rant.

"I got my nigga from Houston coming to make sure you and Diamond land . . ."

Zzzzz . . . zzzz . . . zzzz . . . zzzz

"Safely. Hold on," Tez-Mo said, slightly lifting off the couch, digging his phone out his back pocket. He opened it. One new message.

//: Gloria's dead!

A bead of sweat formed on Tez-Mo's forehead. The message was bold and to the point. That was all Wanda had said.

Tez-Mo looked up from his phone and met his brother's gaze. He sighed and texted Wanda back:

//: Pull up. We need to talk!

He didn't know how he was gonna break the news to his brother. He would have to figure that out later, 'cause bringing that up in front of his mother and niece? That wasn't happening.

"Anyway, the lor nigga should be here in the next few hours. Pack everything you think is a must that you need, want, crave, or desire, 'cause you will never step foot in this house again."

Ms. Brooks gasped in protest but was stopped by Tez-Mo's lifted hand.

"Dang, Ma, can I finish without all the theatrics, please? Me and Kev bought you and Diamond a nice house out in Houston. We put a down payment on the house, so you will have to pay a monthly mortgage, but we also paid your mortgage up for a year so you can get on ya feet until we get down there. Oh, and before I forget—Kev bought you a Chevy Malibu. Also paid for. A 2006 model. Am I forgetting anything, lor bro?" Tez-Mo asked his brother.

Kev looked up like he was thinking.

"Uhhhh . . . I think so. Hold up, that green done burnt my mind slap out. Oh yeah, we got y'all a whole new wardrobe, and some new furniture. I know you loved this spot, Ma, so me and Tez tried to go above and beyond to make this new house your home. We just want y'all safe, Ma. This hustling shit we do—at the end of the day—it's for all of us. Always has been," Kev said, wiping the tears from his mother's eyes.

"We will send everything else that can't fit in your suitcases next week. That cool? I just want y'all as far away from this war as possible. Shit about to get real wicked," Tez-

Mo said, solely with Gloria on his mind. "I can't express how sorry I am, but Momma . . . Diamond . . . I will make it up to you. How? Shit, I have no muthafuckin' clue, but I will. I promise."

Tez-Mo rubbed his goatee—a sign of nervousness for him. But they knew the words he spoke, he meant wholeheartedly.

Diamond walked up to him and hugged him tightly, then looked up. Tez-Mo looked at her innocent soul and smiled.

"Then just stop, Uncle Tezzi. No more people has to die. My mommy—" Diamond began crying at just the thought of Sasha.

Kevin walked over and picked his niece up into his arms. He held and rocked her while she cried her eyes out on his shoulder.

Kev continued to rock his niece like he used to back when she was just an infant. The good ol' days. The days when Sasha was still here. Kev walked out the living room and into the hall that led to Diamond's room. He needed a second as well—to release his own tears. Kevin held onto his niece tightly and wept, finally releasing some of his guilt, heartache, and pain.

Back in the living room, Ms. Brooks looked around the place she once called a home and didn't recognize none of it. Every happy time that had ever taken place in that house was gone, erased, forgotten, and overshadowed by the shooting death of her precious and beloved daughter. The death of Sasha had taken precedence over it all.

Nancy Brooks hated the thought of even sitting in that fucking house—period.

She closed her eyes and took a few deep breaths. She needed to calm herself. She didn't wanna cry. She was so tired of crying. It made nothing better whatsoever. Ms. Brooks had just come to live with the fact that she had to continue going. She had to keep going for Diamond. Some days she just couldn't see how she made it.

Ms. Brooks opened her eyes and exhaled loudly before she began to talk to Tez-Mo about the war that was going on.

"What's going on, baby? Like really? What did y'all do to start a war of this magnitude? For real, tell me—what did you do?"

Tez-Mo looked away from his mother shamefully. He could barely look her in her eyes. He had no real answer for her. All he knew was what he assumed—him and his brother got pulled into some shit that was deeper than them.

"When does it stop, Teziar?"

"You want the God's honest truth, ma'am?" he asked sincerely.

"Yes, son. Yes, I do," Ms. Brooks responded, moving to the edge of the couch so Tez-Mo could feel like he had her undivided attention.

"When me and Kevin are dead."

Tez-Mo's answer sucked the life out of his mother. Ms. Brooks started crying instantly. She now understood this very visit could be her and Diamond's last one with her boys, and it truly saddened her heart. She wiped her face with the sleeve of her Old Navy hoodie.

Tez-Mo could see the answer fucked his mother up, but it was nothing but the truth. There was no reason to sugarcoat anything. Tez-Mo knew any day could very well be his last.

"I better see you and your brother again, Teziar. Do you hear me? I'm not fuckin' playing with you!"

Ms. Brooks cried harder, covering her face with her hands.

Tez-Mo got up and knelt in front of her. He tried to grab a hold of her thigh but was swatted away almost instantly.

"Teziar, please . . . not right now. Please," Ms. Brooks said as she looked up, eyes red from crying.

"Y'all are all I have left. Don't let these muthafuckas kill my baby, Teziar . . ." Ms. Brooks paused for a moment and looked her oldest child dead in his eyes. She wanted to make sure he understood her next words crystal clear.

"I'm serious, Teziar. You better protect your brother or . . . or . . . I will kill you myself. You got him into this gang nonsense–you better get him out of it. And I mean it. Kill whoever needs to be killed, and then you come to me and Diamond. Deal?" Ms. Brooks asked, sticking out her pinky, a gesture she picked up from Diamond.

"Deal," was all Tez-Mo could say in response. A pang of guilt ran through him because he knew that he most likely was making an empty promise to his mother. But it was the only answer he was willing to give her. He knew it would settle her worries.

Tez-Mo got off his bended knee and cuddled up next to his mother, hugging her tightly. "I love you, Momma Bear. I love you with all my heart."

"I . . . lo . . . ve . . . you too, s . . . s . . . son," Ms. Brooks said in between sobs. "I will always love you and your brother forever, you hear me?" she said in reply, pulling her firstborn closer into her.

No more words needed to be spoken—the love automatically transferred from one soul to the next.

Ms. Brooks laid her head on Tez-Mo's chest and cried silently to the rhythm of his broken heart.

***

After Ms. Brooks and Diamond left, the only people left were Tez-Mo and his little brother Kevin, like always. Ever since the pair lost Piru, Stacks, and Hood Ru, they had been out on their own—together—fending for themselves.

Now, as Tez-Mo sat and pondered his thoughts, he stared at the bold letters that appeared across his cellphone. He thought of the best way to address the situation, because he knew that when Kev heard the news of Gloria's demise, he would trip out and want to kill the world. So he had to approach the situation strategically. He knew his brother, and he knew his brother well. They were already at war with every Crip nigga in the county—some even city-wide—so starting yet another war was almost suicidal. They didn't need more issues added to their current ones, but how would he be able to get Kev to understand that?

That was the real question.

Tez-Mo's thoughts were interrupted when Kev came into the living room and sat down, Hennessy bottle in hand.

"Bro, that shit crazy how—" Kevin looked at his brother and sighed.

When does the bullshit stop? Kev asked himself as he sipped from the Hennessy bottle in his hand. He knew the look all too well—something was wrong. Somebody was either about to die or his brother was stressed to the max and had some shit he needed to get off his chest. And being honest with himself, Kev could really care less about either one at the moment. All he wanted to do was relax and drown some of his pain away with the bottle he held in his hand.

Kev acted oblivious to his brother's temperament and sipped on his Hennessy, awaiting the bullshit to begin.

After a few minutes of silence, Kev looked up and stared at his brother. Tez-Mo was looking back at him with fury in his eye.

Kevin: "Why you looking at me like that, lor nigga?"

Tez-Mo: (*laughing*) "No reason, shorty. Just trying to enjoy what down time we got, for real. Feel me? At least now we know Ma and Diamond are safe for sure—we really can turn up now, ya heard. That aside, it look like you got something on your mind. You want to talk about it?"

Tez-Mo didn't even respond. He didn't really know how to, so he just reached his phone over to Kev so he could read Wanda's message himself.

Kev took hold of the phone, curious, and read the message. He handed the phone back just as fast as he received it. The gesture threw Tez-Mo for a loop, because instead of Kev flipping out and demanding blood, his eyes showed signs of recognition.

Tez-Mo: "Ooookay," he said awkwardly, grabbing his phone back from his brother. "Talk to me, my nigga, because I'm lost a little right now. If I know one person in life you loved, it was that woman right there. So—"

Kevin: "She tried to set us up, shorty. I couldn't let her live."

Tez-Mo: "Nigga what? What the fuck is you talking about, yo?"

Now it was Tez-Mo's turn to be at a loss for words. He was speechless, to say the least. It was no way he just heard Kev say that Gloria tried to set them up. No way. *Fuck no,* Tez-Mo said to himself as the information Kevin just told him registered.

Gloria tried to set us up? With who? What the fuck? Tez-Mo's thoughts ran rapid through his head. He looked at Kev dumbfounded, awaiting an explanation.

Kev could see that the information was fucking with Tez-Mo's mental, so he explained . . .

Kevin: "Alright, look . . . that night Gloria came back outta nowhere, that shit wasn't coincidental. She helped set shit in motion with the Puerto Rican bitch—remember the one that the homies said they seen that night having car troubles? Gloria was the one who pointed out our traps and known locations. Unfortunately, that thirsty ass nigga Reese bit, sending Lor Twan to hell with him. The Puerto Rican bitch came through looking for us—me, in particular—because she thought Gloria could most likely sway me into getting in her car and riding with her to Joppa Towne. Gloria had shorty convinced that I was still in love with her or something, and no lie, shorty was right. I've always felt like I was the one that fucked up. When we killed her cousin, shorty never muttered another word to me. The Rican bitch tried to use that fact to her advantage. But you know Gloria green as fuck to this street shit. Because in all reality, if Glo invested any real time in getting back, I would be a dead man, that's for sure. But anyway, Gloria was supposed to take me to the spot I used to beat her shit at—and I'm guessing that's where muthafuckas was gone end me. And probably her stupid ass too."

Kev explained all this nonchalantly as he took another sip from the bottle of Hennessy in his hand.

Tez-Mo couldn't contain himself—he busted out laughing. He laughed at how they almost were caught slipping, big time. The opposition just didn't know what kind of play they had, if they just had patience.

Tez scratched his beard as he looked at his brother, trying to process the information he just gave him.

Fuck . . . Fuck . . . Fuck! Tez-Mo thought.

"So, did she tell you who the fuck these people are that's try'na kill us? Or did your emotions blow the only fuckin' lead we had? Because that's what it sounds like. I'm not trying to tell you what—"

"Yeah you are, shorty! But it's cool, because at the end of the day you right, a nigga dropped the ball. I wasn't thinking logically. You gotta think, shorty, this is my first love we talking 'bout. I know we slimed lor momma's peoples out, but my nigga, we had no inclination that she was of any relation to these niggas. It was a war going on, you asked for my help and I came. Flat out!"

Kev interjected before taking another swig from the liquor bottle in his hand.

"I understand all that, bro, but what the fuck happened?" Tez-Mo asked, confused on what the hell his brother was rambling about.

"Bro, I really can't explain it . . . Okay, look . . . Let me tell you like this. If shorty didn't give me every sign possible that she was on bullshit, I would be dead. You know where the Sheetz gas station is? The one they just built in Joppatowne?"

"Yeah. You talking 'bout the Sheetz that run along Route 40?" Tez-Mo asked, trying to figure out where his brother was going with the story.

"Yup, that's it. Anyway, I had shorty take me there, and on the way out I see her on the phone talkin' to someone. Before I cleared the door, she hangs the phone up, and though it looked mad suspicious, the love I got for shorty made me overlook it. I thought the bitch was . . . as a matter of fact, what time did we leave your drunk ass passed out on that curb?" Kev asked Tez-Mo the question with laughter in his voice.

Tez-Mo shook his head from side to side. He knew his brother was missing some screws, but damn—finding the situation amusing was disturbing.

And I thought I was the crazy one. Tez-Mo looked up indecisively, checking his memory bank to figure the around-about time they arrived at the trap house. He could not remember exactly, but he knew that the time Kev was talking about was in the wee hours of the morning.

"I can't even tell you for real. It had to be between 2:30 and 4 a.m. I had to hear Wanda's mouth all night because of it."

"My fuckin' point exactly! I come out the store and this bitch talking 'bout she on the phone with her grandmother Ru, you hear me? Her muthafuckin' grandmother. I let it slide because she not my bitch no more, to be trippin' over. But my instincts are telling me one thing, while my heart is telling me something totally different. The vibe was just awkward—I really can't explain it. Not one to take chances, I slip my hands slowly to my hip. As we inched closer and closer, I could feel something was definitely wrong. I looked over at Gloria's beautiful face and I just can't see shorty betraying me in no way, shape or form. So I begin to loosen up a bit. I try to at least. When we finally pulled up to the spot behind Sheetz, I wasted no time—I begin to ask questions. Lots of them. Instead of this bitch stalling with her answers, she tells me everything. She explained what was supposed to happen to me at this meeting spot. Before I get to say anything further, she pulls off and hits Route 40. I pull my gun and put it on my lap, awaiting the bullshit. After I realized we were the only car on the road, I relaxed. I began to listen to what she had to say. Gloria starts professing her love for me, but gang, I'm already seeing red. Lor momma ain't stand a chance. I ain't gone lie—maybe if this happened before losing Sasha, just maybe, I might have spared her. If our baby has to rest easy, nigga, everybody has to rest easy. You hear me, Ru? Everybody! I don't know why she thought she had one, like we gone ride off into the sunset together." Kev laughed deeply before continuing:

"I don't know what the fuck she was thinking, big bro."

Tez-Mo reached out for the bottle Kev held in his hand. Kev took a quick sip and handed the pint-size bottle over to Tez-Mo as he finished telling the story of Gloria's demise:

"So, shorty drove us back to her spot in Glen Burnie somewhere. Don't ask, because I have no clue why I drove with her all the way out there. Anyway, as soon as we parked, I looked around to make sure it was no one or anything that could identify me. Once I realized all was well and I wasn't being watched, I sparked her goofy ass."

Tez-Mo chuckled and shook his head as he handed the bottle of Hennessy back to Kev. Kevin grabbed the bottle, sitting it on the table in front of him.

"You good?" Kev asked, tilting the bottle toward his older brother.

"I'm good, bro. Thank you. But my question is . . . how did you make it back to the county without incident?" Tez-Mo asked curiously.

Kev laughed. He didn't really know what his brother wanted to hear, so he just told him the truth:

"I just walked to the bus stop and got on the bus."

Tez-Mo looked at Kev like he lost his marbles. "So hold on, hold on. You telling me that you popped this bitch, then just loaded the bus, lor nigga? What the fuck, shorty—you trippin'."

Tez-Mo thought about the blue light cameras that flooded the corners in the city and asked the most obvious question that was lingering in his mind.

"Did they have any blue's on their corners?" he asked, referring to the blue light cameras strategically placed on every light pole in Baltimore City.

Kev looked at his brother all crazy and responded, irritation in his voice.

"Nigga, fuck no! What the fuck you take me for?"

"A dumb ass nigga! That's what the fuck I take ya dumb ass for. Just drop the shit, man. This shit making my head hurt, shorty," Tez-Mo replied.

Tez-Mo closed his eyes and sighed deeply. He was truly taken aback by it all. Not in a million years could he fathom Kev being capable of killing Gloria Rivera—his first love, shit, his only love. But then again, he also couldn't fathom having to bury his baby sister either. But they did. Eventually.

Just the thought made Tez-Mo cringe with anger. Still to this day, he had nightmares about his sister's funeral being shot up. The dreams hadn't gone away, he just eventually got used to them. He used those very dreams to fuel the fire burning deep down inside his soul.

Well I guess she got what she was begging for, Tez-Mo thought to himself as he took another swig from the Hennessy bottle. He let the liquor bury his pain and wiped his mouth as he continued:

"Fuck that bitch, shorty. But now it's a must that we are on point like no other time before this. You remember when we dropped that lor fat Dominican nigga, Cito? Carlos put them killers on our ass. Granted, we survived, but that was when we had a team—a team of niggas just like us, if not more vicious. And what was yo's name? The lor crazy nigga from over East?" Tez-Mo snapped his fingers together, trying his damn best to remember.

His mind was no good today. The drugs were winning, for sure, because his memory was shot to hell.

“Bro, you know who I’m talking 'bout. The clean-cut nigga, always wore fly ass suits out this bitch. Light-skin, yo, with the waves—he rode with us during that war against Carlos. He was our plug for a minute. He wind up squashing the beef between us and Carlos. You don’t know who I’m talking about?” Tez-Mo tried his best to explain the person he was referring to. The name stood right at the tip of his tongue, but it just wouldn’t come to fruition.

“Byrd? You talking 'bout my muthafuckin’ nigga Byrd?” Kev said, smiling at all the memories of Byrd.

Tez-Mo clapped and jumped out of his seat with excitement.

“Yeah, that’s shorty’s name! I fucked with that nigga, bro. That muthafucka was a live one for real. Back to what I was saying—we don’t have Byrd, Piru, Stacks, or Hood anymore. Even Blaze was about that action, but nigga, they all dead and gone. We the last two of a dying breed. But that dumb ass shit you just did mighta put us on borrowed time. You my brother though, nigga—so you already know how we rockin’, whether you right or wrong.” Tez-Mo laughed as he shook his head from side to side, then he went on: “But I still must admit, you dumb ass for that shit though.”

Kevin smiled nervously. He knew Tez-Mo was mad at the fact he made a decision so crucial without him. But the damage was already done—there was no reason to cry over spilled milk. Kev really ain’t have nothin’ he could say to appease his brother. He knew he had fucked up.

Fuck that bitch, Kev thought, grabbing the Hennessy off the table and taking a drink.

Boom . . . Boom . . . Boom . . . Boom . . . Boom . . . Boom!

The bottle fell from his hand as Kev instinctively grabbed for the Smith & Wesson .40 he held on his hip. He looked over toward his brother—Tez-Mo was already on his feet, running toward the door before Kev could even ask if he was alright.

"Fuck!" Kev cussed as he followed suit, gun drawn, ready to meet his maker.

Boc! Boc! Boc! Boc! Boc!

Tez-Mo stood on the lawn of his property and fired into the all-black Acura Legend as it sped down the residential street trying to escape. Kev opened fire beside his brother, lettin' his .40 bark in rapid succession—

Boc . . . Boc . . . Boc . . . Boc . . . Boc . . . Boc . . . Boc . . . Boc!

Sparks flew off the Acura, indicating contact, but the car never slowed down—escaping unharmed. *What the fuck?* Kev thought as he watched until their taillights disappeared. Kev heard a snap and turned around. *Man, I'm trippin',* he thought.

"Bro, call 911!" Tez-Mo screamed, surprisingly, as he took off running toward the sprawled-out body laying in the middle of the street.

Kev pulled out his phone and dialed 911, jogging after Tez-Mo to see if the person was still breathing and if rescue was even an option. When Kev ran up and saw the tears streaming down Tez-Mo's face, he was at first confused . . . until he looked over at the victim and gasped in horror, almost losing his breath.

Operator: "911, what's your emergency?"

Chapter 9

Earlier . . .

Detective Ramos sat posted a safe distance from the cream-and-beige house in the outskirts of Baltimore County, watching the Brooks family's every move—who came, who went.

The all-black Acura Legend he sat in kept him low and outta sight. Not only was the whip a rental, but the tints were dark as hell—couldn't nobody see in unless they pressed their face to the glass. And even then? They still wouldn't know it was him. Not a single soul—not Tez, not Kev, not even the boys in blue—woulda known it was him. His disguise? Flawless. He looked like a whole hippie—long dark hair, bandana tied tight, glasses sitting low on his nose.

Ramos wasn't out there on no cop shit. Nothing he saw or heard was getting reported, written, or recorded. This little adventure—'cause that's what he'd end up calling it—was really a mission to get answers that had been calling at his soul. He wanted to know who the Brooks brothers were beefing with. Who the fuck really pulled that wild-ass move at Sasha Brooks' funeral. Ramos wanted answers—nah, he needed 'em. This very well could be the connection he needed to begin to solve some of the murders going on in Baltimore City and Harford County. And on top of that, he needed to know who had the balls to spray up Sasha Brooks' whole damn casket, and who had the nuts to greenlight that shit in the first place.

Ramos was also smart enough to know that no police agency would ever be privy to that kind of information unless they hit the trenches and found out on their own, and that was exactly what he was doing.

Ramos took another sip of the coffee that sat in the cup holder. *Ewww!* he thought as he cringed. Every sip of the bitter-ass coffee had his stomach flipping, like he was 'bout to throw up everything he ate earlier. Shit was nasty, old, and ice-cold—like it'd been sitting there since last week. He had been sitting vigil for seven or eight hours now and all he had seen was Ms. Brooks and her niece come and go. To Ramos it looked as if they were packing up to leave for good, the luggage they had between the two wasn't something people took on a regular vacation. *Bout fucking time*, he had thought when he saw the two females hopping into a Chrysler Minivan with their belongings. Women and children should always be left out of the mess that the men in their family caused, because 9 out of 10 times they are oblivious to the things going on around them.

Ramos was disgusted. He moved his tongue around in his mouth trying to dissolve the taste of the bitter coffee that just seemed to linger. Ramos took a deep breath then sighed, sitting the coffee back into the holder and waited for any sign of life. The Feds was on BPD's ass heavy, got all law enforcement in Maryland running round fucking up the peace. Ramos had been telling them over and over who the real players was—but them fools wasn't listening. Ramos knew the Feds and Marshal Wakings were chasing ghosts. Sitting up in their offices talking that political science bullshit, not seeing the real—that this war between the Bloods and Crips ain't about turf. Ain't even about money no more. It was all cycles of revenge. From one killing to the next, Ramos knew if he couldn't just find out who was actually beefing with who he could get closer to solving some of the murders.

Shit was getting heavy. Folks dropping like flies left and right—including his day-one, Kenny Lawson. If Ramos really wanted to untangle this web of lies, betrayal, and bodies, he had to step into a world that wasn't never built for him. He had asked himself many of times, was it even worth it? Was the truth worth dying for? Never could Ramos come up with an answer, but here he sat in an unmarked car, disguised and ready to pry into the lives of two young killers.

The day was proving to be a long one, activity at a minimum, making him second guess the reason behind following the Brooks brothers in the first place. He sighed in pure frustration as he stretched trying yet again to get comfortable in the cramped Acura Legend. Ramos pulled the lever on the seat to recline it further in pursuit of making his night a wee bit easier. He pushed the seat all the way back, then changed his mind. He knew damn well if he shut his eyes, he'd be out cold. Ramos looked at the Brooks home in pure disbelief, he didn't know if he was just missing the action, but since he'd been running surveillance on the brothers, the only action they had were the night Reese and Twan got killed, and they had nothing to do with that. And even then he had to make a choice on what brother he wanted to follow after they split up. Unbeknownst to him, he chose Tez-Mo, the more aggressive one, missing the biggest break and murder of his career. *Fuck it. I'ma just keep sitting*. Ramos's thought was cut short when all of a sudden a shadowy figure appeared out of nowhere, startling Ramos, making him jump out of his seat literally.

Ramos was so consumed with boredom that he hadn't been paying attention to his surroundings. Ramos rubbed his head, trying to soothe the pain; a knot began to form in the spot where he banged off the ceiling of the car. He never took his eyes off the shadowy figure as he slid down into his seat, hoping the person outside the car didn't hear the loud commotion as they walked past.

But by the way the dark figure stopped and looked around, Ramos knew then, he wasn't that lucky.

"Man, fuck!" Ramos cussed. The person had heard him and was now looking for the source of the noise. Ramos wasted no time and reached for the glove compartment. It was where he kept his Rock Island G1 Standard 1911. Ramos opened the glove compartment, illuminating the interior just enough for someone to see inside momentarily if they chose to.

"Fuck!" Ramos shouted out of pure frustration as he tried to shut the glove compartment as quiet as possible.

"Please . . . Please . . . Please . . . Please . . . Please . . ." Ramos begged, hoping he didn't draw further attention.

Ramos looked up, disappointed. He didn't know which action caused the man to turn back around, but he did—and he looked Ramos directly in his eyes before reaching into the pocket of his dark hoodie.

Ramos dare not hesitate. He raised his .45 and fired through the windshield rapidly.

Boom . . . Boom . . . Boom . . . Boom . . . Boom . . . Boom!

A bloody mist sprayed the air as each bullet found its mark. Ramos watched as the figure crumbled to the ground. He kept his gun trained at the windshield a second longer to make sure the man was down for good. Ramos grabbed his ears, trying to stop the deafening sound that rang in his head.

"Ahhhh!" he cried, still clutching his ears.

Boc . . . Boc . . . Boc . . . Boc . . . Boc!

The smell of burnt gunpowder brought Ramos back to reality. The ringing in his ear began to lessen as his adrenaline surged. He turned the key in the ignition, and as soon as the car came to life, he shoved the gear into drive and smashed the gas, hoping to escape with his life.

"Oh, shit!" Ramos exclaimed, speeding through the back roads of Baltimore County. His adrenaline was pumping out of this world.

"What the fuck just happened?" he asked himself, dipping and dodging around every turn, trying to put more and more distance between himself and the Brooks' home. What was he going to do? He couldn't turn himself in—what would he say? Ramos knew he had no true explanation for why he was surveilling the Brooks residence in the first place.

So much was running through his head that he had to stop and think for a second. Everything at the moment seemed to be moving so fast—the car, the street signs, his mind, his heart. Everything was moving at warp speed.

Ramos slowed the Acura down to a crawl as he pulled along the side of the road. He got out, and no sooner than he opened the door, he began to throw up . . . The food and the coffee he had been consuming over the past few days came right up.

Ramos thought about all the shit his late partner had stumbled upon. *This shit isn't safe for one man alone to work*, he thought, wiping his mouth with the sleeve of his shirt. He leaned halfway out the car, not knowing what he was going to do next. For the moment, he just sat back and laid his forearm across his head in deep thought.

Ramos knew he had gotten himself into some deep shit. No matter how he twisted or turned the story, he was royally fucked. He closed his eyes and sighed deeply.

"Fuck! Fuck! Fuck! Fuck!" Ramos yelled at the top of his lungs, beating the dashboard with his fist.

"What the fuck are you going to do now, you fucking dumb ass?" Ramos asked himself out loud. He was vexed. How could he have let this happen? he thought for the umpteenth time.

He looked around the Acura's interior, then stepped out of the car completely into the warmth of the night. It wasn't summer quite yet, but for May it was hotter than usual—or was it just him?

Ramos looked at the damage done to the car. There was no way he was going to get away with what took place that night. The car alone raised red flags—until a thought popped into his head.

He was going to report the car stolen early in the morning and pray the shooting didn't come back to him in any way, shape, or form.

"That's exactly what the fuck I'm going to do," Ramos said enthusiastically.

He ran back to the Acura and grabbed the .45 off the passenger seat. He wiped his prints off the gun thoroughly before breaking it down into several small pieces. Ramos threw the barrel and the two remaining bullets into the shrubs along the side of the road and got back into the car.

He pulled off, tossing pieces of the gun every few miles until there was nothing left. Ramos found a deserted spot to park the Acura within walking distance from his home. With only a thirty-minute walk ahead of him, he made the call—the call that would clear him of all wrongdoing . . . or so he thought.

***

Zach sat the last of the groceries down on the dining table and sat down, he was tired. Those grocery bags had him winded.

"Do you need any help, Momma?" Zach asked, taking food out the bags in front of her.

"No," Momma C said simply. Zach looked at her—the reply had caught him off guard. The cheery demeanor that Momma Kat just had all of a sudden had disappeared.

"Damn, what I do?" Zach looked up, confused. Momma C looked back at Zach, like, *really?*

Zach was lost.

"You tell me."

"We will talk, Zachariah. Now leave me at peace, please." Zach didn't protest. He just got up from his seat and went about his business. He went into the living room and plopped down on the couch and turned the TV on. Zach flicked through the channels frustratingly. The way Momma C just played him made him feel a kind of way.

What the fuck did I do now? Zach thought curiously, as he continued flicking through the channels. He was honestly clueless why Momma C was pissed off at him. Zach wasn't 'bout to keep stressing about bullshit. He shrugged it off and let it go. He wasn't 'bout to be worried about something so minute, when he was having the best day of his life.

"Meme," Zach called out, getting off his ass. He walked to the bottom of the steps and called for Meme again. Zach leaned against the railing and waited on her to respond. The floor creaked above slightly right before Meme appeared gracefully at the top of the stairs.

"Yeah?" she answered, this time fully dressed in a T-shirt and some sweats.

"Whenever you get the chance, holla at me. It'll only take a few minutes. And what that nigga Stoney up there doing?" Zach asked in a matter-of-fact kind of way.

"His little dusty ass in the shower," Meme joked before walking down the stairs to Zach.

"What's up, boo? What's wrong?" Meme asked in a whisper, running her hand along his face. Zach closed his eyes as the chills ran down his spine.

"First off, you better stop. But nah seriously, ya mom's acting weird right now. Do you know why?"

"No, that lady a fuckin' nut, I been telling y'all that. She'll be a'ight. Let me finish getting Liyah ready for her bath and bed, then I'll pull up on you. We got some shit we need to discuss. The dynamics light-weight changed earlier. I feel like my insight should count for something. But like I said, that's for a later conversation," Meme said before leaning into Zach, tasting his lips.

"Ummm . . . Ummm . . . Ummm . . . Nigga, yo' Campbell's good."

Zach busted out laughing.

Meme winked at him before she turned around and ran back up the stairs to tend to her daughter. Meme left Zach stuck on stupid, craving more. Every time Zach saw Meme all he saw was what took place only a few hours ago. Zach still couldn't believe he lived out one of his fantasies. He just smiled and walked back into the living room.

Zach was so caught up in thought of Meme that he was oblivious to someone else watching them.

Momma C was leaning against the living room panel—the door frame that separated the kitchen from the living room. She just watched as Zach diddy-bopped into the living room with not a care in the world. He was so comfortable that he didn't even notice her presence. Momma C took a few steps closer and cleared her throat, startling him. Zach grabbed at his chest for a dramatic pause, before laughing it off.

"Follow me, little nigga." Zach was taken aback by her demeanor.

Oh shit! he laughed to himself. Zach studied her. She didn't look mad, but she did look tired and annoyed. Job shit.

"Damn, follow you though. That shit sound too crazy," Zach admitted as he walked behind her.

"Oh, that sounds crazy? Oh no, wait until I speak my peace," Momma C replied attentively, walking back to the counter where it looked like she was fixing some kind of food.

The mood was normal, Zach felt, so why was he so nervous? Maybe because subconsciously, he knew he had done some bullshit by fucking Meme.

Zach innocently walked up to the counter and laid his head on Momma C's shoulder. She embraced him, bringing him in for a huge and well-needed hug. Though Zach knew Momma C was about to pop her shit, being in her arms may have been the safest he'd felt in a very long time. They both let each other go reluctantly. It was obvious Zach was missed in North Carolina. Momma C looked up and asked:

"How are you doing at home, truthfully? How are your grades? Are you even going to school anymore? Mom? Dad?" Momma C asked each question, face full of worry. The look she held now was that of a worried mother. She reached out and caressed Zach's face. Tears began to cascade down her face without warning.

"Ma, I promise I'm good." Zach grabbed hold of his favorite woman in the whole world and reassured her that all was okay. He didn't need her worrying about his safety.

"Mama, you alright?" Meme walked into the kitchen, concern written all over her face. Meme looked at Zach for answers, but Zach just shrugged. Momma C smiled.

"I just miss this bad ass little nigga. I'm really bout to beat his ass!" All three of them busted out laughing. There goes the Momma C they all knew.

"By the way, you don't go too far either. I got a bone to pick with ya fast ass too."

Meme knew better than to argue, so she rubbed her head in agreement and got back to the task at hand—which was probably nothing, but she made it look good.

"Damn, mama, it's like that?" He shook his head. "That shit crazy, but Mom and Dad are good. Mom's in Kentucky this week taking care of my granny while Dad chills at home—this nigga talking 'bout he wants a bee farm. You know, weird shit white folks get into. How about you? How have you been doing? I know this absence shit isn't like me. Talk to me, obviously something has you scared, baffled, or concerned—if not all three. I ain't never lied to you before, I won't now. No matter how mad you feel yourself getting, ask me anything. Talk to me, Ma. I talk back."

Momma C smiled, picking up the rag out of the sink and rinsing it off thoroughly.

"Well, you know me very well, and I'm just going to get to the point of my concerns. I have a few of them actually. Your young stupid ass has been busy. The most serious of them all is the rumors of you running around shooting at people, people shooting at you, robbing people, and running with known killers. Should I keep going? And don't deny shit, just listen, okay? Look, you my baby, my heart. I love you just as much as I love the bad ass muthafuckas I pushed out myself. But baby, you weren't raised like them. You may kill you a nigga, maybe even two. But you've been loved your whole life. The way you'll eventually have to act to survive in that game you're playing . . . baby, please trust me, you don't have that in you. I'm just being honest about what I know about you. You're not wired like them niggas. Now granted, I could be totally wrong because I haven't been around you in a minute. They could have changed you. The circumstances you in now could have changed you. Shit, life alone could have changed you. Talk to me, because this new you—this new you is too dangerous to be around this family."

Damn, that came out wrong. She threw the rag into the sink and sat down.

"I understand, Ma. I ain't got nothing to really explain. I'm sure Stoney told you in detail what I'm going through in Charleston. But please know I would never, ever bring that kind of static to your door. Just food for thought," Zach replied, in his feelings.

Damn, that was some bullshit, Zach thought, taking the seat beside her.

"I understand, I do. I grew up around killers. Look how Robert turned out. I know you and my daughter made love—"

"Yeah, and I ain't 'bout to sit here and act like I regret it neither," Zach said, cutting her off mid-sentence before she got on a rant and began talking crazy. "Ain't no accident, ain't no mistake. That was me being real with her, not just fuckin' on her. So before you go left, Ma, understand—ain't no games bein' played here."

Momma C looked like she wanted to be annoyed, but his response threw her off.

"Why didn't you think I would find out? Like the smell of pussy wouldn't just linger in the air? That's my daughter. I raised her and cleaned that little coochie of hers. I know her scent.

"But she is grown, with her own responsibilities. She can do whatever she wants, with whoever she pleases," Zach interrupted her again.

"Who said anything about trying to hide or be sneaky about anything? We wasn't trying to be disrespectful at all Momma. To be completely honest it happened out of the blue. I'm still mesmerized by the whole situation. But I swear I meant no disrespect whatsoever."

Momma C threw her nose up before smiling.

"Whatever. All I ask is for you motherfuckers to not wait until before I pull up to do the stinky leg, okay? With that being said, you have shit you need to ponder on, decisions that you need to make. I love you, baby, and it's great seeing you, but Momma is tired as hell. I been on my feet all day and carrying all this around." Momma Cat playfully slapped her ass before finishing her sentence. "That shit fucks my back up. Holla at me before you sneak up out of here, and I'll have my eye on you two nasty motherfuckers. But all jokes aside, y'all look cute together." Momma C teased him.

"Oh, shit." She snickered as Meme walked into the kitchen. Both Zach and Momma C grew silent.

"What?" Meme asked her mother directly. Meme knew her mother well and knew when she was talking shit about somebody. Momma C wouldn't be able to one—keep a straight face—or two, look anyone in their eyes. When her mother didn't look up, Meme knew what time it was and what they were talking about.

Momma C responded innocently: "Oh, nothing. The ravioli for Liyah is in the microwave if she gets hungry. Good night, son, daughter." Momma C joked before leaving Zach and Meme alone in the middle of the kitchen.

Zach's face damn near turned pink from embarrassment. Meme watched her mother giggle her way out the kitchen.

Zach calmed, trying to understand why he fed into Momma C's bullshit.

"She talking 'bout we look good together. Ya mother is a damn mess. I think that's why Stoney been acting weird since he got home too. Momma C said as soon as she walked in, she smelled sex. Ain't no way, but I don't know. Anyway, enough about that. What did you want to talk about that's so important?"

"I'm so scared for you, Zach. You aren't a child anymore, and my days of looking at you as a little brother are over. I look at you differently now. You are so much more than that now. If I was to ask you to put Charleston behind you and move down here to be with me, would you? Would you do that for me and Liyah? Or is the hype about being ran out your own city more important?"

Zach looked at her disappointingly, because no matter what he said she just wouldn't understand.

"Come on, Zachariah. Answer me. Is it?"

The silence broke Meme's heart.

"So you have no words for me? The person you swear you're just so in fucking love with. Man, miss me with that lame ass shit. You got it."

Meme went to get up from her seat, but Zach forcefully pushed her back down into it.

"Nigga, what the fuck! Move, Zach!" Meme exclaimed angrily.

"Hold on . . . Hold on . . . Sweetheart, chill out. I'm not ignoring you, I'm thinking. Understand, I'm never too prideful to live, especially when I know I'm out of my league. You think I like this shit? You think I like playing games with my existence? You sound crazy—I don't. I got in the game to make a little money here, a little money there. I didn't sign up for all the extra's. Niggas are dying on both sides. Okay, look—" Zach wiped the sweat from his face.

Just talking about the shit he was going through made him nervous. "Okay, look. Say I do consider it . . . what would the dynamic of this move be? Because I hear you when you say to be out here with you and Liyah. I'm talking reality, not fantasy, love. Would I really be coming down here as your man, in hopes of starting a family? Or will this move just be for the betterment of my life?"

Meme looked at him annoyed and confused.

"What the fuck is the difference? Please explain."

"My nigga, it's a—"

"I'm not ya nigga. Stop calling me that," Meme interjected seriously, meaning every word.

Zach sighed deeply and continued.

"It's a big difference. One move could mean I come and play family and maybe live happily ever after, while the other means I'm running away and leaving my brother in a foreign city to fight the opposition alone. I'm not into escaping my life to live another. But bro is so much of a real nigga, if I tell him I have a family to raise, he would gladly let me be. Though even then, I still don't know if I'd leave. I don't want you making rash decisions trying to help my cause. God has planned for me what He wants already. There is no escaping that. Now it's possible that I will drop everything at the drop of a dime to come live happily by your side while we raise Aaliyah together. I just don't see that in my future though. I feel like you like me—maybe even love me—but that step you're trying to convince yourself to take isn't smart, and I agree. If it's meant, Ma, it will happen. I've been in puppy love with you damn near my whole life. I don't know what that shit was earlier, why you gave me the opportunity to feel you, be one with you—but thank you. That shit was amazing. I love you, ma. I love you with all my soul. I pray God will align our futures together. I have to go talk to bruh right quick. I can either pull back up on you or just holla at you before I depart tomorrow, that's totally up to you. Just let me know . . ."

Zach leaned over and kissed Meme on her forehead, leaving her sitting there in her emotions. Without any other words or explanations, he walked off without looking back.

***

Knock . . . Knock . . . Knock . . .

"Come in," Stoney yelled from the other side of the door.

When Zach opened the door, it was damn near pitch-black inside the room. The only light came from the monitor that was on Stoney's gaming P.C.

"Nigga, it's dark as fuck in here. What the fuck!" Zach said irritatingly, trying to find his way around the cluttered mess Stoney called a room. "Bro, how do you live like this? That's how I know you not fucking no hoes, bro. This shit nasty as hell." Zach shook his head from side to side, still trying to find somewhere to sit.

"Turn the light on—and that's all clean shit over there." Stoney pointed. "I just had baseball practice for four hours. That's why I came home so late and don't feel like cleaning shit. Be my guest though, bruh—you know you Momma C's favorite child." Stoney joked, pausing his game.

He got up off the bed and walked across the room, flipping the light on, damn near blinding Zach in the process.

"Damn, nigga, what the fuck! That shit bright as fuck!" Zach complained, covering his eyes for a second, waiting for them to adjust.

"I tried to tell ya dumb ass." Stoney laughed, sitting back down on the bed, Indian style, facing Zach. "So what's good, bruh? What's going on between you niggas out there? Oh shit—I almost forgot." Stoney said, getting back up on his feet.

He walked over to his dresser and began searching for something. Zach assumed it was the infamous letter that Rodney had written, but he wasn't sure.

"Bro, ain't shit really going on—regular Charleston shit. Bruh just got caught without his gun on him and got killed," Zach said, trying not to let Stoney all the way into the mix of things going on in Charleston. His friend was a worrying kind of nigga. Zach ain't have time to explain a million things to Stoney. Some shit was just better left unsaid.

Stoney stopped searching his dresser and looked back at Zach stupidly. "Nigga, that shit sounds stupid as hell. When did a motherfucker have to walk around strapped with a gun to survive? Heem wasn't beefing with nobody, and Charleston isn't a city where keeping a gun is a must. You not telling me something. That nigga Rodney said you been running around with some OT nigga robbing people. That's why Haseem got killed."

Damn, Zach thought to himself. He knew that the streets were talking, but he had no clue how accurate and on point they were—though the truth was tweaked some.

"Don't get me wrong, bruh. Whoever told his bitch ass what's been going on may know a little something, but I promise you that nobody but me and Tana know what's really going on for real. This is how everything happened, bruh . . ."

Zach explained to Stoney against his better judgment. He explained everything that took place—from the robbery to walking down Sleeze. It was hard for Zach to relive the night that Haseem got killed, but he still told it, making sure not to leave out nothing.

By the time he was done, Stoney understood clearly why they were going through the bullshit. What still had Stoney confused was Rodney. He didn't understand why Rodney held such a grudge against Zach. They all had grew up playing in apple trees together—the bond they once had got no tighter.

Stoney had finally found the letter and handed it to Zach. He felt like he was betraying Rodney in a way, but he also felt if he didn't bring the letter to Zach's attention, he'd be betraying Zach in a much bigger fashion.

Zach opened the letter and read the words of a nigga he once considered his brother:

What's crackin' . . . Cuz, long time no hear.I pray all is well your way. Anyway, this letter isn't a formal one in the least. I want to catch you up to speed on what's been going on in our beloved city.

Zach has been running around with this OT nigga that got Heem killed. Not only that, but my li'l cousin Bandy also was killed because of a shootout that took place at the funeral. This OT nigga gotta go, little bro. I know Zach will listen to you before he actually thinks logically and listens to me. I'm serious, cuz. Let me slow down and explain a little. The OT nigga talked Heem and Zach into hitting Big Torrey's people. I don't know exactly what they got hit for, but I know it was enough to want them all dead.

Well guess who got killed first—Haseem. I'm not going for that, cuz. And because of you, I still have some love for Zach's bitch ass. So I leave bruh with one chance only. Kill that OT nigga, because if that nigga still breathing when I come home, I'm gone kill both of them niggas. On my soul.

I love you, cuz . . . until I don't. If Haseem was the nigga alive and you were dead, I would be writing cuz the same letter. Let ya peoples know, Stoney—my one and last warning.

—MuddBabi

Zach read the letter two more times before finally balling it up and shooting it into Stoney's trash can like a basketball.

"Nigga, what the fuck? You not gone take bruh seriously?" Stoney asked, astonished by Zach's disregard of Rodney's words. Zach looked at his best friend and busted out laughing.

This nigga must've lost his motherfucking mind, Zach thought as he caught his breath.

"Bro, listen to me. Fuck that nigga and the horse his pussy ass rode in on. What's gone happen is, I'm gone let my nigga know, and we gone proceed from there. All I ask is that you stay out of this and please don't pick sides. I know you fuck with Rodney's lame ass because we were childhood friends, but never forget the fact that we all grew apart from this nigga for a reason—even Haseem. Fuck his weird ass, bro. I'm kind of mad you called me down here to read this. You could've read this to me over the phone. But then again, I needed to see the family. It was worth the trip."

"I bet it was," Stoney replied sarcastically.

Zach punched Stoney in his ribs.

"Nigga, what's that supposed to mean?"

"It don't mean shit, bruh. But you know you was wrong, that's all I'm going to say. You know you are wrong," Stoney said, trying to leave the topic alone by picking his controller back up and resuming his gameplay.

"Bruh, hold the fuck up, what is you talking 'bout?" Zach asked seriously, snatching the controller from Stoney's hands, angering him instantly. Zach stood in preparation of a fight, but Stoney closed his eyes and sighed deeply, clenching his hands into fists. He was vexed, but he wasn't mad enough to fight his brother over it.

"Listen, Zach. Just because you out there in Charleston shooting people and shit now, don't make me scared of you. Nigga, you know what the fuck I'm talking about. The only person who wouldn't know the smell of sex is Liyah. Why would you fuck my sister, gang? You're my brother—you grew up calling her your sister. That shit weird as fuck to me, bro. But you keep yelling this 'you love niggas' bullshit. Nah, what you are is selfish. This shit always has to be about Zach. Zach this, Zach that. All these hoes out here you can fuck, and you choose to fuck the only one that should've been off limits. I don't care about you having a crush on her, blah, blah, fucking blah. I just can't understand it. The love you had for this family should've overrode the lust in both of you. Oh, you don't wear this guilt alone. Jamesa is guilty also—if not more so. I will forever love you. You're my motherfucking brother, but I got to tell you when you're wrong. And you and Meme were out of pocket."

Stoney shook his head in disappointment.

Zach looked to the ground in silence. He didn't know what to say, because in all reality, Stoney was 100% right. He had crossed the line. That he knew for sure.

But that wasn't what bothered Zach . . . what fucked with Zach was the fact that he would cross that same line again and again if given the opportunity.

He couldn't help himself.

That's how much he loved Jamesa Claytor.

"What does what's happening in Charleston have to do with making you scared of me?" Zach said, trying to change the subject. He continued, "I would never bring harm to you, bro. You sound crazy. I may talk my shit, but never physical harm."

Zach sighed, rubbing his hands across his face, tired from the day's events.

"All in all, I do understand your pain. You also need to understand that your sister is grown, Stone—way older than us, by the way. I could understand if Meme was your little sister and you were older, but that's not the case. And come on, bro. Don't act like sis a jump-off. She not just letting any nigga fuck her. I'm surprised and in a state of shock just like you are—still. I'm not making no excuses, because at the end of the day, you're right and you're entitled to your opinion. But bro, no disrespect, that shit to me was a dream come true. I have always loved Mia, bro, and you know it. I meant no disrespect to you or your family. I will fall back if you want, but I want you to know that she just asked me to move down here with her and Liyah. She scared of me living in Charleston."

"We all are, Zach . . . man, fuck."

Stoney sat there a few seconds in thought.

"What did my mother say about all this shit with Meme? Because I know her smart ass used her two cents."

They both started laughing. They could picture Momma C showing her ass.

"To be honest, bruh, she said we looked cute together—and I quote." Zach raised his fingers in the air for emphasis.

"She said what!" Stoney exclaimed, almost choking on the spit in his mouth. "Run that by me again."

Zach laughed at Stoney's reaction, then repeated himself.

"So I guess I'm the only one tripping about this shit then? Ain't that 'bout a bitch," Stoney said.

"I don't think it's that, bro. I believe it's the fact that she grown. No one is going against you—"

Zach paused, putting his index finger over his lips, silencing Stoney as his phone rang.

"Finally, what the fuck!"

Zach pulled the phone from his pocket and answered it:

"Bruh, where the fuck you been? I been blowing your phone up for two days trying to figure out what the fuck is going on. I got hella messages saying you kicking buddies' candles and all type of shit." Zach laughed. He couldn't help himself. "You's a wild nigga."

"You still OT?" Santana asked seriously from the other end of the line.

Catching Santana's no-nonsense kind of mood put Zach on point.

"Yeah. Why? I'm still at Stoney's."

Stoney looked up angrily, but before he got to tripping, Zach put up his finger as if to say he would explain later.

"A'ight, bet. Stay there a few more days. And what that letter say?" Santana whispered into the phone, catching both Zach and Stoney by surprise.

"Bruh, you good?" Zach asked, trying to make out any noises in Santana's background.

"Always. Read me the letter."

"I'm 'bout to put you on speaker," Zach warned, knowing Santana hated that shit with a passion.

"Bet."

Zach read Santana the letter word for word, leaving nothing out. Santana couldn't help but laugh at Rodney.

"Son, ya man's a character. But that's cool—if that's what helps niggas sleep at night, so be it. But I hope you told Stoney at least the truth about what's going on, because if a motherfucker didn't know any better, you would assume Rodney was speaking facts."

"I did. And I also told him not to choose sides—remain neutral. He knew this shit didn't involve him," Zach said loud and clear, making sure both parties understood so there wouldn't be any excuses or misunderstanding later.

"Absolutely. Absolutely. You know any brother of yours is a brother of mine. You better tell that nigga how we out here giving it up over Heem's name. We don't write letters, nigga—we drop bodies, ya heard?" Santana laughed sinisterly through the phone.

"But anyway, stay put. I got a few things I need handled, but the only way I'm going to be able to do that is if I know your lil' ass is safe and out the way. Make sure you're seen, though—and by like cameras and shit. You may need an alibi . . . or two. I love you, son. Protect yourself and stay dangerous."

"You already know, bruh. I love you more," Zach replied.

Santana hung up.

The look on Stoney's face said it all. He wanted no parts of the shit going on in Charleston.

I told you shit was real, Zach thought to himself as he watched the blood drain from his best friend's face.

Stoney's mouth stood gaped and frozen. He hadn't heard much—but he heard enough.

"What's good, bruh? You straight? You over there looking all crazy and shit . . . like you seen a motherfucking ghost or something," Zach joked.

"I just don't know what to say, bro. I don't even know that nigga, or what he looks like. I never even heard of him until that letter Rodney sent. But yet you can hear the love when he speaks to you . . . when he speaks about Haseem. I'm now realizing the severity of things. I hope I never know what it feels like to be living day by day. I'm truly sorry, bro. I had no clue. I didn't know!" Stoney said, wiping away the tears that fell unwillingly down his face.

It was just like yesterday when he lived on Cart Street on Charleston's East Side—having sleepovers with his best friends, playing hide-n-seek and video games until the night fell.

Now Haseem was gone.

And Zach and Rodney were on two different sides of the gun.

In six months, it was no telling whose casket they would be carrying next . . .

Chapter 10

Santana closed his phone as he eyed the gray and black '96 bubble Caprice sitting out of place a few houses back from Zach's Lewis Street home. *Who the fuck?* Santana thought before stopping mid-stride and backing into the nearest cut, which happened to be the first house closest to him. Santana dug into his pocket and pulled his phone back out, calling Zach. It was a must that he find out who was in the car sitting outside of Zach's spot.

"Yooo!" Zach answered, chewing like a cow in Santana's ear.

"Seriously, bro, come on, man, close your mouth. Tell me 'hold on' or something—that shit you doing nasty, my G," Santana replied annoyingly.

"My bad, bruh, I was starving. Nigga, you just hung up. You good? You straight?" Zach asked, concerned.

"Absolutely. But look, it's a whip out of bounds, sitting out front your parents' spot posted. I just wanted to know if you knew who this nigga was or not. It's an all-gray Chevy with black deep dish 4's, I think. It's some clean looking shit too. Too clean to go hunting in, if you ask me," Santana said, looking at the car and trying to explain it the best way he could from where he stood.

"No bullshit, bruh, I ain't got the slightest clue who you could be talking 'bout," Zach said. Then it clicked. "Oh, shit! Bruh, that might be the nigga Nazir's shit. Bruh just came home from doing like 13 in the state. That nigga supposed to be some kind of legend out here. How close are you to the whip?" Zach asked.

Santana scrunched his face up and looked at the phone. All Santana thought at that moment was: *What the fuck kind of question was that?* Santana shook his head back and forth, annoyed. He just didn't understand Zach's line of questioning sometimes. Instead of just telling Santana what he needed to know, he went left.

"My G, listen, stop doing—" Santana stopped and checked himself. It wasn't the right time or place to be frustrated. He let the minor pet peeve go and got back to the task at hand. "Who is this Nazir dude? I've never heard of him until now. If he's such a muthafuckin' legend, why we ain't hear about him coming home?" Santana asked sarcastically.

"Bruh, I'm not for certain. I just happen to see some shit on Myspace about dude coming home a day or two ago. He supposed to be somebody important from back in the day that roamed the East on bullshit," Zach explained. "Oh, and you're going to love this, you know, he's Big Torrey's right-hand man."

Santana thought he was hearing shit.

"Repeat that. What you say about Torrey?" Santana asked, listening intently, making sure he heard Zach correctly.

"That Nazir nigga is Big Torrey's right-hand man."

When Santana heard Zach repeat those words, he tuned the whole world out as his thoughts ran rapid. *Could it really be that easy?* Santana thought, his mind on murder. Santana had been so caught up in playing defense that he never once thought it was possible to touch Torrey's heart—in any fashion. But now, as he stared across the street at the gray and black Chevy Caprice, he saw the opportunity to tilt the scoreboard in his favor. The heartache, the pain, the melancholy he felt when Haseem was killed was now 'bout to be dealt back. Dealt back to the one person who thought that his home front was untouchable.

"Santana!" Zach yelled into the phone, pulling him out of his reverie.

"I'm here. Listen, do what I said earlier. I'm serious. Shit gone be crazy when you get back. You heard?"

"Absolutely. Say no more."

"Love you, bro. Stay dangerous," Santana smiled.

"You already know the vibes, my G," Zach replied.

Santana powered his phone completely off, taking away any possible signals that could ping off nearby towers located around him.

He put his phone away and thought about his next move. He touched his hip and felt the metal that rested there. The Glock he had wasn't right for the kind of message he wanted to send. Santana wanted to send Torrey a loud message. *Let the games begin*, he thought sinisterly as he jogged lightly across the street, hoping not to draw any unwanted attention.

Santana began to pick up speed as he cut through the grass of the first home he came upon, leading him into the alley that intersected with Chamberlain Court. Even with the shadows obscuring him, Santana still had this eerie feeling that someone was watching him. He didn't have time to dwell on his paranoia; he shook that shit off and kept running through the alley. This was a do-or-die moment, and he was taking it no matter the cost.

When Santana finally got to the adjacent alley that ran along Kat's house, he pulled his Glock off his hip and walked along the alleyway leading to Kat's front door. Before emerging from the cut, he surveyed the block thoroughly before walking onto the porch and into the house. Without fail, the door was unlocked and open for anyone to enter. He just didn't understand how anyone could feel safe in such an environment.

Santana closed the door behind him and locked it, locking the rest of the world out.

"Kat! Yooooo, Kat!" he yelled, searching the bottom level, not finding no one in attendance.

Damn, no one is home? Where the fuck is everybody at? Santana asked himself.

The only sound that he heard was the blaring TV coming from the living room, but that wasn't what pegged his interest—it was the sound that wasn't there that was messing with him. Santana didn't have time to think about the silence. He stored the awkward moment in his mental and ascended the stairs two at a time.

When he got to the top of the landing, he heard the unmistakable—but familiar—moans coming from behind Kat's bedroom door.

Santana instantly felt his body grow hot. He didn't know if it was from the anger and embarrassment that jolted through his body or if it was just jealousy coursing through his veins, but what he did know was he was vexed by Kat's sounds of pleasure.

He took a deep breath and calmed himself. He had to remind himself that shorty was for the streets. He knew what kind of woman Kat was coming into it—she thrived off instant gratification. Nobody else's feelings mattered but hers, and Santana refused to get caught up in the drama.

Santana walked into Montez's room and found it empty—Montez was gone. Santana wondered about his whereabouts until it hit him that after Haseem was killed, Montez went to stay with a family member in California, claiming it was too difficult to cope with the violence. Santana rummaged through Montez's closet for his duffle bag. There were no bags in the closet, meaning that the bag was most likely in Kat's closet. Santana gave no fucks. He walked back over to Kat's room and opened the door.

The sight crushed him, but he handled it like a G. Kat was on all fours, getting slayed by the homicide detective nigga Brian Williams. Santana was so mad he had to laugh to remain calm. *This bitch*, Santana thought, clenching his jaw tightly together to suppress his anger. He couldn't watch no more. He turned towards the closet and began rummaging through her belongings in search of his duffle bag.

For a second, Santana went unnoticed—that was until he started throwing things around, making his presence known.

The couple looked up after hearing a foreign noise. Simultaneously, they jumped out of fear of someone else being in the room with them. Kat ran halfway across the bed while Williams reached for his gun. Santana looked back momentarily in disgust. He thought about addressing the situation, but he didn't. Santana just continued his search, looking for his weapons.

Kat cleared her throat as she covered herself.

"Ummmmmm . . . excuse me. What the fuck, Santana?" Kat said, baffled. Kat was sick to her stomach. *How could Santana have caught them?* was all Kat had running through her mental.

"My bad, auntie. I had to grab some clothes. My wife is in the hospital so . . ." he said, letting his words hang in the balance.

"Nigga, get the fuck out!" Kat yelled at the top of her lungs.

At that same moment, Santana felt the familiar straps of his duffle bag. He grabbed the bag and walked out the room, slamming the door shut for dramatic effect.

Santana took his duffle bag and walked to the back room, not really giving two fucks about what Kat was talking about. Santana played tough, but seeing Detective Williams digging in Kat's guts from the back hurt his pride and lightweight took a piece of him. Yeah, Santana knew that she had been fucking the detective and probably many other men, but to actually see that shit firsthand? Now that was a total different story.

Santana knew he couldn't just dwell on the situation, so just like that, his heartless ass brushed it off, kicked Kat out of his heart, and got back to business. He was sure he was running out of time as is.

Santana closed the door and locked it, giving him the privacy he so badly needed. He unzipped the side compartment and removed the all-black Nike baseball gloves and laid them across the bed. He thought better of it and put them on instead—he couldn't afford to lose track of the things he touched.

He then unzipped the main compartment and pulled out the mini choppa—his AK-47, equipped with an adjustable shoulder stock and a green beam attachment. The baby K was his love. Santana used it often when Doug took them to Kanawha Forest and taught them the ins and outs of target shooting. That was before Haseem was killed. Now Santana just practiced by his lonely self.

The AK-47 was the illest gun he had ever possessed. Now it was time to let Eleanor off the leash.

Knock . . . Knock . . . Knock . . .

Santana jumped for a second but calmed when he realized Kat most likely was the person on the other end banging. Santana ignored her and went back to what he was doing. He didn't have much time—the Caprice could possibly be gone. Time was of the essence.

Santana hurried himself along, pulling two magazines from the bag.

"Ahhh, fuck!" Santana yelped as a sharp pain shot through his back. He rubbed his back and felt the bruised spot. He felt it for a second and thanked Allah again for coming to his aid—making sure that the bullet that hit his vest the afternoon of the shootout didn't penetrate, harming him any further.

Santana felt as though it was something that he was missing. He thought long, he thought hard. Then Santana glanced in the mirror and it instantly clicked. He needed to change his clothes.

He had had the same clothes on for multiple days. He could've easily been identified by what he had on, so changing his attire was an absolute must.

Bang . . . Bang . . . Bang . . . Bang . . .

"Santana, open the door please. I want to talk to you," Kat said tearfully through the door.

Santana put on all-black, ignoring Kat's pleas. His body ached, but he continued to change without complaint. *No pain, no gain.* Santana laughed at the corny thoughts running through his head. He looked himself over in the mirror once more before grabbing the tools he needed to perform adequately.

He pushed the bag under the bed and unlocked the door, but before he exited the room, he turned to make sure that everything he took out was put back in its rightful place.

Satisfied, Santana opened the door and walked out into the hall, nonchalantly passing Kat on the way.

Kat sat bolt upright against the wall, with her feet pulled to her chest, tears streaking down her face.

"Why are you acting like this?" Kat scurried to her feet and began to grab at him as he passed by.

Santana pulled his shirt out of her grasp and kept walking.

"Santana!" Kat whined.

He ignored her, but stopped at the top of the stairs.

"Where the detective nigga at? He still here?" Kat shook her head, no. "Good. He doesn't need to be here right now. I'll be back. Clean yourself up. Fuck you crying for? You weren't crying a minute ago, when that nigga was digging ya muthafuckin' guts out." Santana just shook his head in disgust. "Don't let that nigga back into this house, Kat, period! Do you copy?" Santana said firmly, tucking the last of his hair into his ski mask. Santana looked at Kat and sighed deeply. He was at a loss for words. Santana really didn't have nothing further to say, so he didn't say nothing at all. He descended the stairs and walked into the night with murder on his mind.

***

"911, what's the emergency?" the operator asked calmly from the other side of the phone.

"Somebody just jacked me for my car . . . Fuck!" Ramos yelled nervously into the phone.

"Sir, please just calm down. Can you give me a description of the assailant? Are you in any danger? Hello? Sir . . . Hellooooo, sir?" the operator asked fretfully. "Sir, are you okay?" she asked, listening intently to the breathing coming from the other end of the phone.

"I'm a police officer . . . I'm a police officer!" Ramos shouted in short spurts, rubbing the phone against his flight jacket to cause a static-like sound.

"Sir, please calm down. Sir, are you in any danger?" the operator asked rapidly.

"I'm good . . . I'm good . . ." Ramos answered, out of breath.

"Okay. Just breathe, sir. Can you tell me where you are? Are you safe?"

"I am. Give me a second. I'm trying to catch my breath."

The operator agreed and gave Ramos a few seconds to gather himself. The information that Ramos had to give was crucial, because his location wasn't showing on the operator's GPS system.

"Sir?" the operator finally asked after a few minutes passed by.

"Yes, I'm here. My name is Detective Ramos, badge number 3045. I'm an off-duty BPD officer from the robbery-homicide unit," Ramos answered quickly, still out of breath.

"Okay, sir, just try to labor your breathing. Calm down—"

"Calm down . . . calm down . . . how the fuck am I supposed to calm down when I just had a gun in my face, over a fucking rental car. Huh? Please enlighten me. How am I supposed to remain calm, ma'am? A damn rental car."

Ramos sighed deeply for dramatic effect.

"The license plate number is Delta, Stacy, Mark, 4, Alpha, 67. I'm sorry, I didn't mean to—oh shit!"

Ramos yelled before gunfire erupted and the phone disconnected.

"Hello . . . Hello . . . sir? Are you okay? Sir?" the operator asked repeatedly, yelling into the phone promptly, but it was of no use—the caller was gone.

***

Santana pulled the ski mask over his face as he slowly crept along the alleyway behind Zach's house. Santana was looking for the best possible escape route to use when he was done with his task at hand. The weather was comfortable out, so he knew there still would be plenty of people lingering out enjoying the spring air, so he proceeded with caution. Santana took these witnesses into account, but the price of sending one of Ty's main niggas to hell was a chance he was willing to take.

Santana walked along the alleyway behind the row of homes that sat on Lewis Street until he spotted the Chevy Caprice still sitting in the same spot. The smoke that drifted out the ajar window told Santana that there were still people inside the vehicle. Satisfied that he made it back in time before Nazir ventured off excited him—but puzzled him at the same time. *Why is this nigga just sitting in this one spot?* It was a question Santana asked himself but would never know. Whatever the reason, it cost Nazir his life.

Santana chambered a round into the barrel of the AK-47, hitting the beam all in the same motion. Santana pointed and waved the gun up and down until the green dot appeared on the wall of the house in front of him. Santana smiled. It was his time to shine. He took a deep breath and exhaled slowly. He did that a few times until his nerves calmed. Santana inhaled nervously one last time before walking out of the shadows looking like the reaper. He walked up as if he belonged, AK-47 gripped firmly, hidden behind his back.

The window rolled down, stopping Santana dead in his tracks as he approached. The man behind the wheel smiled intoxicatingly, showing a mouth full of diamond-encrusted gold teeth. His smile instantly disappeared when his mind grasped the severity of the situation.

Before Nazir got the chance to protest, Santana raised the choppa and said, “Welcome home, nigga!” He squeezed the trigger callously.

Boc . . . Boc . . . Boc . . . Boc . . . Boc . . . Tatttt . . . Tatt . . .

The choppa shells banged in succession, knocking chunks into the Caprice and blood onto the interior as each bullet found its target. When Santana finally stopped shooting, all he could hear were the piercing shrieks from the woman in the passenger seat. The woman was curled into a ball against the passenger-side door, shaking like a leaf.

“Please . . . please . . . please . . . pleeeaaassssse don’t kill me. I have . . . I have . . .” The sobs choked her. “I have children.” The woman begged, hands outstretched as if they would protect her from the bullets.

“Aye!” Santana yelled. “Who else in the car?” He pointed with the nose of the gun.

The woman shook her head from side to side as she whimpered into her hands uncontrollably. Blood splatter covered her body. The blood was so thick, Santana couldn’t tell if she was wounded too or if it all belonged to Nazir.

Santana let the gun drop to his side. There was no imminent threat near. He knew letting shorty live could bite him in the ass in the long run, but killing women and children was an absolute no-no.

Though Fatty and Torrey crossed the line first, he wouldn’t—period. He was going to make them pay for Darla in other ways. He didn’t need to catch up—he tilted the scoreboard. He was up. Plus, Santana had enough shit he had to answer to God for; killing innocent people wouldn’t be one of them.

"Ma, you good?" Santana asked as he quickly opened the driver-side door.

The woman stared at Santana with fear written all over her face. She just shivered against the passenger-side door, not saying a word in return.

Nazir's body laid slumped between the steering column and middle console. His body laid awkwardly against his radio system, eyes wide open, with a grayish-blue film beginning to form over top of them.

Santana reached into the car and grabbed Nazir's Gucci belt with his left hand. While holding the AK firmly in his right, he made sure his grip was secure before yanking Nazir's lifeless body out of the car forcefully, causing Nazir's head to hit flush against the concrete.

Santana looked up once more at the woman balled into the fetal position, wondering if she was capable of carrying out a message for him or not. The woman's teeth clattered together violently—she just wouldn't stop shivering from fear. She was scared to death.

Santana shook off any emotion that he held within him for the woman. He had a task to do, and he needed to get it done—and done quick. Santana began to speak.

"Tell that fat bitch he next, he keep playing with me! Flat out!" Santana lifted the assault rifle without any notice and squeezed two rounds into Nazir's face, knocking two large holes into him, making it impossible for anyone to recognize him.

Santana made sure they would close Nazir's casket and be forced to remember him by pictures. He wasted no more time. He ran away with a smile on his face, upping the score yet again—3 to 1.

"That's for you, gang. I'm gone keep sending these niggas, son. I just wish you would have listened, bro," Santana said, running back the same way he came. "Rest easy, family," he stated proudly, momentarily stopping to look back at his latest work.

A calm feeling washed over him, sending chills through his body. Santana ran off, disappearing into the shadows of the night.

Chapter 11

Williams sat silently in the unmarked sedan as he watched Kat's front door jaded He had no clue what he was doing still sitting in his car watching Kat's home. Williams had it bad, he knows he should have pulled off minutes ago, but for some reason he just couldn't. He couldn't bring himself to do it. He was embarrassed, hurt, angry, horny and flat out confused Not only did he feel like what just transpired seemed weird, but he felt like he was missing something, something his heart recognized, but his mind couldn't register. Williams sat there puzzled deep in thought. He knew Santana, Justice—whatever the fuck his name was— heard them having sex; he was in the room for God's sake.

Once he opened the door and saw what was going on, he should have shut the damn door and got the fuck on, Williams at least knew that much. But no, the little bastard decided to enter the room and make his presence known killing the mood All to retrieve some clothes? Really? Williams questioned the logic and it just didn't add up to him. He was losing his fucking mind This Santana kid has been a thorn in his side since his arrival in Charleston. Williams shook his head and sighed at the thought.

"Oh shit, speaking of the devil," Williams said out loud as he leaned forward to make sure he wasn't seeing shit; Williams watched the door to Kat's house open and out stepped the man of the hour, Justice "Santana" Torres.

Williams ducked low in his car, sliding down as far as humanly possible. He was stocky for his six-foot statue, so the task was seemingly difficult, but he made it work. Being only fifty yards away made him an easy target to spot, especially if you were looking/or him. Though the car was an "unmarked" sedan, the police issued Crown Victoria stuck out like a sore thumb.

Williams looked on, not blinking once, afraid he was going to miss something of importance.

Santana stepped onto the porch and looked up and down Jackson Street before closing the door behind him; The miniature AK47 dangling from Santana hand, left Williams at a loss for words. What the hell? Detective Williams thought to himself. Santana looked around once more before pulling the ski mask over his face and turning into the alley and disappearing behind Kat's home.

***

Ring . . . Ring . . . Ring . . . Ring . . . Ring . . .

Detective Williams sat in his car for a few more seconds before finally hanging the phone up yet again. It felt like the 20th time he'd called Kat and got no answer. It was no way Kat was asleep—especially after what had just taken place only an hour or so before.

"Man, what the fuck," Williams cussed stressfully.

Tap . . . Tap . . . Tap . . . A light knock tapped against the window, drawing Williams's eyes upward. It was Schooner.

Detective Williams looked up at his partner, homicide detective Daniel Schooner, and held his index finger up, asking for a moment to gather his thoughts. Schooner reluctantly nodded, frustration written all over his face. He walked away from the window without saying anything further—he was pissed, and he made no secret of it.

"Come on . . . come on . . . come on . . ." Detective Williams begged, as if he was pleading with the universe.

Kat's phone rang countlessly in his ear, taking away any hope he had.

"Brian! Are you fuckin' serious? What the fuck, are you just gonna keep calling me until I fucking answer?" Kat yelled into the phone, blatantly agitated with him.

Williams laughed a deep, gritty laugh before answering her.

"Man, shut the fuck up! And you goddamn right I was gonna continue to call until you answered your motherfucking phone. You tell that stupid muthafuckin' nephew of yours to call me right the fuck now, or he will be going to jail for this muthafuckin' body he left mutilated on Lewis Street. And you better stay by your muthafuckin' phone too, 'cause if I call and you don't answer, that little nigga is going to jail. Play with me if you want," Detective Williams said bluntly, the biggest smile plastered across his face.

Kat sat silent on the other end of the phone, taking in what the detective was saying to her.

"And what if I tell you that I don't give a fuck and that weird shit between y'all?" Kat replied, calling his bluff.

Williams laughed out loud before finally replying.

"You won't," Detective Williams stated firmly, then hung up, leaving Kat on the other end at a loss for words.

Williams looked at himself in the rearview mirror and smiled—he was happy that the power had finally shifted. He placed his phone in the middle console of his car and got out. Schooner looked over at his partner, shaking his head in disgust.

"Have you looked at the vic yet?" Schooner asked Williams, spitting sunflower seeds into a Ziploc bag he held in his hands.

"Nah, is there something I should see?" Detective Williams asked, stepping out of the car and walking past the yellow crime scene tape that corded off the block from the public. "Whoever this is, he must've been someone of importance," he added, watching the crowd of people continue to grow by the minute.

"It was Nazir Howard," Schooner stated, kneeling down and pulling the sheet back, revealing Nazir's body from the shoulders up.

"Oooohhhh, shit!" was all Det. Williams could muster before turning away.

The sight was gruesome. How they knew who the person was under that sheet was beyond him—recognizing any kind of features would damn near be impossible. The bullets that struck Nazir's face had disfigured him terribly. One of Nazir's eyes was caved in and hollow. For better words to describe it, Nazir had no facial structure left to identify. Yeah, this was personal.

What could this man have done to Santana to make him do this? Detective Williams asked himself as he made his way to the parked cruiser that held their only eyewitness—well, besides himself.

Williams opened the door to the cruiser and squatted so he could be eye-level with his witness. The girl was visibly shaken, wrapped in the warmth of a blanket provided by the Charleston Police Department. The blood splattered across her face was still evident and mixed with the tears that streamed down her cheeks.

Williams adjusted himself until he was comfortable. He took out his notepad and pen that he always kept with him for times like this, ready to jot down notes as they came.

"I'm not even gonna ask you if you're okay, 'cause that would be the dumbest question I could ask. But are you feeling better now that you know you're safe?" Det. Williams asked, trying to get the witness to feel a sense of familiarity.

She nodded, pulling the wool blanket up to her face.

"Did you get the opportunity to see the killer's face?"

"No," she said, barely audibly.

"I'm sorry, sweetheart, you gotta speak up. There's a lot going on behind me. Can you please speak a little louder? Thank you. What's your name?"

"Fantasia Mitchell," the witness replied.

"That's a beautiful name," Williams complimented her, without even meaning to.

Fantasia smiled faintly. "Thank you."

"Can you tell me what happened tonight, Fantasia? Can you tell me what led to this happening? Has Nazir been into any kind of arguments or altercations with anybody tonight that you know of? What about since he's been home? Did Nazir have any enemies before he went to jail? What about while he was locked up? Can you give us any kind of info that can lead us to the person who killed your friend? I'm sorry about the 21 questions, but of course, you know it's routine," Detective Williams asked, trying not to leave any stones unturned.

"Nothing happened. This was random. We were just chillin', smoking, and a masked figure came from behind them houses right there." Fantasia pointed at the row of homes that lined the 1500 block of Lewis Street.

Williams followed her finger and looked at the place where the shooter emerged from. He knew the alley Fantasia was talking about—it was the same one he saw Santana turn into with the assault rifle in hand. Williams was almost sure Santana was the shooter, but he didn't understand his motive.

He wasn't willing to bet his life on a hunch. Santana just killing a random person he couldn't see? Nah, there was more to the story, and he needed to know what the hell was going on.

"Was you able to see a build, height, skin tone—anything?"

Fantasia paused for a second and shook her head no.

"Ooookay . . ." Williams scratched his beard, thinking of anything else he could ask. *Anything.*

"Did he speak to Nazir at all before he . . . you know? Did he say anything to you?"

Williams immediately saw the fear rise in Fantasia's eyes when he asked that question. She shook her head no quickly.

She's lying, Detective Williams thought, excited. *She knows who did it. Did she see his face?*

It was something this witness knew that she wasn't telling. Detective Williams paused for a second. He needed to think of a different way to approach the situation.

"Look, do you want us to catch this man, or are you just going to let him walk free and give him another chance at harming you? Help me take this man off—"

"No disrespect, officer, that man let me live. I'm not going to cooperate and put myself in jeopardy. You will not protect me or feed my family if I'm killed. So please, as a Black man, I ask that you understand. I will not give you any more information. I don't know nothing. You see what this nigga is capable of. I'm not trying to be that man's next victim," Fantasia stated emotionally. The tears sat at the brim of her eyes, threatening to fall.

"I understand. I understand. Can you tell me off record what he said that spooked you? It had to be something, because when I asked you specifics, you turned a shade lighter. I won't write anything down. I won't ever repeat it. I just need it as food for thought. I want to know what I'm dealing with, ma'am. I don't want this to happen to anyone else, sweetheart, so please help me—help me connect what dots are missing," Williams explained, desperation laced in his tone.

Fantasia looked at him solemnly. She wanted to help the detective, but she just couldn't. Fantasia knew the police couldn't be trusted. But if she knew that giving him the information off record would get him off her ass, then why not?

"I swear I will deny anything you say if you repeat this. I'm serious, Mr. Williams. Please don't get me killed."

The detective nodded in agreement, flabbergasted by Fantasia's sudden change of heart.

"I promise I won't! I swear! Thank y—"

Fantasia knew she was signing her death certificate if she spoke the words that were lying heavy on her heart. She sighed deeply before finally speaking them out loud.

"He said something about telling Big Torrey that he will be next if he keeps playing, or something to that effect. I told you I didn't know shit. That was all he said before he ran off."

Detective Williams stored the data in his mental and stood up, legs wobbly as hell.

Damn, I'm getting old, Williams thought, rubbing his aching knees.

"Thank you very much. Look, if you really don't want to talk, you don't have to. You hear me?"

Fantasia nodded.

"Tell the detective you want a lawyer. You won't be forced to talk. Again, thank you. Here's my card if you change your mind."

Detective Williams placed the card on the leather seat before closing the door to the police cruiser.

Williams sighed and looked over the crowd for familiar faces. He recognized many—drug dealers, gang members, informants—some he had used before and some he knew would never budge. But it wasn't the dealers, bangers, or informants he was looking for. It was one man in particular that he needed to speak with: Big Torrey. But as he scanned the crowd, he realized Charleston's most sought-out criminal wasn't in attendance.

Williams swiped his hands down his face as he searched the crowd again, this time looking for anyone he could squeeze for information. He was starting to become frustrated with the situation as a whole. The night was becoming a trying one, to say the least.

Zzzzz . . . zzzzz . . . zzzz . . . zzz . . . zzzzzz . . .

Detective Williams's phone vibrated, causing him to temporarily take his eyes away from the crowd of mourners. He looked down and flipped the phone open. It was a message from Kat.

Williams smiled as he opened the message. But as he read the contents, his face grew hot with anger. He pressed his eyes shut and took a deep breath. He reopened the text and read the message a third, then a fourth time. He had to make sure what he was reading was real.

You fucking bitch! Detective Williams cursed, staring at the words looking back at him:

*//***:** *Santana told me to relay this message to you . . . don't shoot the messenger. LOL. Anyway, he said send who you are going to send, he said something about the matter being frivolous because he has an alibi. A solid one at that, by a state official. Because at the exact time of the shooting, he said that he walked in on a homicide detective having sexual relations with his aunt. He is also saying that his recollection is accurate with the time the shots rang out. LOL. That boy is so funny. The ball is in your court, Brian; you can play this how you want. Talk to you later. I love you.*

Detective Williams closed his phone and cursed under his breath.

He was back to square one all over again.

Fuck! I'm going to get you, you little bastard, Detective Williams vowed as he walked back to the crime scene, with his mind on everything but the deceased.

A new fire burned inside him. He wasn't going to stop until Santana was buried in the penal system for the crimes he had committed. It didn't matter what it took—he wasn't going to stop until that boy's body turned cold.

***

Wanda gargled tragically on the blood rushing into her mouth at a rapid pace.

"What the fuck . . . Keeeevvvvvv, call 911 . . . Nigga, call 911!" Tez-Mo yelled, looking down the street both ways, making sure the threat was gone.

Tez-Mo put the Glock 17 down on the ground and intertwined his fingers on Wanda's chest, and began giving her chest compressions.*1 . . . 2 . . . 3 . . .* Then he put his mouth to hers and blew air into her wounded lungs.*1 . . . 2 . . . 3 . . .* Again, pressing his mouth to hers.

"Breathe, shorty, breathe . . . please breathe. Baby, we need you," Tez-Mo begged, tears running down his eyes.*1 . . . 2 . . . 3 . . .* He blew air into her lungs. The fear in Wanda's eyes brought uncontrollable tears to his.

"Please Wanda, don't leave me. I need you, Ma! Baby, stay with me."*1 . . . 2 . . . 3 . . .* Mouth to mouth.*1 . . . 2 . . . 3 . . .* Mouth to mouth.

Tez-Mo frantically pushed on Wanda's chest and blew into her lungs. It did not seem to be helping. Tez-Mo wiped the blood from his mouth with the back of his hand.

"Kev!" Tez-Mo yelled.

How the fuck could this happen? Tez-Mo thought as he cried silently, tears streaking down his face, weakening by the minute. He did not know what to do. He wanted to hold Wanda to let her know that everything would be okay, but he knew the gesture would be futile. Wanda was dying. Tez-Mo could feel her slipping away.

"Keep fighting, Mama . . . keep fighting," Tez-Mo said to Wanda as calmly as he could. He was not ready to let Wanda go.

What the fuck was she even doing here, anyway? Tez-Mo thought to himself. That was until he remembered the message he had sent her, telling her to pull up because he needed to talk to her regarding the rumors surrounding Gloria's death. But he had no clue that she would be driving out so soon.

Tez-Mo began looking around for Kev. He was nowhere in sight.

"Kevin! Shorty, where you at?" Tez-Mo yelled angrily.

Wanda started coughing, choking on the blood that rapidly filled her damaged lungs.

What do I do . . . what do I do? Tez-Mo asked himself, looking around for anything or anyone that could help keep Wanda breathing until the ambulance came.

"Kevin, where . . . the . . . fuck . . . are . . . you!" Tez-Mo yelled as loud as his lungs would allow. He was furious. He felt alone in the middle of the road. He could only imagine how Wanda felt.

Tez-Mo looked defeated.

"Stay with me, Ma, please. A nigga need you," Tez-Mo sniffled. "We have so much life to live, baby girl. God, please save her . . . save my soulmate. Please."

Tez-Mo bent his head until it touched Wanda's chest. He broke down when the familiar smell of Wanda's body wash caught his nose.

"Why . . . God . . . take me. Please why . . ."

"Sir, push her onto her side!" a woman said as she emerged from the crowd that began to form only feet away from Tez-Mo and Wanda.

Tez-Mo looked up in confusion at the lady in the gray robe and black slides. Instinctively, he grabbed for his weapon. The woman saw Tez-Mo grab for his gun, but she paid him no mind and continued on her path so she could offer him a helping hand.

"Baby, look. Put her on her side. She shouldn't be laid like this, honey. That's why she keeps choking on her blood. Trust me, please. Let me show you," the woman said seriously, touching Tez-Mo's hand as she slowly turned Wanda onto her side.

"Go call 911, baby. I got her," the woman assured him, holding Wanda's body in place.

Tez-Mo did not answer back automatically. He just shook his head frantically from side to side.

"I can't leave her. You . . ."

The woman wasted no time. She got up immediately, cutting his words short, and took off up the grass and back into the house she came from.

Tez-Mo heard the sirens from a distance. It was music to his ears. He wiped away the tears that streaked down his face and said:

"I told you, baby, I told you. God got us. You survive, I survive, we survive—I promise! I will quit, love. On Sasha," Tez-Mo said as the sirens grew closer. "I love you, baby, stay with me. I love you so much, Momma. Keep fighting a little longer," he said as he squeezed Wanda's hand tightly, hoping it reassured her that he was still with her.

The flashing lights lit up the night as the EMT rounded the corner and pulled into the residential block.

Tez-Mo rose from the ground, gun in hand. The crowd of onlookers gasped in fear.

Tez-Mo put the gun on his hip once he became aware of what he was doing.

Oh shit, I'm bugging. He waved to the paramedic frantically.

"She over here! She over here! She got multiple gunshot wo—"

"Sir, we got it from here," the female paramedic stated calmly, dismissing him.

The anger that built in him almost got the best of him, but he knew it would only slow them down, so he said nothing and stepped aside.

"I'm right behind you, baby. I love you, Wanda. Fight! You hear me? Fight! Till the end, right?"

Tez-Mo ran along the stretcher until it was lifted off the ground and put into the ambulance.

He rested his hands above his head and closed his eyes. Tez-Mo had never spoken to God before, but he was in a time of need. He wanted to at least speak on Wanda's behalf. He dropped to his knees.

"Dear God, I know I'm one of the people that you hate with all your being, but I come to you humbly and tired. I need a way out this shit. These niggas are not playing fair. They've took Sasha and maybe now Wanda. Too many innocent people are losing their lives over this bullshit . . . Man, I still don't even know what started all this shit. I have no just cause for nothing that I'm doing. I'll leave this shit alone, I promise. Please just save my baby. I can't live without her, God. Please, I'm begging you. Please forgive me for the sins that I have committed. I'm not perfect. Please, God, forgive me for my sins. Please, I beg you."

Tez-Mo wiped his face and got off his knees slowly. Small pebbles stuck to his knees as he rose to his feet.

"Here, let me help you," the woman said as she reached her hand out for Tez-Mo to grab.

He looked at her hesitantly before grabbing her hand.

Tez-Mo got up and dusted off his True Religion denim jeans. He peeked at the woman as he dusted the rest of his clothes off, knowing he did not need to. He just wanted to steal glances.

Tez-Mo had never seen the woman before. The only reason he was not on high alert about her was because she was a dark mocha color. The bitch his homies and Gloria described was a Puerto Rican redbone. Tez-Mo still proceeded with caution.

"Who are you?" Tez-Mo flat out asked. He did not have time for the games.

"I'm one of your neighbors. I've been one of your neighbors since you moved Nancy out here a few years ago. Me and Sasha were very close. I have an 11-year-old daughter that went to gymnastics with Diamond's bad ass. Hi, my name is Angel. I'm sorry about what happened to Wanda. She was . . . I'm sorry . . . is also a good friend of mine."

Tez-Mo looked at Angel like she was crazy.

How the fuck . . . was all Tez-Mo could think to say at the moment. He was flabbergasted.

"So you been a friend of my family all this time and I've never seen you? How? No disrespect, you too beautiful for a nigga to casually miss. How—"

"I've been to a lot of functions that your mom and Sasha have thrown. I was present, but you and your brother were not," Angel said sarcastically, lightweight joking.

Angel shivered at the brisk air. The nightly chill made her tighten her robe and rub her arms.

"I was actually able—"

Angel's words faltered when she saw Kevin walk up.

Tez-Mo followed her gaze and turned around. He looked into the eyes of his younger brother, then sighed deeply.

"Nigga, how dare—" was all Kev was able to say before Tez-Mo took off on him, punching him dead in his face.

Kev stumbled and backed out on him before Tez-Mo had the chance to pounce on him.

"Bitch ass nigga, I called you crying in need. You ignored me, nigga. You were there, then you wasn't. I should keep beating your ass, lor nigga. You motherfucking deserve it, bitch ass nigga. You fucking deserve it," Tez-Mo said venomously, trying to shake the pain out of his hand from hitting his younger brother.

Kev did not say nothing. He just kept the gun raised, eye level to Tez-Mo's face.

"Don't hesitate. What you just waving that bitch around for? Nigga, use it. Pull that bitch, use that bitch. I'm not afraid to die. Is you?" Tez-Mo taunted Kev. "Nigga, I motherfucking dare you."

Angel stepped in front of Tez-Mo, hands raised.

"Please, young man, this is your brother. Whatever is going on, you both can get past. A split-second decision can change everyone's life forever. So please," Angel pleaded, for the sake of the both of them.

"Nah, watch out. This nigga want to kill me. Let this bitch ass nigga do what his heart feels. Man, fuck this nigga, I'm out. He bluffing. Bitch isn't going to kill nothing, or watch anything die," Tez-Mo said as he pushed past both Angel and Kevin.

Tez-Mo locked eyes with Kev, and all Kev could see was disappointment written all over Tez-Mo's face. Kev didn't give no fucks.

"Coward," Kev said loud enough for Tez-Mo to hear as he walked by.

Tez-Mo laughed. "Says the nigga holding the gun," he replied swiftly.

"You didn't beg God for Sasha's life. You didn't promise to change for her. But you going to now, tender dick ass nigga. I motherfucking hate your bitch ass." Kev laughed. "You really going to save this bitch—"

Tez-Mo turned around quickly and advanced toward Kev. Kev raised the gun again. Only this time they were closer, and Kev raised the gun to Tez-Mo's chest plate.

Angel just could not believe her eyes. Everything she had ever heard about the infamous Brooks brothers was proving to be a myth. What Angel was witnessing was sad, and she instantly began to regret even getting involved whatsoever.

Kev continued, "But you not going to beg or change for our sister?"

Tez-Mo just looked at Kev. He really couldn't believe he was staring down the barrel of a gun—ironically, a gun he paid for. The betrayal hurt, and it hurt bad. This was his baby brother. The nigga he shot and killed someone for as kids. The nigga he checked under the bed to fight the boogeyman for. His heart, his other half. How could he ever? Tez-Mo thought, brokenhearted. The tears that ran down Tez-Mo's face were unwilling. He didn't mean to show any emotion.

"That was your fault, Kev. They followed you home. Those bullets were meant to bury you, my nigga. Not me. Not Sasha. You! You were supposed to beg for her life, not me. By the time I was told, she was already dead on arrival. Don't forget that. And take me serious when I say this, please, because I am not playing, laughing, or joking around. I mean this shit whole heartedly, gang. You get no more passes, nigga. Raise another motherfucking gun at me, to me, or around me . . . on Sasha, I'm going to end your life. Or I will force you to end mine. You my flesh, my blood—how could you threaten me in such a manner? I just don't . . . huh . . . I don't know, man. You got it."

Tez-Mo threw his hands in the air, in surrender. He looked at Angel and mouthed "thank you" to her before walking away to his truck sitting in the driveway of their home.

"Nigga, where you going?" Kev called out to Tez-Mo, putting his gun back on his waist.

Tez-Mo didn't have no time to argue. He wanted so badly to make it to Harford General that all that could wait. Especially the bullshit with Kevin.

"To the hospital to make sure my bitch is still breathing," Tez-Mo replied sarcastically.

Angel ran to the truck before Tez-Mo could get in. She grabbed his arm caringly.

"Look, no matter what happens, when you finally do get there, you will have to wait. She will be in surgery. You look crazed. You have blood smeared all over you—your face, your neck, arms, clothes . . . shall I keep going to point out the obvious?

"You can come take a shower in—"

"Ma, no disrespect, you pretty and all, but come on shorty. My wife not even cold yet and you acting hella disrespectful right now."

Angel's hand dropped from his arm as her face contorted upwardly, like she was trying to search her mind for something.

"Listen, if you took what I offered as a sign of thirstiness or anything sexual, you read me all wrong. If you would have let me complete my sentence, you would have known I was going to open my home to you—courtesy of me and my husband. I saw what just took place because I have eyes. I know that is your brother, and I'm sure you love each other. But right now . . ." She looked over at Kev, then whispered so that only Tez-Mo could hear, "He is not to be trusted right now."

"Thank you, Ma, but I'm straight. None of that other shit matters right now. I apologize too, man. I truly meant no disrespect."

"None taken. Just know our door is open. Just knock."

Angel casually walked off, instinctively looking both ways before crossing the street.

Tez-Mo opened the door to his maroon-colored Ford F-150. He grabbed the handle inside the car and lifted himself into the truck, ready to find out about his wife. But before Tez-Mo got the chance to close the door, Kev yelled angrily.

"Bro, what the fuck! We got work to do. We got to find who the fuck did this!"

Tez-Mo stared at his brother with a blank stare. He got out the car and walked back to Kev, standing in the middle of the street. Tez-Mo was pissed. Kev couldn't tell if he was red from anger or from the blood smeared all over him.

"Listen, Kevin, this shit is your motherfucking fault. All of this shit has been your motherfucking fault with your soft ass. When are you going to realize your stupidity is killing all of our loved ones? I'm serious, bro. At this point, I'm just riding with your hot-headed ass. Me and you, bruh—we switched places a long time ago. If my wife doesn't survive, I'm going to make the city feel Momma's blood. If she does make it, I'm done. Take it how you want."

Tez-Mo turned around and hopped back into his F-150. He just sat there, thinking about everything—Hood, Stacks, Piru. He thought about Sasha, Tijuana, Wanda, Reese, and Twan. All the people that he knew, that left Earth earlier than attended by God.

Tez-Mo shed tears for them all. He wiped at his face, but to no avail. Tez-Mo's heart had been broken for a long time now. This breakdown was inevitable.

Tez-Mo took out his phone so that he could call his mother and update her on the problems going on in her absence, but Tez-Mo stopped in his tracks. The proof was in the pudding—his phone displayed the last incoming message from Wanda.

The message read as follows . . . in all caps:

//: GLORIA'S DEAD

Tez-Mo jumped and upped his pistol as the door to his F-150 opened. It was Kev. Tez-Mo lowered his gun. It was evident that the words Tez-Mo spoke hit home.

"Can I?" Kev asked before getting into his brother's truck, especially after the stunt he just pulled. Another thing Kev knew for certain was Tez-Mo was extremely unstable, so he knew it was a must that he watched what he said or how he acted.

Tez-Mo nodded for Kev to join him.

"What's up, man, what do you want?" Tez-Mo asked, getting straight to the point. "What is your aim, gang? Why are you in my truck, bro?"

"Damn, Ru, what did I do? All I ever had was your back, bro. I have followed your lead—"

"Until you didn't. What made you kill Glo, Kev? Like what the fuck, bro? Nigga, you didn't think we'd be at the top of this nigga's most wanted list? At least give me clarity and not that bullshit you told me earlier. Because that shit was some bullshit."

"After them niggas at the trap got killed—"

Tez-Mo laughed at his brother's blatant ignorance.

"What do I do now, bro?" Kev asked, confused.

"Your niece's father was amongst those casualties, nigga. Have some damn respect. Plus, that was your main nigga, not mine."

"Fuck that hoe ass nigga. His thirsty ass got himself killed."

"As far as Glo, bro, I already spoke my peace on that. I had to do what I had to do. I didn't want to go, you insisted that I went with her to right your wrong. I was trying to stay with you while you were drunk. The last thing I was worried about was Gloria. As soon as I sat in that car, I knew she wasn't the person I had fell in love with at Edgewood Middle. There really wasn't nothing to speak about. I really don't know why I even went, because I had changed myself. I wasn't the same nigga that she had grew to love. Don't get me wrong, I'm not going to sit and act like at first I wasn't excited to see shorty, because I was. When I spotted her in the crowd, I didn't want to let her out of my eye sight." Kev leaned against the door for comfort, then continued. "But anyways, bro, I changed. I changed for you. I knew Hood and them loved you, but I also knew nobody gave a fuck about you like I did. I doubt this shit with Glo got sis hit. It was too soon. Too fast. It doesn't add up. But then again, I don't know. I know we put in enough work to warrant retaliation. Don't forget, we didn't start this. We weren't beefing with no Washington Park niggas, bro, so why they kill Sasha? Why did they even want to kill me? I never dropped nobody from that side, unless you did and didn't tell me. They sent shots first, period. Mom's house, then Sasha's homegoing. We did what we had to do. Now you telling me you going to leave me in these streets alone? That's whack, nigga. You supposed to be big bro. I understand you hurt about your girl. Chalk that shit up and let's go opp hunting. Don't let her die in vain. That's your girl, not mine. Whenever you stop acting like my sister and more like that savage nigga I know, then holla at me. Until then, I'm cool on you. In the meantime, I get caught lackin' by myself, this body on you, nigga. My blood will be on your motherfucking hands, coward ass nigga."

Kev looked at Tez-Mo disgusted. He no longer had shit to say to his older sibling. From that day forward, Tez-Mo was dead to him. Kev got out the truck, slamming the door behind him.

Tez-Mo watched his younger brother through the rearview mirror. Kev had walked away and hadn't looked back. The gesture hurt Tez-Mo's feelings, but he knew he would have to let it go. Tez-Mo could understand Kev's point of view, but Kev had to also understand his. He was tired of killing the innocent in the name of getting back.

Tez-Mo thought about what his life would have to be if he squared up. Did he really have the dry life in him? If he really wanted to leave the game, Tez-Mo and Wanda—if she lived—would have to move far, far away from Maryland. Could he really live with the fact that he left Kev out in the trenches by his lonely, when in all actuality, the reason Kev was so deep in the game in the first place was because of the pressure him and Hood Ru applied?

Only time would tell, Tez-Mo thought to himself as he revved the engine up.

The events of the night ran through his mind as if on repeat. His momma and Diamond leaving them. Wanda choking on her blood. Kev pulling his gun on him—not once, but twice. All of it replayed over and over and over again, breaking his heart. It was then he knew this life for him was over. This life that he chose for him and his brother had single handedly ruined his family.

Tez-Mo loved Kevin unconditionally, and that would never change. But he knew that his fate relied solely on the outcome of the night's events.

Tez-Mo erased everything from his memory bank—Gloria, Carlos, Kevin, Sasha, Reese. He erased it all. At least for the night, all he wanted to focus on was the survival and future of Wanda Dawson. The love of his life. She needed him more than anyone in the world, so everything else had to take back seat while Wanda's situation took precedence.

Tez-Mo pulled out and raced to the hospital in hopes his other half was still alive.

Chapter 12

FB Freezo sat in the driver seat leaned up against the door as he ate Planters Roasted Cashews. It was one of Freezo's favorite foods in the world—let him tell it. Him and Za'Leek Edler, better known to the streets as FB Leek, sat outside of Tha Carter waiting on the crowd of mourners to clear out so they could get back to chasing money.

"Let me get some of those, Fully," Leek asked, reaching his hand out towards Freezo.

Freezo looked out the side of his eye at Leek and sucked his teeth dismissively. "Nigga, stop playing, and this my only bag too. You buggin'. I can drive us to the Sev and we can buy you whatever, but you won't be getting none of these, player." Freezo laughed, shaking the blue Planters bag in Leek's face. "I still love you though, Fully."

Leek stuck his middle finger up at him, trying to snatch the bag all in the same motion. Leek was too slow, causing both of them to bust out laughing.

"Wit' yo' stingy ass," Leek said after he caught his breath from laughing so hard.

"Nah, Fully, I just love these bitches. I'd share my bitch before I share the chews, bro."

Leek smiled devilishly. "I might have to take you up on that offer with Mikaela fine ass. You know I been waiting to—"

Leek looked over. Freezo had stopped chewing the cashews in his mouth—it damn near looked like the nigga stopped breathing altogether. Freezo eyed Leek, daring him to finish his sentence.

"Breathe, mad dog. You the one talking crazy. I was just taking advantage; you feel me?"

Freezo snarled his nose and began chewing again slowly as he eyed his comrade seriously.

"Don't make me fuck you up, little nigga, Freezo said."

"You know it's all in love, big bro. I'm too loyal to ever do some shit like that. It was a joke anyway. Well, I got something that's been weighing on me since Darla got shot the other day."

"Talk to me," Freezo replied, giving Leek his undivided attention.

"So what do you think of this shit with Lil' Gleek, bro? Motherfuckers got to start seeing that this Fatty Man nigga isn't what this team needs. Especially not as no leader. Heem would still be here if it wasn't for them back door ass actions. Bandy . . . shall I keep naming niggas that has lost their lives from a result of Fatty's decision making? This bitch ass nigga in the way, bruh," Leek said bluntly.

He was tired of hiding in the background while Fatty Man single handedly destroyed their *Full Blooded* clique.

"Bro, I know. I feel your pain. Haseem was like a brother to me. Nigga, I slept head to feet in the same bed as that nigga. But we already been through this with Fatty, and look at what happened. In the end nothing changed. We remained dysfunctional as fuck so—"

"Hold on, Freeze. Hold on," Leek said, cutting him off mid-sentence. "Bro, I mean no disrespect, I swear. But gang, you over there sounding soft as hell as if this nigga put fear in your heart. Ain't nobody worried about that lame ass nigga, bruh. I will end him where he stands. He not the only nigga dropping shit. My bodies don't come from a bunch of niggas I once loved. Other than them, what confirmed kills does he have? Think . . . exactly. Every single one of them friends of his. Rayo . . . Remy . . . Von. Even Nessy was once cool with Fatty. That nigga is a fucking dirt ball, bro."

"Za'Leek, listen, bro. That shit you speaking on isn't facts, bro. But believe me, I understand how you feel. Bruh has given niggas reason not to trust him. But still, can't nobody prove that Fatty killed any of tha homies."

Leek busted out laughing, causing Freezo's face to turn crimson red. Leek couldn't tell if he was embarrassed or mad, but his light complexion did nothing to hide the slight he felt. It really didn't matter no way, because one thing about Leek—he was going to speak his truth regardless. The only reason he hadn't brought his thoughts to the table yet was because of Sleeze's untimely death. And since then, they had no real place to host their meetings or hold the weight that Torrey was feeding them. They were all waiting for the final touches to be made for the new spot.

"Nigga, you playing, right? Bruh, fuck making sense, it's a fact. The world knows. He already admitted to doing Remy bold. You were there for that admission—the last meeting we had at the old spot, the same night Sleeze got killed—you don't remember?" Leek asked, astonished by Freezo's sudden lack of memory.

"I do, bro," Freezo answered nonchalantly, putting another handful of cashews in his mouth.

"Bro, I was about to say, because when he asked us to raise our hand if we felt like he killed Remy, a lot of us raised our hands, including you. Shit, how he acted that night, it was like you hurt him for raising your shit. Anyway . . . bro, you talking 'bout making sense . . . hmph . . . it's the only truth about this lame ass nigga I know. I'm a real nigga, and I truly understand why Fatty did Remy and Von slimey, but why the fuck did he kill Gleek? I'm still hella lost behind that one. It wasn't like he was fucking Darla. And what really pissed me off about this shit—we were all just about to leave literally, until we heard a creak come from the back of the house. You know what I'm talking about, like when a door is being opened after being shut for a grip."

Freezo nodded in agreement, and Leek continued.

"Alright, so at that point we all get to clutching. Gleek the only one with his gun out. All I can remember is girlie got to panicking, explaining that the person walking down the hallway was her son and to please not shoot. This the problem with that—Darla had literally just said that she didn't want her son to come back from the movies with her sister and see them there, guns drawn and what not. That statement was the whole reason we were about to leave. But now she talking about her son was really taking a nap? Shit sounded sketchy as hell. Next thing I know, she took off full speed, trying to make it to the hallway, and Gleek didn't hesitate, popping shorty all in her neck and back. Don't get me wrong, bro—I feel bro made a bad choice. But come on, bruh. All he knew was to protect us at any cost. And he did just that. Little bro didn't know what was going on. Even still, why kill your own brother over that?"

Leek got choked up just thinking about Gleek's death. He looked out the window at the crowd of mourners that gathered in Nazir's memory. Another Black soul claimed by the ghetto. Leek just shook his head in disappointment. The beef that was going on between Santana and FB was superficial as hell.

"Bruh," Freezo sighed.

The situation was a hard one for many reasons. One, he really didn't care too much about Remy, Von, Nessy, or even Gleek. He had told Fatty that he didn't agree with prematurely letting Gleek into the pack, but Fatty being Fatty, he did it anyway.

Yeah, Gleek had been known around Charleston to bust his gun, but he was also known for his reckless and dismissive behavioral flaws. In other words, the nigga was a loose cannon. But after Gleek saved Fatty as Santana advanced on his car, it was no longer a conversation. He was FB.

Now, as the second in command, he was left with the mess to clean up like always. Secondly, he knew Leek was right—Fatty needed to fall back for the betterment of their hood. But damn, he wasn't trying to go through the bullshit of watching his back and all that other whack shit. So for now, all he would do was eat his cashews and just go with the flow.

Leek looked back at Freezo with disappointment written all over his face. He just couldn't let it go that easily.

"Aye, bro, Fatty really did little man bold. He did Gleek dirty, bro. Do you know he shot that man in his face four times? He made sure Ms. Claire had to close bruh's casket. Before we left, Gleek was no longer recognizable. It just was so uncalled for. Bro didn't deserve that. You talk a nigga into joining your gang, to kill him a few days later? In whose world does that happen or make sense? Please tell me. I almost killed Fatty Man's ass right there. For real. The only reason I didn't was solely based on the fact of not knowing how Buddha and Roscoe would feel about the whole shit. I didn't know if I would have had to kill them, so I just kept my feelings to myself. I just couldn't fathom killing my sandbox niggas for real. Plus, I wasn't trying to die myself. This shit all fucked up, man. I can tell you that this shit isn't what it's supposed to be, that's for sure. I took an oath to love and protect thy brother—not to kill them in a time of mutiny. We are not the CPD. I don't need a jury or a judge to convince me Fully sour. I can hear that nigga hiss every time he talks," Leek said, hoping Freezo would understand his stance in the matter.

Freezo sat still for a second, not saying a word. He just looked out the window, down the street at the flashing lights and crime scene tape. Death and funerals seemed to be the only time the Black community gathered together in unison. Shit was sad, Freezo thought, before looking over at Leek.

"So what you think we should do about it then? Tell me. Give me a solution and be realistic, little bruh."

"Happily," Leek said and sat up excitedly. "Kill that coward ass nigga," Leek responded seriously.

It was Freezo's turn to laugh. Leek was talking crazy.

"Bro, you trippin'. Now you just talking out the side of your ass."

Leek looked at Freezo seriously. Wasn't shit he was saying a joke. Leek was dead ass serious.

"Am I? I bet if we took a vote, everybody besides a handful, maybe, would agree that Fatty's a snake that needs instant termination. I'm serious. I will kill that man myself."

"No. But we have a meeting coming up tomorrow—I mean today. Make your feelings, issues, and concerns known. And see if you're not alone on this. If niggas feel like you do, we'll go from there. You cool with that?" Freezo asked, extending his hand in agreement.

"Shit, of course I'm cool with that." Leek leaned over and dapped Freezo up, doing their signature handshake. Leek was excited. He rubbed his hands together in anticipation.

The night turned into morning before Charleston PD got Nazir's body off the ground. Nazir had only been home for a matter of 24 hours before he was killed in cold blood. The message Santana sent was loud and utterly clear.

Torrey upped the ante on both Zach and Santana for the grief he had caused. It was now thirty thousand apiece to capture or kill the pair.

With nothing to lose but sleep, Za'Leek Edler stayed up pondering—pondering what he was going to do, or maybe even what he was going to say. Whatever it may be, it was going to be brought forth that day, in front of their whole squad.

Za'Leek relished the moment when Fatty Man's cards would yet again come tumbling down and he would be an outcast. Only this time, the story would be written with a different ending.

***

Tez-Mo stirred. The delicious aroma that filled the air captured his senses. Somebody was in the kitchen throwing down, that was for sure. The thought of a home-cooked meal made Tez-Mo's stomach growl with hunger. He hadn't eaten any real food in days. All he had been consuming was drugs and alcohol, literally.

Tez-Mo yawned and opened his eyes, instantly shielding them from the rays of the morning sun. *What the fuck . . . that bitch bright as hell.*

Tez-Mo cracked one eye open and realized he was on the couch in his mother's house. *I must have been dreaming,* he thought at last. He had to be. Tez-Mo opened his eyes fully once he got adjusted to the brightness in the room. He just laid there, looking at the ceiling, trying to figure out what last night's dream could have meant. Was it a sign from God? Was he being warned to keep his family safer and secure?

What could a dream of that magnitude mean? Tez-Mo had never had a dream so vivid in his life. The feeling that coursed through his body, the sound, the people, just everything—it all seemed so real. Too real, if you asked him. Wanda had gotten killed, and Kev had pulled a gun on him, all in one night.

Tez-Mo shook off the chills that ran through his body just thinking about it. He swiped a hand over his face and sighed deeply.

Last night's dream was literally the only thing running through his mind as he laid there staring at the ceiling. He had so many questions that needed to be answered—but who would he ask? Everyone would think he was losing his mind. How would he be able to explain? He could never remember a time he had a dream like that.

"That shit was crazy . . ." Tez-Mo said, trying to laugh it off.

He sat bolt upright and stretched, eyes closed. He twisted his body from one side to the next. After his neck cracked, his back followed suit. Tez-Mo got off the couch and picked up the blanket, then proceeded to fold the quilt. He was so gone last night he didn't even remember falling asleep—let alone being covered up.

Tez-Mo prayed that his mother wasn't the one who covered him up. He could hear the argument coming. Ms. Brooks had warned him and Kev about sleeping on her couches. He had heard it enough, and he really didn't have the patience. Tez-Mo shrugged the thought away as fast as it came.

After he folded the quilt, he laid it to the far left of him and fluffed the pillows back out like his mother liked. Tez-Mo sat back down, searching his mind. Something wasn't right—he could feel it. But he didn't know what it was. It was out of place.

The scraping of a spatula told him that either his mother or Diamond was in the kitchen going crazy in front of the stove.

Diamond was only ten years old, but she was already a force to be reckoned with on the stovetop. Before Nancy Brooks had gotten pregnant with Teziar, her true love was cooking. Ms. Brooks would have gone to college and majored in culinary arts in Silver Spring, Maryland, but she never got the chance.

It was Ms. Brooks' dream to be a world-renowned chef. Shit, she would have even settled for running her own restaurant—but with a new child and a broken dream, she did the next best thing. She passed her love for the art to her beautiful and intelligent granddaughter, Diamond Carter-Brooks.

Tez-Mo knew that when either one of them was in the kitchen, magic was being made. His stomach growled again just at the thought. He was starving.

"Ma!" Tez-Mo called out as he got off the couch and walked a few feet before stopping.

He had to be tripping. He began looking around for the first time that morning. He was lost. Literally.

Where the fuck am I? Tez-Mo began to panic. Instinctively, he reached for his hip. His gun was gone. He was not armed.

Tez-Mo ran to the couch and felt around—in between the cushions, under the pillows. He even looked in the folded clothes on the floor in front of the couch.

Tez-Mo tried to breathe—deep, long breaths—but nothing seemed to work. He thought of any scenario that could have led him to someone else's house. He never left bars or clubs with females, because he was too far into beef and wasn't willing to take that chance of being backdoored.

"Yo!" Tez-Mo yelled, trying to grab the attention of anyone in the home.

He heard the sound of heels clanking against the floor, setting him a little at ease. Tez-Mo watched as Angel walked from the back, where he assumed the kitchen was. Angel was definitely dressed to impress. She had on a beige skirt suit with matching three-inch heels. She looked like she was on her way to work—at least that's what it looked like.

"Everything okay, Teziar? What's wrong?" Angel asked, concern written all over her face.

Tez-Mo was confused by her demeanor—you would have thought he belonged there. He got straight to the point.

"No disrespect, but why am I here? And who are you? What the fuck happened last night that I ended up—"

Tez-Mo stopped midsentence and rubbed his temple. Almost on cue, the memories rushed back into his head—but in pieces. Tez-Mo sat down, feeling like he was getting dizzy.

Angel came closer and touched his shoulder. Tez-Mo looked up into her hazel eyes and felt comfort.

"Baby, are you okay? Do you need me to do anything, like what's up, talk to me? But be fast, I'm cooking. I was making me and you some quick shit before I went to work. My children already ate and left for school. It's only a few more days left, so they may come home early. You're welcome to stay until you get yourself together," Angel said in a friendly tone.

Tez-Mo nodded in appreciation.

"What the fuck . . . where is my gun?" he asked, looking up at Angel.

"Oh, I left that in your truck, under the driver's side seat. Sorry, but I have curious children," Angel replied, standing there with a spatula in one hand and her other hand on her hip.

"How did I even get here?"

"Hold that thought. I will answer any questions you have, but I have to go before the food burns. I'll be right back, sweetie," Angel said, jogging back into the hallway that led to the kitchen.

Tez-Mo looked around. The house was almost identical to the one he had bought his mother. The only difference was the taste in appliances. The house was immaculately clean and equipped with some of the latest appliances on the market.

He knew something was off earlier—he could feel it. And damn, was he right. He was in a stranger's house. A stranger that Tez-Mo had only met just the night before. But even that, he had no recollection of.

That's when it hit him. *Oh, shit. Please say it isn't so . . . please say it isn't so,* Tez-Mo thought, pleading.

What he thought was a dream . . . was reality.

Wanda was dead, and Kevin had come close to taking his life.

Before he began to freak out or ask himself a million questions, Angel reappeared with two plates of food in her hand.

"Please sit with me at the dining table. I try not to make a habit of eating in the living room," Angel said, waiting to see if Tez-Mo would make an issue of her request. Thankfully, he didn't. He grabbed one of the plates and followed her into the dining area. The table was already set. There was orange juice, milk, and water sitting in pitchers in the middle of the table. Angel didn't know what kind of beverage Tez-Mo liked, so she laid out a few options.

After they were seated, Tez-Mo grabbed his fork and began scooping at his eggs, as if he was about to take a bite of food without saying grace. Angel looked at him perplexed. She cleared her throat loudly, stopping him in the middle of lifting his fork to his mouth. Tez-Mo looked up. Angel reached her hand over to him so he could join her in prayer. Without any kind of fight, Tez-Mo smiled, placed the fork back on his plate, and grasped Angel's hand.

"God, I thank you for this food we are about to receive, the love I know you will give. I ask that you look over us in these days of pain and confusion. Please don't lead me astray. Please forgive us for what we do not know and understand, and please have patience for what we do. Again, thank you, God. Amen," Angel prayed, then slowly released Tez-Mo's hand.

They both picked up their forks and dug in. Angel could tell that Tez-Mo hadn't eaten in days—the way he devoured the plate of eggs in front of him said so. Luckily for him, she had made enough eggs, toast, and turkey bacon to feed a small army. Her kids usually ate breakfast at school, so their portions usually stayed wrapped up until she either ate it herself or threw it away. Well, that was the case most of the time. Sometimes, on a rare morning, they would get up early enough to eat.

Now, as far as her husband . . . well . . . Angel didn't have one. Ever. She had just said it as a quick reply to Tez-Mo's insult. All she was, was a family friend—and that's all it would be.

The silence was so awkward that Angel began to feel uncomfortable—and awkward—in her own home. She couldn't help but watch Tez-Mo. She felt bad for him. He had lost his girlfriend and brother all in the same night. Angel knew it had to be a hard pill to swallow. The creases in his forehead when he frowned let her know that he wasn't young, but she could see that he wasn't old either. The years of the streets had aged Tez-Mo. His facial features showed years of worry and years of stress. Angel didn't know what to say. She was intimidated by Tez-Mo's presence, but she didn't know why. He had never said or done anything to her. They had never even met before last night. Angel couldn't put her finger on it, but there was something about Tez-Mo that scared the shit out of her.

Tez-Mo looked up from his plate. He could feel Angel staring at him. Surprisingly, she didn't look away. They just locked eyes for a second. Neither looked away. They studied each other closely.

Tez-Mo busted out laughing as he looked away and began eating again.

"What?" Angel asked curiously, trying to figure out what he found so funny.

"Nothing, ma'am. I'm trying to figure out how I ended up here this morning. Can you tell me what happened last night?" Tez-Mo asked in return, wiping his mouth with the paper towel that sat beside his plate.

"Which time? Man, a lot happened last night. A lot," Angel replied, making sure she put emphasis on *a lot*.

"Man, all of it. My brain doesn't want to register what happened so bad that I woke up thinking it was all a dream. A vivid ass dream. This shit is crazy. So everything I thought was a dream really happened?"

Angel nodded.

"Okay . . . so when I came back from the hospital, what happened?"

Angel wiped her mouth, drank another sip of orange juice, and began explaining to Tez-Mo the events of the night.

"When you came back from the hospital, you banged on my door. I didn't expect it, but I was still up because I was shaken from seeing Wanda sprawled out on the ground bleeding from gunshot wounds. I couldn't get none of that shit out of my head long enough to fall asleep. I opened the door, I asked you what happened, if Wanda was okay—you stumbled in and began crying, mumbling something about Wanda dying on her way to the hospital and how it was all your fault.

"I took you over to the couch and laid you down. I took your shoes off, took your gun off your waist, and then draped one of my favorite quilts over you. When I left to put your gun in your car, you were still crying. I came back a few hours later after you were sound asleep and turned you on your side. You know, just in case you threw up. But after a while, I walked to my bedroom and fell asleep until my alarm woke me."

"Damn, man. That shit is so crazy, man. Why Wanda? She was too good of a person to deserve to be killed like that. Did anybody see anything? Like what the hell happened? I told her that I was sending my mother and Diamond off, but that was it. We spoke briefly through text . . . well, actually she hit me about a family issue, I replied, and that was it. She never hit me back."

"So why did you and your brother return fire?" Angel asked, confused.

"Shit, this our block. Ain't nobody 'bout to be coming over here harming nobody, fuck no! I don't care who it is. Plus, I thought we was protecting a neighbor—not my wife. Man, fuck!" Tez-Mo banged the table with his fist, making everything on it rattle. He realized where he was and apologized. "My bad, Angel. I just can't seem to protect none of my family from the reaper. I've lost Sasha, Reese, now Wanda. That's not even counting three of my best friends. I want out this shit, shorty. Dead ass, I want out."

Tez-Mo covered his face as the tears rolled down his cheeks. Angel grabbed Tez-Mo's forearm and moved his arm away from his face.

"I don't know why you hiding your face now. I've done seen you cry multiple times already. And I'm not going to lie, your face hell of ugly when you do," Angel joked, trying to change the mood in the room.

Tez-Mo couldn't help but laugh. She was silly as hell for that, but he definitely appreciated the effort.

"You got that one, you got that one," he laughed, turning his frown into a smile. "Let me ask you another question about last night that's foggy but still lingering."

"Shoot!" Angel replied immediately.

"Did my brother pull his gun on me or did I make that up in my head?"

Angel just sat there, looking at Tez-Mo disappointedly.

"By the look on your face, he pulled the gun . . . but was I tripping and he had to? Or did it look like he was on bullshit and really wanted to end my life?"

Tez-Mo turned his chair towards Angel so that he could look into her face and see the truth. Because something in him felt like Angel might fabricate the truth just to keep him calm—and he didn't need that right now.

Tez-Mo wanted to know the truth. He needed to know—had it only been them, would Kev have pulled the trigger?

He needed the answer from an unbiased source. And right now, Angel would have to serve as that unbiased source.

"Teziar, please. I'm not trying to get involved with any family matters. Especially one of that magnitude," Angel explained, desperately trying to get out of answering Tez-Mo's question regarding Kevin.

"Please shorty, because what that nigga did was foul. One. Two, I don't want to go back around that nigga if my life is in the balance. You know what his face looked like last night, I don't. I can't remember. Did he pull his gun out on me in defense or did he pull his gun out on me maliciously?" Tez-Mo asked sincerely.

"He did." She paused, then continued. "I do believe at first it was to get you up off him, but he let the moment linger for too long. Then when he yanked the gun off his hip for the second time, I thought—"

"Hold on, hold on. That nigga pulled his gun on me twice?" Tez-Mo asked in shock, not believing what he was hearing. That revelation broke his heart, and Angel saw it almost instantly. The hurt came and went. It was now replaced with anger.

"Yes, he pulled his gun twice. It was the reason I told you that if you needed somewhere to stay for the night, you could come here. Look, Teziar, I'm sorry for the death of Wanda. She was someone that I was growing to love, like Nancy and little Diamond. I want nothing but the best for your family. We've leaned on each other for years. But I don't want to get any further involved in the rift between you and your—"

"Okay, look, listen . . ." Tez-Mo said, cutting Angel off mid-sentence. "Answer this with a simple nod or yes or no. That would be good with me. If you and the rest of our neighbors weren't out there when the situation happened with me and Kev, do you think he would have . . . you know . . . pulled the trigger? I'm not saying in a way to kill me; I'm just talking about period. Would he have squeezed that trigger and wounded me?"

Angel sighed deeply, releasing the air through her mouth. She knew she shouldn't be getting involved at all, but what if the shoe was on the other foot? Wouldn't she have wanted to know? She thought hard, she thought long. Angel closed her eyes, trying to remember what Kev's initial demeanor was when he pointed the gun at Tez-Mo. The image of Kev's snarl and the way he bit his bottom lip in anger said enough. Angel opened her eyes and replied in the most serious tone of her life.

"He would have killed you, Teziar. The look on his face said it all. The snarl, and the—"

"Way he bit his bottom lip," Tez-Mo finished her sentence, saddened. Those were the signs he couldn't remember seeing. Ironically, those were also the signs that made Angel feel the way she did. Tez-Mo didn't know what he was going to do with the information, but he stored it in the back of his mind. He got up from the table and grabbed his plate. Angel watched in confusion.

"What are you doing, sir?" Angel asked.

"I'm about to wash my plate. I have a lot that needs to be done today. Plus, you're about to go to work anyway. I'm not sitting in your house while you're not here for one, and for two, I'm not too much of a stay-home kind of nigga. Talking about stay-home nigga, where's this husband of yours? I didn't hear you say shit about him at all this morning. Is everything okay? I haven't caused any kind of friction, have I? If I did, shorty, I sincerely apologize about that," Tez-Mo said sincerely, meaning his words.

Angel looked up in the air for something complex to say so that Tez wouldn't ask again, but she came up empty, so she said the next best thing.

"It's a long story, best told at a different time," Angel replied with a smile.

"Damn, Ma, you asking me out on a date already? My shorty hasn't even been dead for twenty-four hours yet." Angel's mocha complexion turned a dark crimson from embarrassment.

"TEZIAR! Stop doing that," Angel protested before she busted into tears. Tez-Mo didn't know what he did wrong—he was only playing. The joke was at his expense, not hers, so he was lost. He definitely wouldn't have said it if he knew Angel would begin to cry.

"In light of my apology, I just want to point out that I'm not the only ugly face around here when they cry . . .

ewwwww . . ." Tez-Mo responded with a wink and a stuck-out tongue, praying that he lightened the mood.

Angel sat there speechless, mouth gaped open in surprise. *No, this negro didn't*, she thought to herself. He had got her back in a big way. Angel couldn't do nothing but respect his reply—she had started it.

Angel wiped away her tears and laughed.

"Oh, okay, you got it, sir. You got me." It was all Angel could say as Tez-Mo disappeared, dishes in hand.

Chapter 13

With the violence plaguing the city of Charleston, making money was at an all-time low, and Big Ty was taking notice of the hit to his pockets. Fatty knew he had to figure something out fast, because the low prices that him and Sleeze were promised came with strings attached—those strings being Santana Vasquez and Zachariah Taylor.

So far, the only person that hadn't stood true to their word was Fatty. Shit, even Sleeze had contributed from beyond the grave. Though it was ill-mannered, he still contributed nonetheless. Fatty's main problem was the fact he thought Santana and Zach would be an easier task than ever, but he had to admit—he slept on them. And it was proving to be costly on his part.

In all actuality, it may even have been easy if they would have just listened to Freezo and gunned for the head—Santana.

But no . . . the thirst of Sleeze's broke ass lured him to hit Haseem, setting off a chain of events—a body that they all had agreed FB wouldn't take. Even Big Ty understood Fatty's stance. Haseem was a friend of the family, and killing him was off-limits . . . until it wasn't. Fatty had made it known to everyone that attended Torrey's meeting.

Not only was FB Bandy Haseem's first cousin, he was also Freezo's friend. They had grown up in the juvenile system together.

As Fatty sat comfortably on a stack of multi-colored milk crates, he thought about everything that had went wrong since the day of Haseem's murder.

Was all this shit my fault? he asked himself over and over again. *Could I have changed the outcome if I did better at keeping Heem alive?* Those questions ran through his head like wildfire.

He looked around the newly rented warehouse that served as FB's new meeting spot and stash house. Since the death of Sleeze, the gang hadn't conducted any meetings—or more so, hung around one another. They had a lot to discuss, because a lot had happened since that fatal night.

Fatty had to address a few issues that he knew he couldn't just sweep under the rug—Gleek being one of them. Fatty knew that many of his comrades didn't like what happened, and in truth, he had no words that would soothe their hearts. He just had to be real and move on. If what happened had to be discussed beyond the warehouse walls, so be it. But it wouldn't be with his mouth that he spoke with—it would be with violence.

Fatty watched as members of his gang slowly began to show up. The silence in the warehouse was awkward, but understandable to say the least. It was the reason they had pow-wows: so that they could address any and all bullshit.

He looked at his watch. His G-Shock read **11:52 AM**. Fatty had called the meeting a day in advance so no one would miss or be late. But by the looks of the crowd already in attendance, one of the two was bound to happen. Many would either be late or no-shows, and every FB member knew there was no tolerance for either action.

So Fatty sat back and waited. He waited to see who would test his gangster by not showing. Being late is one thing . . . not making an appearance was a whole other issue within itself.

Fatty tapped his back pockets for the box of wine-flavored Black & Mild cigars that he had. He reached into his pocket and pulled the box out. He opened it. He had two cigars and half a blunt inside. Fatty looked at the joint for a second and thought better of it—he needed his whole mental capacity. Fatty knew he had to be assiduous within his duties on this particular day, so smoking a mind-altering drug was out of the equation. He settled for one of the cigars instead.

Fatty lit the flavored full cigar as he watched the warehouse begin to fill. He looked down at his watch again—**11:58 AM**. With one look, he glanced around the warehouse and noticed that his now second-in-command wasn't present, causing Fatty to sigh in frustration. If anybody knew better than to be late, it was Freezo. But Fatty had hella love for Freezo, so awarding him a few extra minutes wasn't about nothing.

Fatty wanted to finish the black anyway. If he wasn't in attendance by then, *that's* when they would have an issue.

Just as the thought left Fatty's mind, Freezo busted in through the double doors.

"My bad, my bad. Police was out there looking like they were following me. I had to park and slide through on foot. How my niggas doing though?" Fatty could hear him say to the group of FB members as he greeted them with their signature handshake.

Fatty wasted no more time. He stubbed out his cigar and rose to his feet. It was time to start the meeting.

Fatty walked to the front of the pack and greeted his men.

"What's banging, Fully! Glad to see all in attendance on such short notice. Very much appreciated. As everyone knows, Sleeze's funeral will be a few days from now. I expect all to be present to send bruh off right. Also . . . I know some may be mad, confused, or hurt about the shit that happened with Gleek. I have no words that can make you feel better. Bro was in the wrong for shooting Rayo's baby mom. Not only that, but he was told to chill out and calm down multiple times that day. He didn't. There is no excuse, because I have none. But if anybody feel some kind of way, now is the time to speak. Please speak now or forever hold your peace."

Fatty looked around to see if anyone was going to challenge him. His eyes grew wide when he heard someone speak from the crowd.

"Someone say something?" Fatty asked.

"Yeah, nigga, I got something to say," a voice said from the middle of the crowd.

Fatty could see the crowd begin to part. Za'Leek stepped forward.

Fatty smiled, lip twitching in anger.

"Speak what's on your mind, Fully," Fatty said, trying to maintain his anger.

"Nigga, you're a bitch! And you deserve to get your ass whooped, bitch ass nigga! Somebody hold the clock!"

People in the crowd began to mutter to one another in disbelief. No one had ever challenged Fatty like that before—besides Von and Remy—and both of them were dead.

Za'Leek bent down to tie his shoes. He didn't even attempt to look up because he dared Fatty to try and sneak him. It would give him more of a reason to do him dirty.

Fatty sat there, not moved by Leek's antics.

"You done, little nigga?" Fatty asked, not impressed one bit.

"Bro, tie your shoes. I want my fade," Leek replied seriously, getting up from the ground, ready for whatever.

"Nigga, is you done?" Fatty asked again.

Za'Leek said nothing. He squared up with Fatty.

"Nah, bro, you killed my little nigga over a weak ass bitch. You need your ass whooped. You a bitch! You lucky that's all a nigga on with your hoe ass. I can see through your act, nigga. You catching this fade or not, hoe ass nigga? If not, I'm going to take my place outside this warehouse, because this FB shit over for me. You ain't no leader of mine. You can suck my—"

Fatty swung.

Leek weaved his punches with ease.

"Yeah, that's what I like." Leek put his hands up and advanced toward Fatty Man. Fatty put his hands up and bounced around, trying to avoid Leek's assault.

Leek turned toward Freezo and pointed at him.

"Fuck that, this nigga ain't my muthafuckin' brother. Put that clock away. I'm going to beat on this nigga until he quits," Leek said in a matter-of-fact tone.

Freezo didn't respond. He just shrugged and put his hands inside his pocket. Fatty looked over and glared at Freezo, making a mental note of the gesture.

Leek's 6'2", 180-pound frame advanced, closing in on Fatty. Fatty backed up, trying to stay out of Leek's reach.

"What you running for, pussy ass nigga?" Leek spat at Fatty.

"I'm going to show you pussy, nigga!"

Fatty rushed Leek out of frustration and anger. He took Leek into a bear hug. Without hesitation, Leek quickly brought two elbows down to the sides of Fatty's head.

"Aaargh! Bitch ass nigga!" Fatty exclaimed, breathing hard, trying his hardest to squeeze the life out of Leek.

Leek struggled to get loose but was able to bring another elbow down on Fatty again.

"Bitch!" Leek swung his right fist as Fatty lifted him in the air and brought him down as hard as he could. The punch landed wildly across Fatty's eye as Leek slammed into the ground hard, knocking the wind out of him temporarily.

Freezo stepped forward. He wasn't willing to let his little man get done dirty. But surprisingly enough, Fatty backed up. He didn't rush him.

"Nah, nigga, get up. You got so much mouth, catch these hands, nigga."

Fatty advanced, punching Leek in his face as he regained his footing. Leek skillfully rolled with the punch and smiled. Leek banged his knuckles together.

"That's exactly what I like. Finally, you pulled your panties up. Now pick this nigga up."

Leek rushed Fatty. He faked a right—Fatty went for it—and got hit with an uppercut to his body. Fatty stumbled, grabbing at his rib cage. His anger got the best of him, and he rushed Leek swinging wildly, hoping to connect with flesh.

Leek sidestepped Fatty and swung, catching him flush on the chin. Fatty's legs gave out—he dropped like a sack of potatoes. Leek was on him before he could even think about getting up. He stood over him and punched him in the face repeatedly.

"Bitch . . . Bitch . . . Bitch . . . Bitch . . . Bitch . . . Bitch . . ." Leek said with each hit that landed to Fatty's face.

Leek didn't stop punching Fatty until Freezo grabbed him and carried him away.

"That's enough, bro! You tripping! What the fuck, gang? You made that stupid ass shit into war. Man, fuck!" Freezo shouted, pushing Leek further and further away.

"Fuck that hoe ass nigga! That nigga deserves death!" Leek shouted for all to hear.

Fatty got up—mouth bloody, eye swollen. He watched as Freezo led Leek away. He didn't even wipe his mouth; he just smiled and shook his head up and down. Everybody that knew Fatty knew what was running through his head at that moment.

Leek was a dead man walking.

"Nah, Fully, bring bruh back. It's all good. You win some, you lose some. But you live to fight another day. Something some niggas can't do. Fuck that nigga Gleek. Tell that nigga's momma you're going to pay for that closed casket. Fuck you talkin' about."

Fatty began clapping loudly.

"Everybody give little Leek a round of applause. He proved he can fight a little dirtier than me. I could've did the same shit, but I spared you. Fuck you talkin' about."

Fatty laughed, wiping his mouth off before spitting blood onto the ground.

"Nigga, you a bitch, and I'm going to bury you next to the rest of them dick-sucking niggas!" Fatty said venomously.

Leek tried to run past Freezo to get to Fatty, but Freezo wouldn't budge. Leek turned his attention to the rest of the team and spoke his peace.

"I love all you niggas, but if you not with me, you against me. That goes for everybody. There isn't no nigga excluded. This nigga is a snake—he killed every nigga we ever loved. Von, Remy, Gleek, Heem, Bandy. Shall I keep going? This nigga going to get his day—even if I gotta go team up with opp niggas. That fat bitch going to die. We screaming we love Heem, we love Bandy—but this fat bitch the reason they are dead. The only nigga riding for Heem is that OT nigga. Niggas should be ashamed of themselves. I'm out. Hit my phone and tell me whose side you on, because I'm telling you—by later tonight I'm going to be out this bitch hunting for that nigga right there."

Leek pointed at Fatty.

"And if your name isn't in my call log, it's on sight. And that's on my pop's soul, gang. Nigga, I'm FBK. Fuck *Full Blooded*."

Leek pushed his way through the double doors, disappearing into the morning sunlight.

Fatty gritted his teeth and closed his eyes, trying to take in everything that just happened and process it. His protégé had just gone rogue.

The chatter that ran through the warehouse didn't go unnoticed. Fatty snarled as he watched Leek rush out the building.

Bitch ass nigga . . . wait till I catch you. I'm going to make them identify you by your dental, Fatty thought, knowing he wouldn't be able to sleep until Leek was six feet deep.

Fatty smiled sinisterly. He had murder on his mind, and everybody in attendance knew.

Fatty turned his attention back to his remaining soldiers. Silence fell over them.

"So who else is with that nigga? Huh? Who else is with that nigga? Buddah? Roscoe? What you niggas on?" Fatty asked, staring at the two in particular because of the relationship they held with Leek.

"I'm rocking with you, big bro," Buddah said proudly, like the question was one of stupidity.

Roscoe looked at Buddah like he lost his fucking mind.

"Nigga, what did you just say, gang?" Roscoe backed up to make sure he heard what Buddah said.

"I said I'm rocking with Fatty, nigga. Did I stud—"

Roscoe wasted not another second before he punched Buddah in the face with all his might.

Buddah stumbled and looked at Roscoe before squaring up.

"Nigga, you a bitch! That's our muthafuckin' brother. Fuck you mean. Dick-eating ass nigga."

"Nigga, fuck you and that nigga! Soft ass niggas," Buddah replied through a bloody mouth before he began to attack Roscoe with a flurry of punches.

The crowd parted and gave the men the room they needed. Buddah swung wild, but he caught Roscoe in his forehead and jaw, dropping him. Buddah advanced toward Roscoe to finish his business, but the door to the warehouse swung open and Leek walked back in—Glock in hand, ladder sticking out the bottom, ready to take a soul.

"What's that shit, huh? Nigga, what you say, bitch ass nigga?" Leek looked at Buddah standing over Roscoe, and he stopped. Leek held his Glock at his side. "Fuck is you doing, bro? Get up, Scoe."

Roscoe got up and socked Buddah in his shit again. This time Buddah gritted his teeth and just looked at Roscoe.

"What's going on, bruh?" Leek asked Roscoe, lost as hell about what was taking place.

"This bitch ass nigga going to tell Fatty he rocking with him over us, so I punched that nigga in his shit. Like what the fuck—nigga, it's always been us and only us. I don't know what's up with this nigga, gang."

"Leek!" Freezo exclaimed. "Gang, what are you doing? You trippin', Fully," Freezo said, walking toward Leek with his hands raised, trying to calm him before things got out of hand and Leek started a war—one that they might not be able to win. And truth be told, Freezo knew it was probably too late, but he tried anyway.

"Bruh, stop! You know I love you, big bro, but don't come any closer, please. I don't know who you rocking with," Leek said honestly.

Freezo stepped back, hands still raised. He could tell that Leek wasn't playing—he was dead serious.

Once Leek realized Freezo wasn't a threat, he went back to the situation at hand.

Leek looked at his longtime friend with anger in his eyes.

"That true, bro?" Leek asked simply.

Buddah looked at the ground. Leek laughed, lifted his Glock, and fired once, hitting Buddah in the chest. The impact took Buddah's breath, dropping him instantly. It felt as if time had stood still. Leek was at a loss for words. The tears that ran down his face said everything. He was hurt—his heart was broken.

Suck that shit up, nigga. He chose them over you, Leek's inner voice spoke to him as he wiped his tears away.

The warehouse erupted into mayhem. The remaining members of FB took off toward the exit, leaving Buddah sprawled out on the ground fighting for his life. Leek walked up to Buddah and raised his gun again.

"You were willing to kill me? The nigga you called your brother since kindergarten, huh? Talk, nigga. I said talk, nigga!" Leek exclaimed, fresh tears running down his face.

Buddah looked up, fear written all over his face.

"Don't look all scared now, nigga. Tell Heem I send my love." Leek raised his gun.

"No!" Roscoe exclaimed, pushing Leek's hand down, saving Buddah from his demise.

"Let that bitch ass nigga live, bro. We gotta get out of here—Freezo waiting on us outside."

Leek just stood there, staring at Buddah with hate in his eyes.

"Come on, bruh! You know the fucking police beating these streets heavy right now, nigga, come on! What the fuck!" Roscoe yelled, pulling on Leek's arm.

Leek clenched his jaw tightly and nodded. He wanted to end his so-called friend's life right where he stood—but it came with a cost. A cost that he just couldn't afford.

This shit ain't over, nigga. I'm gone catch you, Leek thought to himself as he ran off, following Roscoe out the warehouse into a new beef with a certified killer.

***

Drew pulled up and looked at the Victorian structure. It was old, unpainted, and beat to hell. The home that Drew knew all too well looked foreign to him. Though he had grown up in the home with Rocc and his friends, Ms. Inez had kept the maintenance up on it—until she didn't. And as the years went by, it deteriorated from lack of care.

Drew sat outside and thought about what he was even doing there in the first place.

Carlos had put a BOLO out on anyone that had information leading to the capture of the individuals connected to Gloria—his daughter's death. The revelation that Glo was not only related but the daughter of Carlos "Los" Rivera was insane. He had known Gloria for years. She had been hanging around Washington Park since her high school days.

The money Carlos was promising was money that would change a person's life, but Drew had no intentions of turning Rocc in. He was there to cut the ties to the only person leading to Simfany. Drew knew if Rocc ever got caught by Carlos, he would tell him everything that had taken place—and that wasn't a risk he was willing to take. Not with Simfany's life. He had already lost Tijuana; he wasn't about to lose Simfany too.

Drew shut the engine off and hopped out his royal blue Dodge Ram. He dusted off his clothes and straightened himself so that he could look presentable. Drew looked around as he walked up the steep but short hill leading to Ms. Inez's house. He knocked loudly and waited. When no response came from within the house, he knocked again—this time louder. No luck.

What the fuck? he asked himself, confused as hell. Someone was always home. Ms. Inez had been smoking crack since the beginning of time. She was known for letting local hustlers come and trap out her house, so seeing no activity whatsoever concerned him. Drew pulled the Smith & Wesson off his hip and banged again.

"Ms. Inez! Rocc!" Drew called out as he tried to look into the house through the blinds. He could see barely, but it didn't indicate anything foul. It was Drew's gut feeling that something bad had went down. Not one to ponder long on any situation, he booted the door until it gave. The door flew open. A stench that was unmistakable hit his nose. Drew instantly knew somewhere in the house there was a dead body. He knew the smell all too well.

Damn, Drew thought as he slowly made his way through the house. The living room was empty, but as soon as he entered the kitchen, he saw Ms. Inez sprawled out on the floor.

Drew bent over and checked her pulse. He knew she was dead, but checked anyway. Ms. Inez was cold to the touch. She had been gone for days.

"Damn, momma. I'm sorry this had to happen to you," Drew said as he closed her eyes.

Drew got up and walked through the rest of the house—nothing else was amiss. He closed the door as he left.

Drew pulled his phone from his pocket and called Simfany. She answered on the second ring.

"Yooooo!"

"What's good, shorty? You got time to kick it?" Drew asked nonchalantly.

"For you, you already know," Simfany replied in a sing-song kind of voice.

"Alright, so look, that shit you wanted me to do with Rocc . . . that shit a no-go. I think Los sent his men through here and grabbed that nigga. I'm leaving his mom's crib now and shorty not amongst the living."

"What about Rocc?" Simfany asked cautiously.

"He not here," Drew replied subsequently.

"FUCK!" Simfany yelled into the phone.

Drew knew that she would be sick at the revelation.

"Okay . . . okay . . . look, make sure you pull up on me later. That nigga will be here later at some time. He hasn't called me, so Rocc must have held water."

"I wouldn't get my hopes up on no shit like that. That nigga couldn't hold a secret if his mouth was cemented. I'm only saying this because I know this nigga. He the type of nigga that hear something from one side and can't wait to tell the other. Look, Simf, from my experience with the nigga, depending on what kind of tactic they have used, Carlos knows everything. Shorty a talker. That's one of the reasons we not how we supposed to be."

"I always wondered what the apprehension was for. If a nigga saved my life, I would feel in debt. But it makes sense why I never see you niggas together."

"Be on point, Simf. I tried. I'm gone send Peedi ya way," Drew tried to reassure.

"No! I mean, no need. I'll be prepared. Thank you, baby. I love you. Stay dangerous, you hear me? Just be readily available if I need you."

"Always, beauty. Always." Drew laughed before hanging up. It was obvious that something was going on between Simfany and Peedi, but it wasn't his place to speak on it, so he let it go.

Drew hopped in his car and started the engine. Before pulling off, he opened his phone to place another call—this time to Peedi—but thought better of it. Instead, he sent him a simple text:

//: Shorty need you to be present tmrw, so be on standby. And you bet not hurt my lady lor nigga!

Drew sat in place for a second as his mind ran rapid. It was the first time in his life that he was left speechless with no answers.

Gloria was Carlos's daughter. That shit was real live crazy. Out of all the people in the fucking world this woman could have been related to, she happens to be related to Carlos muthafuckin Rivera. Drew laughed at the irony of the situation. He took a deep breath as he put his SUV into drive and pulled off into the beautiful morning sunlight.

***

Carlos pulled into the cul-de-sac that he bought for Carmen years prior to their divorce. Though Carmen no longer lived there, he still kept and used the home for his extracurricular activities. At the moment, his henchmen occupied the space, and the news he received earlier that day made him speed to his old stomping grounds.

As Carlos pulled up, memories of Gloria swept through his mind. He missed his daughter tremendously. The fact that he never got the chance to restore their relationship only made her death more and more difficult to handle. Carlos wiped the tears from his eyes before he began talking to Gloria as if she was sitting in the seat beside him.

"Chula, I love and miss you more than you can imagine. My heart bleeds for the what-ifs. I don't blame your mother no more for taking you away from me. She did it to protect you. Somehow you still ended up being hurt by this side of the game. I promise I will get to the bottom of this, Glo, and make it right. I love you with all of me, chula . . . till my dying day. Rest easy, mommas. Rest easy."

Carlos looked at the picture of Gloria hanging from his rearview mirror. It was a picture of Gloria as a growing teenager—before all his chips fell and he lost the loves of his life.

Carlos wiped the fresh tears as they trailed down his face. He needed to get himself together for the task at hand. Carlos opened the door and stepped out of the Rolls-Royce. He hadn't driven himself around the city in years, but today was an exception because of the circumstances. He had sent every henchman on his payroll to scour the city and surrounding counties for Brandon Rockwell, better known as Rocc. He was the last person seen with Gloria alive. And Carlos needed answers—so he had him blitzed. He told himself that he would release Rocc if the answers he gave were substantial enough, but his heart spoke a different tone.

Carlos entered his old home detached, his Beckett Simonon's clicking against the marble floor with each step he took. He navigated the home by memory until he reached his destination.

Juan and Jose were present at each end of the basement, watching Rocc twist and turn, trying to fight his way through the ropes that held him in place. The twins were the only people besides Simfany that Carlos trusted—and that said a lot because Carlos wasn't one to trust easily. It was his only way of survival. The smaller the circle, the smaller the chance of betrayal.

Carlos nodded. On cue, Juan walked up to Rocc and untied all the ropes that secured him. Rocc tenderly rubbed his wrists as he looked up at Carlos for clarity. He didn't have the slightest clue why he was tied up in someone's basement.

"Cuz, what the fuck did I do?" Rocc asked, still rubbing the rope burns on his wrists.

"I'm asking the questions here, sir. Do you understand? The answers that I ask ain't up for discussion. If you give me the answers that I need, I promise I will let you go. Do you hear me?"

Rocc nodded in agreement.

"Okay. But if you lie one time or think you're going to bullshit me, I'm going to kill you. Do I make myself clear?"

The blood drained from Rocc's face as he nodded again.

"Now that we have this understanding, let's begin, shall we?"

Carlos turned and locked eyes with the twins. Without any words being exchanged, the pair walked out of the basement, leaving Carlos alone with Rocc.

Carlos waited until the twins were completely gone and the door was closed before he started his line of questioning.

"Are you good? You hungry? Can I get you anything? Because I don't need no interruptions until this shit is over. I have a dinner date with a dear friend in about eight hours. I expect this to be done before then, right?"

Rocc looked on in bewilderment at the boss-like nigga in front of him. *Who the fuck is this nigga and what does he want?* Rocc thought to himself as he sized his situation up.

"I'm going to explain who I am and what I want," Carlos stated simply, as if he could hear Rocc's thoughts. "My name is Carlos Rivera."

The name alone frightened him. He knew the legendary story of Carlos "Loso" Rivera.

What would the plug want with me? Rocc thought in disarray. He was truly at a loss for words.

"You mean like *The* Carlos Rivera?"

Carlos laughed slightly before nodding.

"What the fuck . . ." Rocc thought out loud.

"My temperament exactly. But many don't know that the woman you called your girlfriend is—well, actually *was*—my daughter before someone murdered her. That reason alone is one of the reasons you are sitting here. I want to know who is responsible for the demise of my daughter. Whether it's rumors or factual information, I want to know what happened and who the players are. If you can lead me to the person who killed my daughter, I can and will make you a rich man," Carlos explained, giving Rocc an option to live and prosper for the information he may know.

"So, papa, what is it going to be?" Carlos asked, hands outstretched in anticipation.

Rocc sat and contemplated what he really wanted to do. He knew the kind of money Carlos could offer would change his life, but he also knew that the opportunity Carlos was offering could be a hoax. And he wasn't willing to die over some shit he didn't do.

Rocc had tried to plead with Simfany, Peedi, and even Gloria about the idea they had come up with. It was a dangerous one—one that could backfire—but none of them listened to him. His opinion never mattered to Gloria when Peedi and Simfany were around.

Rocc looked up at Carlos, who waited patiently. He sighed heavily before he finally spoke.

"Do you know a gang that goes by the name of Tree Top Piru, 400 block, Spruce Street?"

The look that washed across Carlos's face told Rocc that he did—and in a big way. Carlos lost a shade of color in his face at the mention of the gang. The thought of his late protégé crossed his mind. It had been a long time since he last thought of Byrd, a man he bred to be great, but who got caught up in the lure of chasing money and being the man. Just as fast as Carlos's emotions surfaced, they disappeared.

The business he was in didn't allow one to act off emotion. Emotions got many men and women killed.

"I do. What do they have to do with this? With my daughter being killed?" Carlos asked, confused. He knew Gloria was present the night his little cousin was killed in Harford County years prior, but they had let her live—so why double back years later to kill her?

What Rocc was trying to insinuate made no sense to him.

"What would they gain but a war from doing this?" Carlos gave Rocc a peculiar look.

"Well, Gloria was telling me about them and the situation with your cousin from a few years ago—"

"What does my little cousin's murder have to do with my daughter?" Carlos interjected.

"Everything! Your daughter wanted revenge, sir. Gloria wanted Tez-Mo and Kevin's head—the remaining members of TTP."

Rocc anticipated the consequences that might come if he revealed the names of the people who played puppet master in Gloria's death.

"I'm lost. Who would she seek help from to do such a thing like that?" Carlos looked at Rocc with a different set of eyes now.

"Don't look at me like that. I had nothing to do with this—and I mean not even the smallest role. I had no clue until I heard that Gloria was dead," Rocc pleaded.

"So how did you come to stumble across this information, Rocc?" Carlos asked, tone cold and matter-of-fact.

"I was told because I was out in the county busting my gun trying to find answers about my wife," Rocc said, lying through his teeth—scared he had fucked up.

Carlos closed his eyes and rubbed his temples with his forefingers. He remained silent until he calmed himself. His temper was trying to get the best of him, but he knew if it did, he would never find out what happened to his daughter . . . or why.

"So did you ever find the people that is responsible or played a role in this get back mission?" Carlos asked Rocc.

"Yes."

"Then who?"

"A man that I grew up around named Darius Royals, and some Puerto Rican bitch named Simfany that my homie Drew knows."

"Simfany? Where is she from? Why do I think I heard that name before?" Carlos played dumb, not believing his ears. "Can you describe what this woman looks like?" he asked.

Rocc nodded.

"Shorty is beautiful. She thick as fuck and she 'bout that action."

"What else do you know about this woman named Simfany?" Carlos was getting sick to his stomach with each mention of his longtime friend.

"I just know that she was asked by Gloria to aid and assist her in killing yo' and them. Why do you keep asking all these questions about shorty? Do you know the bitch or something?" Rocc asked curiously.

Carlos considered telling Rocc the truth. *Fuck it, why not?* Carlos thought to himself as he rose from his seat.

"As a matter of fact, I do," Carlos replied as he pulled the .45 caliber 1911 from his backside and aimed it at Rocc.

"Hold on, hold on! What the hell, yoooo . . . Don't do this, man. Pleassseeeee. I swear I—"

Carlos pulled the trigger unapologetically, hitting Rocc in his face, sending his soul up for Allah to handle.

Chapter 14

"What do you want us to do, boss?" Juan asked as he pulled into the parking spot in front of Simfany's townhouse.

"I'll call you when I'm ready to go," Carlos replied, looking out the window of his 2006 Rolls-Royce Phantom.

"I'll be close by if I'm needed."

"You won't be needed, Juan." Carlos laughed casually at him.

"You sure?"

Carlos nodded in agreeance. Nothing else needed to be said.

Juan got out the car and walked to the rear passenger side, opening the door for Carlos to exit. Carlos stepped out of the Phantom looking like a million dollars—only if he felt like he looked, his day would have been a good one. He had a lot on his mind. His world had been turned upside down only hours prior. Rocc's words still haunted him as he approached Simfany's front door: *Some Puerto Rican bitch named Simfany that my homie Drew knows.*

Carlos just could not shake the feeling of being betrayed again. He sighed, trying his best to hide his feelings. Carlos didn't want to expose the hand that he was given.

Before Carlos was able to lift his hand and knock, Simfany opened the door with a big smile on her face, showing her beautiful pearly white teeth.

"Hey, papi, good afternoon," Simfany greeted, then leaned in and planted a kiss on Carlos's lips.

The moment their lips locked, Simfany felt the tension. *Something isn't right,* she thought as she pulled away from Carlos.

"Good afternoon, Chula. How has your day been?" Carlos replied ambiguously.

"My day? Oh, it's been okay. Just got a lot on my mind. How about you? And where are the groceries I asked you to buy? Your ass must not be hungry. Come in."

"Oh, my bad, Chula. It's been a long day," Carlos replied, brushing off Simfany's words like they meant nothing. The gesture definitely didn't go unnoticed.

Carlos stepped into Simfany's house for the first time.

"Please take a seat, relax yourself. Why are you so tense?" Simfany asked.

Carlos ignored the question again. He just walked into the plush living room and sat down. Simfany rolled her eyes and followed, sitting directly across from him.

"So what's your problem, Carlos? Talk to me—I talk back," Simfany said with an attitude.

"I don't know. You tell me. What was the purpose of this meeting?"

Simfany had to laugh just to keep from getting angry.

"Sooo . . . that's what this is called now? A meeting? Oh, okay. Well, let's get straight to the point. This is regarding your daughter. Gloria came to me and a man named Peedi for help in killing Kevin and Teziar Brooks. They are members of Harford County's Piru chapter. They hail from Harford Commons to be exact. You already know about me and my son killing Piru, Stacks, and Hood. Well, in the midst of that, we started a huge war—which eventually linked us to the Crips in the city. Anyway, Gloria came up with an idea that got her killed."

Simfany started from the beginning of the night before Gloria was killed. She explained everything to Carlos without leaving out a single detail.

Carlos sat in place and listened without interruption. When she was done, she looked at her longtime friend and waited for a response. Carlos's expression was blank. He showed no sign of emotion. He was more so lost for words.

He didn't know how to feel. The person he had grown to love had played a role in his daughter's death—or did she?

Carlos's mind was playing tricks on him, that was for sure. *What am I supposed to do now?* Carlos asked himself as he put his face in his hands.

"Say something, Los, please. You're scaring me. I had no clue that, that was your daughter. No one did. I can almost bet my life on that," Simfany pleaded, hoping he understood where she was coming from.

Carlos looked up, face red from frustration and hurt. The only thing running through his head at the moment was the vision of his daughter's casket being lowered into the ground, forcing a lone tear down his face.

Carlos was truly stuck between a rock and a hard spot. He felt that if he let Simfany live, he would be betraying Gloria. But in his heart of all hearts, he knew Simfany didn't really do anything to warrant death.

Carlos sighed deeply before replying.

"I really don't know what to say, Chula. I'm sick to my stomach, that I can admit. But what am I supposed to do—kill you? Because that's the only answer to this. But it's also the wrong move. I don't think you knew she was my daughter. Because coming to me to kill these men would have been a way easier task in itself. But what hurts me is the fact that I may never get retribution for my child."

"And why is that?" Simfany interjected.

"Because there is no one to blame for her death," Carlos replied, disappointed.

"Oh, yes the fuck it is!" Simfany exclaimed. "The last person that Gloria was with was the Piru nigga, Kevin Brooks. She was supposed to be meeting me at the Sheetz gas station located on Route 40 in Joppatowne. I guess it was the place she used to have sex with him back in her high school days.

"The only person that could've killed her is Kevin. He was the last person I knew she was with. I talked to her minutes before pulling up and they weren't there. According to the news, Glo was found the next morning. She had been dead close to 8 hours by the time they found her. Do the math, Los."

Simfany let that linger in the air for a second before she continued.

"Don't get me wrong, I can't tell you one hundred percent that he did do it. But there is no other explanation. Right?"

Simfany asked, unsure of her own answer.

Carlos shrugged and interlocked his fingers together, bringing them to his forehead like he was about to pray.

"You alright, Los?" Simfany asked with concern.

Carlos didn't reply. He just looked up, face bloodshot from the tears streaming down his face. It broke Simfany's heart to see him that hurt.

Simfany got up from the loveseat and sat on Carlos's lap. The gesture took him by surprise, but it calmed him nonetheless.

"Look at me, papi."

Carlos didn't budge. He just stared through blurred vision at the floor, letting the tears roll down willingly.

Simfany used her forefinger to lift his chin so their eyes met. There was an energy that passed between them that neither could explain. All they knew was—it was there.

A pulse ran through Simfany's vagina, causing her to grow wetter and wetter by the second.

Bitch, stop! Simfany thought, pulling her finger away from his chin. Only this time Carlos didn't break eye contact. He continued to stare deep into her eyes.

Simfany's heart raced. The electricity surging between her legs . . . she hadn't felt that in a long time. Crossing that line with Carlos wasn't something she wanted to do, but the throbbing between her thighs was telling her different.

What are you doing, bitch? Simfany thought, trying to get up.

Before she got the chance to rise, Carlos wrapped his hand around her waist and pulled her in for a kiss.

"Los, we can't—" Simfany tried to protest, until their lips locked in a passionate kiss.

The butterflies going crazy in her stomach told her everything she needed to know—she needed him, and she needed him bad.

Simfany's body loosened. She was not going to fight what felt so right. She sucked on Carlos's tongue, sending him into his own state of passion.

Reality hit hard when they finally pulled away. Carlos leaned back in, lips brushing hers again, but within seconds Simfany was pulling away.

She tried to catch her breath, licking her lips and staring into Carlos's eyes. Simfany cussed herself out in her head.

She wanted to fuck Carlos's sexy ass so bad, but she wanted it to be a sound decision—not one made in guilt, not because she wanted him to forget the role she played in Gloria's death.

"You sure this is what you want to do, Los? Because you know once we cross this line, shit won't be the same between us. And me not knowing what that means scares me. I love you, and besides Santana, you know you the only other person I share my heart with. I haven't been fucked in a long time, Los. This will make me hate you if you do me dirty. I can make you forget if that's what you want, but I'ma do it my way. This passionate shit you doin', you can stop, 'cause you don't need to do it. It'll only complicate shit," Simfany said earnestly.

Carlos pulled Simfany closer into his lap and looked up into her eyes.

"Look, chula . . . this shit that I feel for you may come with a price one day, but right now, you all I may ever need. I done snatched soul after soul in a quest to figure out what happened to my daughter, and now that I know—I wish I didn't. I love you, Simf. I believe the words that you speak, momma. I believe you didn't know Gloria was my daughter, and that's why I'ma spare you—and the company you keep. But this can't be excused or forgotten, chula. She my only child. Excuse me . . . she *was* my only child. No disrespect, but if I let you live, somebody else gotta pay."

The words Carlos spoke sent chills through Simfany's body. He tightened his grip on her, rubbing his hand up and down her back, trying to bring her comfort.

"I promise, chula, you got nothin' to worry about. You hear me?"

When Simfany didn't answer, he grabbed her chin lightly and pulled her face until it was directly in front of his.

"You hear me, Ma?"

Simfany nodded in reply. Carlos leaned in and kissed her lips passionately. Time felt like it stood still.

Carlos pulled back and released his grip from around her waist. He wanted her to know she was free to go if she pleased.

Simfany thought about the pros and cons of messing with Carlos, and the good definitely didn't outweigh the bad—and she knew that. But that was the *smart* way of thinking. Right now, Simfany was thinking with her hormones, and she wanted some dick.

"I love you, Carlos," Simfany finally said before rising from Carlos's lap and bending down in front of him.

"What are you doing, Simf?" Carlos said, pulling on her arm. Simfany looked up seductively from her knees into his eyes.

"What you mean? You know what I'm doing. I'm tryna suck on this dick of yours."

Carlos's face turned beet red, and he knew he was about to regret what he was about to say—but it had to be said.

"I don't want you this way, Simfany. I don't want you sucking my dick lustfully. If we gon' take it there, we takin' it *all* the way there. I don't see you as that—I see the queen you possess. Don't get me wrong, I'm hatin' myself for even sayin' this dumb ass shit, but you mean more to me than some pussy love. As bad as I want you to eat on this anaconda—"

They laughed in unison.

Carlos continued, "We got something more pressing to talk about. So please, Ma."

Carlos reached his hand out. Simfany grabbed it with a smile, thinking to herself: *This nigga think he got all the sense.*

For the first time since arriving at her townhouse, Carlos took notice of her attire. Simfany was dressed to the nines for their dinner date. She wore an all-black Abercrombie & Fitch tennis skirt, with a matching Mara Linen black vest, complimented by the latest black and white Jordan Retro 5s. Carlos loved the sleek look on her. He was just so used to seeing her dressed in her signature Juicy Couture attire, it fucked him up seeing her in casual clothes.

Simfany already knew what needed to be discussed, and she was beyond ready to enlist Carlos's help in killing the Brooks brothers.

"So what do you think we should do about these Piru niggas?" Simfany asked, taking her seat back on Carlos's lap.

"I think we should hit home and make them come looking for us," Carlos replied, with a menacing look on his face.

Simfany gave him the side-eye, like, *Nigga . . . what the fuck are you talkin' about?* Carlos laughed.

"Elaborate, Los?"

Simfany wanted to know what extent he was willing to go for revenge in the name of his daughter.

"I promised myself that when I found out who was responsible, I'd eradicate them and they whole family—and I'm standing on that. I'd love your blessing, but I can't expect that from you. But that's my plan with the Brooks family. I already tried my hand at endin' them little niggas before, but the men I sent acted off emotion and shot the funeral up instead of confirm the kills like I paid for them to—"

Carlos's words began to fade in her ears as everything started clicking.

Simfany's heart raced. *Oh shit!*

Carlos was responsible for Tijuana's death. He sent the blitz that got her friend killed.

"Hold on, Los . . . what are you talkin' about? I'm lost as hell," Simfany played dumb, hiding her hand. She didn't know how she felt yet about the bombshell Carlos had just dropped.

Carlos smiled wide.

"You remember the night you had to speed through Bond and Preston?"

Simfany searched her memory bank. Blank. Then it hit her like a ton of bricks. The night Paris tried to get her killed.

Now the memory came back clear.

"I do . . . but what does that got to do with what we talkin' about now?"

She was genuinely lost this time.

"Because the same men that saved your life that night are the same men that shot up Sasha Brooks' funeral."

"Why?" Simfany blurted out.

"To be honest, chula, there's multiple reasons. One—Tez-Mo killed Byrd. The hit was sent down from their big homie, Stacks," Carlos said sarcastically, using air quotes. He continued, "Second—they killed my cousin while my daughter sat inches away. And last, one of the shooters that flipped Sasha's casket was raised by Byrd, and he wanted to seek revenge. Shorty came to me with a plan—one I felt could be useful if played right—so I hired them. Would've killed two birds with one stone. But emotions got involved, and the mission wasn't carried out like it should've been."

"I understand," Simfany said simply.

She didn't know how to feel. Her whole reason for wantin' the Brooks brothers dead was because of what they did to Tijuana. So to hear *Carlos* was the puppet master pulling strings? That shit fucked her up.

Because unlike Carlos . . . Simfany wasn't so forgiving.

"So where do we go from here?" she asked, rising from Carlos's lap.

Ring . . . Ring . . . Ring . . .

Simfany jumped at the sound of her phone. Instinctively, she patted her pockets. Nothing. She ran into the kitchen, hoping she left it on the charger.

Luckily, she had.

She picked it up just in time.

"Hello?" Simfany answered, halfway out of breath.

"What's poppin', shorty! How you livin'? Did yo slide through there yet?"

Her nerves calmed at the sound of Peedi's voice. He hadn't called her all day—and honestly, she didn't expect him to, not after their dispute the night before.

"Yes . . . and this nigga knows *everything*," she exclaimed. "He got to Rocc before we could. But to my surprise, the nigga wasn't mad."

She lowered her voice, purposely leaving out the part about her intimacy with Carlos.

Peedi paused. She heard him sigh deep. She knew he was concerned—but in time, he'd see he had nothing to worry about.

Oh shit—before I forget, she reminded herself.

"I almost forgot some shit. Make sure you remind me to tell you something *very* important when I call you back. Cool?"

"Yeah, I got you. Hit me as soon as that nigga leave your house."

Simfany laughed to herself, hearing the jealousy all through Peedi's tone.

She hung up and walked back into the living room where Carlos stood waiting.

"Everything okay, chula?" Carlos asked, genuine concern all over his face.

"It is. Why you ask that?"

"The look on your face says it all. You seem high-strung, ready to flee like you got somewhere more important to be. Is it about your son? He okay?"

Carlos fired off questions, trying to figure out what was going on.

"Yeah . . . it actually *was* him," she said nervously. "He in the middle of a huge war in West Virginia right now. Don't ask," she added, trying to head off more questions. "Not to change the subject, but what we gon' do about these Piru niggas?"

"We're gonna hit the mother and niece. Or at least threaten they lives so Tez-Mo and Kev come for us. That's when we end them all."

"What!" Simfany shouted, shocked. There was no way she heard him right. Kill a woman and her grandchild?

This nigga lost his marbles.

"Carlos, now think about what you saying right now. You *really* willing to kill a child and her caregiver in the name of revenge? Los, that's takin' shit too far."

"Nah, I'm not takin' anything too far. My daughter lost—"

"Your daughter chose her path, Carlos. She wanted to seek revenge over what happened to your cousin. That's understandable. But takin' it to Tez-Mo and every *man* in their family is fair. Woman and children? Nah. You know the rules. Follow 'em."

"First off—I don't need to follow shit!" Carlos shouted so loud spit flew from his mouth. "Don't tell me what the fuck I can and can't do, Simfany. You lucky I'm not takin' what you did as a sign of—"

"Of what, nigga? I'm *glad* you not taking this as a sign of what, Carlos? You know what? You can leave. You not gon' keep making me feel like I'm your muthafuckin' enemy just 'cause I don't agree with your ass."

Without another word, Carlos rose to his feet, face red from irritation.

"Say something, Los," Simfany pleaded, already regretting her words.

"What is there to say, Simfany? You spoke your piece. You chose your side."

"Did I?" she asked venomously.

"Yeah . . . yeah, you did," Carlos said, cold and final.

"Well, if that's the case, you need to take all of the shit that I have of Gloria's with you."

A lone tear slid down Simfany's face as Carlos turned to walk away, but he didn't get far. Simfany's next move stopped everything cold.

With his back still turned to her, Carlos was thinking, *Who the fuck does this bitch think*—when his thought got cut off by the cold barrel of a Glock 26 pointed dead at him when he turned to face her.

"Whoa . . . whoa . . . whoa . . . Chula, what are you doing?" Carlos asked, his eyes pleading.

"I'm ending this chapter of my life, Carlos. I'm not with killing old women and children. Especially not over something you started. If you never sent them little niggas to shoot that fucking funeral up, we wouldn't be here. That one scenario set off a chain of events—events that got someone I held dear to my heart killed. I put my love and loyalty on the back burner to appease you, because I felt like if the roles were reversed, you would have done the same. But I see that holds no truth any longer. I'm not looking behind my back no more, Carlos. I loved you. I loved you in more ways than one. But at this point, we can't co-exist, baby boy."

Simfany pulled the trigger unapologetically.

Boc . . . Boc . . . Boc . . . Boc.

She hit Carlos in the chest four times.

Simfany watched as Carlos took his last breath and fell to the ground.

Confirm the kill, Simfany thought to herself as she walked up to Carlos's lifeless body and pulled the trigger three more times, making damn sure his death was certain.

Chapter 15

Ring . . . Ring . . . Ring . . .

The blaring of the phone woke Santana out of his slumber. He was tired as hell. He had stayed up all night waiting on the cavalry to come and get him, but to his surprise, no one showed up. Kat had finally come through for him. She had hand-delivered Detective Williams to him by the balls, at least for the time being.

Santana sat bolt upright, stretching his torso to the max, cracking his backbones in the process.

Damn I needed that, Santana thought as he twisted from one side to the next.

He let his phone ring until the voicemail picked up. At the moment, he needed to be as low-key as possible—even if it included hiding out. As long as Zach, Darla, and Melquan were safe, nothing else mattered. Besides his mother, those was his only obligations that he was taking seriously. They were the only family he had left.

When Santana's phone stopped ringing, he picked it up and called his voicemail.

"*Baby boy, call me ASAP. We need to talk. This cannot be put off; this is very urgent. I'm serious—do not ignore me, Santana. I love you.*"

Santana didn't need to hear no more. He deleted what was left of the message and hit one—the code to speed-dial his mother.

"Damn, that was fast," Simfany laughed, answering his call on the first ring.

"What's going on? You good?" Santana asked apprehensively. He knew his mother was about to throw some bullshit into the game, so he just sat and listened to what she had to say.

"I killed Carlos."

Santana laughed hysterically. He knew his mother did some dumb ass shit, but this—this he couldn't fathom. He couldn't see her killing Carlos. From what he knew of the pair, they were the best of friends. He had even suspected that they were fucking each other at one point. But of course, that wasn't something he cared to worry about, so he didn't. So to hear that she took Carlos up through the wringer threw him for a loop.

"Why did you do some dumb shit like that for, Ma? We got enough issues as is—now we gotta worry about the whole state getting on our ass, and for what? What the fuck could that nigga possibly have done that coulda made you go to that extremity? Please enlighten me," Santana stated, annoyed with his mother and her constant bullshit.

"Man, fuck that nigga. He the reason Tijuana's dead. It was his actions that led to her demise. Since I've linked with your lor homie Drew, I've found out a lot about the war between Carlos and the Piru niggas that was running with Byrd. After Big Cito—Carlos's cousin—got killed, him and Byrd squashed their beef with promises of going their separate ways. But as you know, Byrd disappeared shortly after, almost sparking the war back up. Days turned into weeks, and weeks turned into months before Byrd's body popped up along the Chesapeake. Niggas made all kinds of shit up about what happened to Byrd, but all the rumors amounted to nothing. I got blamed, Los got blamed, and the Piru niggas got blamed, but nothing was ever concrete for real. Fast forward a little—Carlos found out about Piru and Stacks smokin' Byrd. How? I have no clue, but they did. Byrd had a protégé that approached Carlos about settling the score. And you know Carlos, just being Carlos, he agreed to help and supply whatever was needed to exact revenge. Now this part I can only speculate, 'cause I don't know the whole truth—but I assume that the niggas Los sent botched the hit. Granted, they shot up the funeral, but to my knowledge they didn't hit shit but shorty and her casket, which was what sent them niggas into a murderous rage. This is where Tijuana comes into this twisted-ass shit. Tez-Mo and Kev thought that Drew and them was responsible for the shooting, so they sped straight to Washington Park and shot the first person that they saw. Unfortunately, that person was Tijuana."

Simfany had to take a breath for a second. Her head was throbbing. The emotion of losing Tijuana came rushing back to her. She could only imagine how Santana was feeling at the moment, especially after hearing the story that led up to Tijuana's death. Tijuana wasn't supposed to die—especially not by the hands of Teziar and Kevin Brooks over some gang shit that she had nothing to do with.

Simfany contemplated at that very moment if she should tell Santana about the children that was growing inside of Tijuana at the time of her death.

"Baby boy, are you there?" Simfany asked, looking at her phone, making sure that he was still on the line. Her phone indicated that he was still there, but his silence was loud. "Are you okay, Tana?" Simfany asked sympathetically.

"Yeah, I'm good. This shit just crazy how Ma went out. She went out over some shit she didn't even condone. She hated that gang shit with a passion. The irony of the situation just . . . I don't know, man. I hate even talkin' 'bout this shit, Ma. No bullshit. So what do you think is gonna come of this shit with Carlos? Did anyone know that you were meeting him? If so, who?"

"Peedi knew that Carlos was supposed to come over to my house. But other than that, I don't think anyone else knew."

"Good. Who the fuck is Peedi?" Santana asked curiously.

"You bein' serious?" Simfany replied, confused.

"Uhhhhhhh . . . yeah."

Simfany ignored Santana's sarcasm and just answered his question.

"It's one of Drew's childhood friends."

"Oh, okay. That makes sense. I thought you done had you a new boo," Santana joked, trying to lighten the mood a little.

They laughed in unison.

"Nah, little nigga, that's the last thing I'm worried about at the moment," Simfany said seriously.

Knock . . . knock . . . knock . . .

"Pretty Lady, let me call you back—someone knockin' on bruh's door," Santana said as he rose from the comfort of his bed.

"Okay, baby boy. Make sure you do that. We have to finish this discussion. Love you."

"Love you more, Ma. Stay out of the way. Please. If you need me, make sure you call—I'm only a call away. I'm serious, Momma. Stay dangerous."

"I got you, baby boy. And where is Darla? I haven't heard from her in what feels like forever," Simfany asked, stalling.

"Maaaaa . . . I have to go. I love you. I'll explain everything later."

Simfany laughed, returning the gesture before finally hanging up.

Santana grabbed the Glock from the nightstand before making his trek down the stairs.

Who the fuck could be knocking on the door? he asked himself as he descended. Santana popped the clip out of the new Glock 21 he had just purchased from a fiend only days prior. He had 7 shots. It wasn't many, but he knew he would make them count if he had to.

Santana walked into the living room and peeked out of the curtains. The person standing on Zach's porch confused him to the core. If his memory served him right, FB Freezo was standing on his porch—with his shirt off, spinning in a circle—showing Santana that he was unarmed and wasn't there on no bullshit. As a precaution, Santana looked around the porch for any surprises, but Freezo was the only person present.

"What the fuck you want, nigga!" Santana yelled loud enough for Freezo to hear.

"I come in peace, bruh. I'm not here on FB time. That's on Heem."

The use of his nigga's name pissed him off, but he also knew this was a nigga Haseem loved dearly. It was one of the only reasons Freezo was still amongst the living.

Santana closed the drapes and walked to the door—against his better judgment.

What the fuck could this nigga want? Santana thought to himself as he unlatched the locks on Zach's door.

"Nigga, this shit better make sense," Santana said, serious as a heart attack.

Freezo walked into the foyer, hands still raised in the air. He didn't want Santana to take him as no kind of threat, especially right now. He came unarmed—and on a mission. Freezo needed to be heard, and heard *now*.

"What you want?" Santana asked through clenched teeth, gun at his side.

"I'm gone get straight to the chase. Me and a couple of my niggas not feeling the shit that fat ass nigga on, and we tryin' link to end this nigga and them hoe ass niggas runnin' with him. I know this shit sound crazy as fuck, but bruh, Fatty Man gotta go. And in truth, I don't got the manpower to get it done without making this a suicide mission. That nigga Zach can tell you how me and Heem rocked since the sandbox. The reason gang even still alive is because I know for a fact he had nothin' to do with Haseem bein' killed. That was the work of Sleeze—and Sleeze alone. That I just found out also. As you can see, my nigga, I come in peace. I want no smoke. I've had you dead to rights a few times, and I never sent shots at you. You more valuable to me alive than dead—believe that. Can I put my hands down now?"

"Nah. Keep talking," Santana said maliciously.

"Nigga, what the fuck else you want me to say? If you not tryin' put this nigga to sleep, say that, and I'll get the fuck on. I'm here 'cause I need ya gun, little nigga. You gone fuck with niggas or not, bruh?" Freezo said, becoming frustrated by the second.

Man, how the fuck I let this nigga Leek talk me into this lame ass shit, Freezo thought, sighing deeply.

"Nah, I'm good, my nigga. I don't need no help takin' that nigga off this earth. His time coming. If what you say is real, just stay out my way. I'm gone get that shit done. Flat out," Santana said confidently, before opening the door, signaling Freezo to leave.

Freezo laughed, then shook his head up and down.

"Stay dangerous, bruh. Tell Zach hit me if you change ya mind."

"I won't, bruh," Santana responded sarcastically, slamming the door—barely missing Freezo as he cleared the threshold.

This bitch ass nigga had the muthafuckin' nerve, Santana cussed as he ascended the stairs, pulling his phone from his pocket. He needed to call Rashad. He needed to know what was going on between the FB niggas that had FB Freezo knockin' on his door trying to link with him against the opposition.

***

Simfany paced the floor—back and forth, back and forth.

What the fuck I'm supposed to do, what the fuck I'm supposed to do, Simfany thought to herself as she continued pacing anxiously. She knew she had royally fucked up this time—by killing Carlos Rivera. Simfany still had her gun in hand as she ran scenario after scenario through her mind, looking for a way to fix the shit she just caused. Every outcome came up blank.

She started doing breathing techniques, trying to calm her nerves.

"Fuck! Fuck! Fuck!" Simfany exclaimed, wiping the sweat from her forehead.

An idea popped into her head as she looked down at Carlos's lifeless body. She tossed her Glock on the couch and ran into the kitchen, frantically searching for her phone. Peedi was the only person on her mind—her best bet at making this current situation disappear. But like always, her phone wasn't where she thought she left it.

Simfany stopped and tried to retrace her steps. She remembered grabbing it minutes before Carlos came into her home. Running into the living room, she checked around the loveseat. Within seconds, she found the phone sitting on top of the armrest. She opened it with trembling hands and dialed Peedi's number from memory.

Peedi answered on the first ring.

"Shorty, what's good? What that nigga say?" he asked, referring to the conversation he knew she was supposed to be having with Carlos that evening.

Simfany laughed at the irony of his words.

"Well, he took the shit with his daughter pretty well . . . but it was the shit about Tijuana that I didn't take well. I killed that nigga," she replied nonchalantly, looking at Carlos's sprawled-out body on her floor.

"You did what?" Peedi exclaimed.

"I FUCKIN' KILLED CARLOS!" Simfany yelled at the top of her lungs.

"Where? Why?" Peedi asked simply.

Simfany's silence told him everything he needed to know.

"Fuck, shorty. I'm coming now. Don't move nothin'. Get in the shower and be ready for me by the time I get there. You hear me?"

Simfany nodded like he was standing right in front of her.

"Simf, do you hear me?"

Bzzzzz! Bzzz! Bzzz! Bzzz! Bzzz! Bzzzzzzz!

Carlos's phone vibrated in his pocket.

Simfany looked at the body and stepped back. Should she answer it? Or just let it go to voicemail? That was the question racing through her head.

"Simfany, do you—"

"Yes. Just shut up and get your ass here!" she snapped, hanging up and tossing her phone back on the loveseat.

Before she could walk away, it rang again. The ringtone told her everything—Santana was calling back. She turned and picked up.

"Hey, baby boy."

"Hey, pretty lady. You good? You need me to make that trip tonight, come make sure everything's straight?"

"Nah, I should be good."

"What about them bodyguard niggas Los be with? How you gone get around them?"

"He came by his lonely self. Neither one of them niggas was with Los this time around."

To confirm, she walked to the window and peeked out through the blinds. Panic kicked in almost immediately. All the cars out front looked regular. Nothing flashy. That was off. In all the years she'd known Carlos, nothing about him was ordinary.

She closed the blinds and continued.

"I just looked out the window and I don't see a car that stands out, so that means he was dropped off."

"Damn, okay. Well, that means they know where he at, and now you need to figure out what you gone do from here," Santana said.

"What the fuck! I didn't think of none of this shit in advance."

Santana laughed at the irony of her confession.

"That's obvious," he said out loud.

"Shut the fuck up, Santana. Please."

"Okay, look. I got an idea. But call Drew and that Peedi nigga—run it by them first. I need you protected in case anything go wrong. You hear me?"

"I do."

"Bet. Call Juan. Tell him Carlos had too much to drink and that he need to come get him from your house. They trust you. You been part of their inner circle for a long time—well, until this shit happened—but still. They trust you.

"Tell him you got a prior engagement you can't miss, and go from there. You think you can handle that?"

Simfany smiled, surprised at how quick Santana's mind worked.

"I like that idea. I don't know where Drew is, but I already called Peedi to come over here to help with this mess I caused," she said sheepishly, rubbing her arm like she was trying to warm herself.

"You good, love. Just get this shit handled and then finish tellin' me what happened. Fair?"

"Fair. Love you, baby boy. Thank you. You hear me?"

"Siempre, pretty lady. You already know the vibes. Stay dangerous and let me know if you need me. Bye, beauty."

"Bye, baby," she replied, hanging up.

***

Big Ty sat in silence, rubbing his temple, trying to get the headache pulsing behind his eyes to calm down. He'd been up all night dealing with the death of his closest friend, Nazir Howard.

Ty couldn't believe it. His brother was gone.

How the fuck could this have happened? Ty questioned himself. He was at a complete loss. He had underestimated Santana in a big way—and now it was costing him more than just money.

"Torrey . . .? Torrey!" Ms. Nautica called out as she walked toward him.

At the sound of his name, Ty looked up, face hard with anger. But his features softened when he saw the pain in Nazir's mother's eyes. It shattered him to see her like that.

"Hey, Ma. How you holding up?" Ty asked softly.

"How you think I feel, Torrey? My son been away from me all this time . . . As soon as I get the chance to get him back, I lose him again. Only this time . . ."

Ms. Nautica's voice cracked.

"He's gone, Torrey. He's gone . . . Some . . . body . . . took . . . my baby . . . from . . . me."

She finally got the words out through sobs.

Ty lowered his head, ashamed. She didn't know the full story—but he did. And the guilt was eating him alive. Nazir's blood was on his hands.

"Ma, you know I'm going to handle this. Without question. Just give me some time. Please. I gotta wrap my head around this shit too," Ty replied, just as his phone started ringing.

He lifted his hip and pulled out his *Motorola Razr*. Flipping it open, he looked at the caller ID.

Took you long enough, lil nigga, Big Ty thought as he answered.

"Fuck took you so long, nigga? I sent you a message to hit me last night. What you on, nigga?" Ty bellowed through the phone, clearly annoyed at Patty's tardiness.

"Whoa, whoa, big homie. I got a lot of shit goin' on in-house right now. That's for another time though. What's good though? What's so urgent anyway?" Fatty asked, confused by Big Ty's sudden change in demeanor.

"That bitch-ass nigga killed my brother last night. I'm done playin' with this little nigga, bruh. What the fuck am I feeding you niggas for if you not gon' do the job you promised to do? I need that nigga dead ASAP. I don't care who does it. If you can't get it done, then say that. Either way, I'm uppin' the bounty on both those niggas. I got a fifty ball for whoever send them bitch-ass niggas to hell."

Ty saw Ms. Nautica re-enter the room and changed his tone slightly.

"I understand what you're sayin', and I'll do my best, Fully, but I got some in-house shit that's puttin' a halt on all that shit right now. I know how you feel about this lil' nigga, bruh, I want that nigga dead too. I'll hit you back in—"

"What you got goin' on? Maybe I can help you help me," Big Ty interjected, cutting Patty's words short.

Fatty explained the whole situation—starting from the shooting at Sleeze's vigil, ending with what had happened only an hour prior to their conversation.

"Has anyone went and checked on ya lil' nigga Buddah?" Big Ty asked, as if it was a real concern of his.

Big Ty watched as Ms. Nautica paced her home miserably. The death of her son had truly fucked her up. He felt her pain. It was crazy how Nazir did all that time locked away just to get killed the same day he came home.

"Yeah. That lil' nigga just got outta surgery. Bruh got hit in his chest, but the wound was superficial. He gon' live," Fatty replied nonchalantly.

"So when do you plan on meeting with ya men again?"

"I'm out huntin' right now as we speak. Give me a few hours and I'll let you know what's up. All this happened out the blue, Fully, so you gotta bear with me. I'll personally dead that OT nigga myself. All I ask is for understandin', big bro."

"And all I'm askin' is for you to keep up your side of this deal. I done gave you everything you asked for—shall I say more? These niggas shoulda been dead, bruh. I'm not gon' say this shit is your fault, but Nazir's death do fall on you and them niggas you call your homies. Before you go MIA, send me all the addresses you got on hand for them niggas. I'm done waitin' on you to handle your business. This shit shoulda been done by now."

Fatty Man scoffed before replying.

"Yeah, yeah, yeah . . . I'm sending them to your phone as we speak. Hold on . . . I know that's not who I think that is."

Fatty Man laughed at the irony.

"I think I see one of those niggas right now. I'ma hit you back in a minute," he said, rushing Big Ty off the phone.

"Handle your business," Big Ty replied, rubbing his hands together in anticipation of Nazir's killer meeting his maker.

***

Zach pulled off the interstate, back into his stomping ground. Though it was a good relief to get away, he missed his home state. He hated the fact that he felt like he was running away from his issues at hand. Santana would be mad at his return, but he wasn't about to be the one just hiding out of state like a coward.

Little did Zach know, a lot had transpired in the hours since he last spoke with Santana. Nazir had been killed, Buddah had been shot, and the core of Full Blooded had been dismantled. Zach didn't know he wasn't coming back to the same city he had left only days before. He was coming back to the middle of a war between the masses.

Zach chose to exit the interstate near the 35th Street bridge so he could sneak back into the city without bein' seen. He knew Santana had inquired about Nazir the night before, and when he woke, he saw that there were "Rest in Peace" posts all over Myspace. Though he didn't really know if Santana was the one responsible, he at least had a clue. Zach knew, nonetheless, that he needed to be careful on the way back in.

His gas light began to flicker as he pulled down the ramp off Greenbrier Street, back into Charleston's East End.

"Man, fuck!" Zach exclaimed.

He knew he could make it home with the tank on E, but he also knew he'd eventually have to stop at a gas station to fill up. He looked to his right and saw the 7-Eleven sittin' at the corner of East Washington Street.

Fuck it, he thought.

This gas station was the polar opposite of what the Shop-N-Go was. There weren't no groups loiterin' outside, and there wasn't no drug activity whatsoever. Maybe 'cause the Capitol building was literally across the street. Zach had no clue, but he knew that if there was a gas station where he'd be safe for a second to pump gas, it was this one. So without a second thought, Zach pulled in. Still thinking cautiously, he parked the rental in line with an easy escape route—just in case.

Zach opened the glove compartment and grabbed the Glock .27. One thing Santana taught him was always be cautious, no matter what the circumstances. You never knew what God had planned for you. So Zach took heed and stayed prepared at all times.

He popped the magazine out of the Glock .27—another habit he picked up from Santana's genius. The double-stacked factory clip showed he had a full mag. Ten shots to give if shit got tweaky.

Zach tucked the gun on his hip and stepped out the rental. The parking lot was relatively empty, besides a few gas company workers sittin' outside their truck, parlayin' while the gas gauges filled. Zach nodded at the men as he walked past. They nodded back, returnin' to their convo like nothin' happened.

Damn, I wish life was still that simple, Zach thought as he opened the door to the 7-Eleven.

There was nobody inside but the clerk. They made eye contact and nodded at each other.

Zach walked toward the back by the refrigerators and grabbed a Lipton Long Island Iced Tea. He cracked it open and took a sip. He closed his eyes as the chill from the drink hit.

Damn, this bitch cold as hell, he thought, fighting a quick brain freeze.

Zach headed back to the front, drink in one hand, digging in his pocket with the other. He pulled out $30 and laid it on the counter.

"Bruh, can you give me $25 on—" Zach turned to look out the window at which pump he was parked at, but before he could finish, the cashier was already handing him his change.

"Thank you, bruh. Have a good one," Zach said, backing out the door of the 7-Eleven.

***

"Don't move another step, bitch ass nigga," Fatty Man said through clenched teeth as he pointed his P229 Legion 9mm Ruger at Zach's face.

"Whoa . . . whoa . . . whoa, bruh. Calm down. What's—"

"Shut the fuck up, lil' nigga. Move!" Fatty Man exclaimed, pushing Zach forward, trying to conceal his gun as he pressed it into Zach's back.

"Bruh, you trippin'. I ain't—" Zach tried to plea his way out of Fatty's grasp. Fatty stopped in his tracks and smacked Zach upside the head with his Sig Sauer.

"Arrrrggghhhh!" Zach yelled, grabbing his head, trying to figure a way out of his current predicament.

"Mooooooovvvvveeeeee!" Fatty yelled, shoving Zach toward the car parked on the side of the gas station.

"All right . . . all right . . . all right . . . damn, bruh." Zach followed Fatty's instructions and walked to the end of the walkway and into the alley beside the 7-Eleven. Fatty's Chevy Impala was parked horizontally in the alley for a quick getaway if needed.

"Now go to the driver side door," Fatty demanded.

Without argument, Zach did as he was told. Fatty Man looked around to make sure the coast was clear. From where he stood, it was. Then something caught his eye.

Is that Freezo's whip? Fatty Man thought to himself, but he wasn't a hundred percent sure. He cussed to himself.

These niggas got me lookin' over my muthafuckin' shoulder. I'm gon' kill ALL them bitch ass niggas, Fatty promised himself.

Zach watched as Fatty drifted off into his thoughts. He wanted to make a run for it, but the distance he'd have to cover without gettin' shot was impossible. He looked around nervously for some kind of escape route. There wasn't none but the straight stretch.

Man, fuck it, Zach thought as he looked back to see what Fatty was doing. The dark eyes looking back at him screamed *I dare you.*

Zach's heart dropped. The plan he was just trying to build died right before his eyes.

Man, I gotta get the fuck outta here, he told himself as his mind raced.

"Bruh, what do you want? If you just wanted to take my soul, you would've killed me already. What can I do to stay alive? Nigga, we grew up under you—how you gon' take up a bounty on my head from an OT nigga? Ain't you the same nigga who preach—"

Fatty hit Zach across the face with the butt of his gun without remorse.

"Nigga, I said shut the fuck up and move."

"FUCK! Where the fuck can I move to, nigga? You got me stuck in the fuckin' driver side door," Zach replied, spitting blood from his mouth.

"Pull that lever right there and step back."

Zach didn't want to take his eyes off Fatty, but he knew if he didn't follow instructions, it could end bad for him. He was still alive at the moment—and he wanted to keep it that way. So he did as he was told.

The trunk popped open with the tug of the lever.

Hell no! Zach thought as it all started to make sense.

This nigga wants me to get in the trunk. If I get in this trunk, I'm for sure gon' die. Please, God, protect me from this crazy muthafucka.

"Get yo' ass in the trunk," Fatty demanded.

"Nigga, hell no! If I get in that trunk, you really gon' kill me. You got me fucked up. You might as well kill me n—"

That was all Zach got out before Fatty raised his gun and cracked him over the head with all his might, knocking Zach unconscious.

"After you give me the whereabouts of your fuckin' boyfriend, I'm definitely gon' kill your stupid ass now," Fatty Man mumbled to himself as he picked Zach's body off the ground and dumped him into the trunk.

Boc . . . Boc . . . Boc . . .

"Oh shit . . . what the fuck!" Fatty Man shrieked, raising his gun in defense.

Fuck . . . fuck . . . fuck! Fatty thought as he ran to the driver side, tryin' to get the Impala into gear. He didn't know where the shots was comin' from—then it clicked.

He wasn't seein' shit after all. That car that rode by? That was Freezo's.

Boc . . . Boc . . . Boc . . . Boc . . . Boc!

Fatty Man heard the bullets smacking the body of his Impala, making him duck instinctively. He raised his gun and started busting back wild, even busting out his back windshield trying to back Freezo off him.

The gunfire stopped—only momentarily—but it was enough time for Fatty to finally get the Impala in gear.

Fatty Man sped off, wheels screeching, kicking up dust and leaving the shooters with empty clips and nothing to claim. *Bitch ass niggas*, Fatty Man laughed to himself nervously, as he looked in the rear view to make sure that he wasn't being followed.

***

"Bruh, what the fuck are we going to do now? That bitch ass nigga just took Zach!" Leek yelled, out of breath. He had just got through chasing Fatty Man's Impala down the street.

"I don't know, fully," Freezo said in reply.

Leek looked up at him, hands on his knees still trying to catch his breath. The look he gave Freezo said it all.

"What?" Freezo asked, dumbfounded, like he didn't know what the fuck was going on.

"You know what. Stop playing stupid, my nigga. Don't fucking call me that!" Leek said without anything further. He wasn't trying to get into it with Freezo over some bullshit—especially not right now. Shit just had hit the fan. Zach had just been kidnapped by Fatty Man. The city was about to bleed over this one. Neither man didn't want to be on the wrong side of the fence when shit got real.

"What do we do now, gang?" Freezo asked in a haste, pulling into traffic.

"Nigga, you know what we have to do," Leek smiled. This was the kind of action he prayed for. Leek didn't know Santana, besides what niggas brought to the table. From what he could see, all Santana was doing was sliding on behalf of the niggas that he loved. That shit was respectable in the lifestyle he lived. Leek liked the loyalty Santana possessed for the people he claimed he loved.

"And that is?" Freezo asked, curious to say the least.

"We gotta go back to see Santana. At this point, it's Zach's only option."

Freezo looked at Leek like he had lost his mind. Leek wasn't present when he talked to Santana earlier that day, so he wouldn't know the man's demeanor when it came to the two teams linking. But Freezo said nothing regarding the matter. He wanted Leek to see it for himself. Santana wasn't siding with them. They were his enemies. His team was the reason Haseem was in an early grave—no matter if they were indirectly responsible or not. They were responsible nonetheless.

"I see the way you're looking and you're wrong, bro. This is totally different than when you came at him earlier. The one other person on earth that this nigga loves has been taken, and I'm sure he would gladly team up with us to get that nigga back. If I'm wrong, I'm wrong. But I just don't see him saying no. Pull up at that nigga's spot. I'll go in there by my lonely. Trust me, bro," Leek said confidently.

"I hear you. We gone see. And I'm not letting you go in that muthafucka by yourself, lil' nigga. It ain't that type of party. I'm not saying that because I'm scared, I'm saying this because I already saw that man's reaction regarding this. I'm hoping you right, because Zach's life depends on it. This is a whole different situation in itself. We gone see what Allah got in store for us all."

"Alhamdulillah!" Leek replied as they pulled up to Zach's home on Lewis Street.

Leek barely waited for the car to stop before hopping out and running to the door.

"Nigga, what the fuck is you doing?" Freezo shouted at Leek as he rushed from the car.

Leek hopped the steps and started banging on the door with all his might.

Boom! Boom! Boom! Boom! Boom!

He kept banging until finally the door opened—and he was staring down the barrel of a .40 caliber Glock 27.

"Son, this shit better be good!" Santana said, face set like uncertain stone. "Y'all niggas ain't gone be satisfied until I body one of you niggas."

"Man, fuck all that shit you talkin' 'bout. That nigga Fatty just took Zach! Zach was at the Sev whe—"

Santana heard Leek's words and saw his mouth moving, but the words were lost in Santana's vision of anger. He had to be hearing shit.

His hand tightened around the grip of his Glock. All that ran through his head at that precise moment was his loved ones, hoping they were all safe. Santana gritted his teeth in anger before lowering his weapon and moving to the side to let Leek in.

Leek looked back at Freezo. Freezo, surprised by the gesture, put his gun away and walked up the stairs into Zach's house—a house he had been in a million times as a child.

Freezo closed the door behind him as he entered last.

Santana was visibly taken aback. He was at a loss for words. All he could seem to do was pace the floor in the foyer. He looked up at Leek and began to speak.

"Tell me what you talkin' 'bout, son. Where my brother at?" Santana demanded, gun still in hand, clutched firmly.

"Look, I'm gone make this shit fast, but first put that gun away, bruh. I told you I come in peace. Nigga, I'm in this predicament because of you, my nigga, and the morals that I stand on as a man. Now hear me the fuck out, nigga!"

Santana just stood there, stubbornly.

"Nigga, you wasting muthafuckin' time."

Santana looked over at Freezo, then at the gun in his hand. *Fuck it,* he thought, putting the gun on his hip.

At this point, he had no choice but to enlist the help of the niggas who knew Fatty Man's hoe ass in and out.

"Speak," Santana said arrogantly.

Leek laughed to himself at the cockiness Santana possessed. It was obvious Santana had a little man's complex. But he didn't let that dissuade him. Leek started from the time of FB's entry into Darla's home to the shooting that took place at the warehouse that morning, to the shootout they just had trying to save Zach.

"I just don't see us getting this little nigga back. Unless y'all have a designated spot to stash niggas in times like this. What the fuck are we supposed to—"

Santana's words were drowned out by the ringing of his phone.

If you my nigga / you my nigga till the end / fuck a bill, fuck a bitch, fuck a Benz / it's toast till we die / Roll up the weed and blow the smoke in the sky / la la la.

Santana ran to the kitchen counter and grabbed his phone.

"Yoooo!" Santana answered, putting the call on speaker.

"Listen, you already know who this is, so no need to play games. This how we about to do this. I'm gone give you a choice that you will either live with or die with—but either way, a choice has to be made," Fatty Man said through clenched teeth.

"Fuck you want, nigga?" Santana said, with hate laced all in his words.

"I want you, bitch ass nigga. You can trade your body for his," Fatty Man said, laughing disturbingly.

The look on Leek and Freezo's face was grave. They all knew the mission would be suicide if carried out the way Fatty had planned.

Santana snarled his face up. It was official—Fatty had lost his muthafuckin' mind.

"Where do we gotta meet?" Santana said simply. He wasn't 'bout to argue, go back and forth, or sit and debate with Fatty.

Fatty Man said what he said. Now it was time to get this shit on the road so he could get his partner back.

"My G, look. I got close to $30,000 for you and a little over a half a block for you. You can have all that shit right now. Just give me my little nigga back. This shit not personal, son. You let that nigga Sleeze take Heem, so I snatched back. We even. Shit, to my understanding, you blatantly told niggas that he was off limits. Right? A'ight nigga. Your homie that was with you broke the code of conduct you set forth. If this is about money, keep it like that. You caught gang slippin', okay bet. Fuck that little $15,000 that fat bitch got for you and take this chicken I got for you and let son go. And my word—I'm gone," Santana assured Fatty Man.

"As a matter of a fact, I'd consider a payment for this nigga back, but I want a hundred thousand instead of that weak ass thirty you trying to give me."

Fatty's reply took the air from Santana's body.

"My G, you buggin'. Where the fuck am I going to get that kind of money from?" Santana asked, clearly vexed by the impossible request.

"You got two options, little nigga. Pay me what I want or exchange your soul for his. There is nothing else to negotiate. You got until 8 o'clock tomorrow night. Hit my phone when you're ready to meet. You know what it is. If I don't hear from you, they gone find ya little boyfriend floating in the Kanawha River."

Fatty Man hung up. It was nothing else that needed to be said between the two. Santana had his mission, and the time frame he had to complete it in.

Santana closed his phone and stared at Leek and Freezo. The look on Santana's face told them everything they needed to know. Getting Zach back was most likely going to be an impossible task.

"What he say?" Leek asked, breaking the silence.

Santana explained to him and Freezo what Fatty wanted in return for Zach. Freezo walked off as he ran his hand through his head. The mission was suicidal to say the least, but for the love of his nigga, Santana was willing to give it a try.

The only thing about it . . . where the fuck was he going to find that kind of money?

"Where the fuck we gone find that kind of money at?" Leek thought out loud.

Freezo nodded in agreement. "Between me and Zach I got close to fifty, but knowing Fatty bitch ass . . . it ain't enough."

Santana took a deep breath and sat down. He needed time to think.

How the fuck am I going to get that kind of money by tomorrow? Santana asked himself. He was drawing blanks.

"I got an idea. One that neither one of you niggas may like, but it's the only option at this point."

Both men looked at Leek with curiosity.

"Speak, nigga. We don't have time for the suspense," Santana said, annoyed.

"We gone have to hit a bank. I know that shit sound crazy, but it's our only—" Leek said apprehensively.

"OK . . . OK . . . OK . . . OK . . . I see a nigga mind moving!" Santana said as he got off his ass and rose back to his feet with a new founded hope.

Boc . . . Boc . . . Boc . . .

The sound of shattering glass made each person grab for their waist.

What the fuck! Santana thought as he crawled along the floor trying to get out of the direct line of fire.

Boom . . . Boom . . . Boc . . . Boc . . . Boc . . . Boc . . . Bang . . . Bang . . . Boom . . .

Freezo pointed towards the staircase.

"I got you!" Freezo yelled. "On three, I'm gone cover y'all. Hit the stairs as fast as you can. Keep ya head low."

As soon as the shooting let up, Freezo yelled, "Go!"

Leek ran up the stairs as directed. Santana stayed in place. He locked eyes with Freezo.

"Go, bro, I got you. When you get up stairs, hit at them from the first bedroom to the left. When the shooting stop I'll know to—" Santana said.

Boc . . . Boc . . . Boc . . .

Santana's words were cut short by another round of bullets.

What the fuck! Santana thought as he lifted his gun and fired back, giving Freezo and Leek the cover they needed.

Boc . . . Boc . . . Boc . . . Boc . . . Boc . . .

One, two, three, four, five. Santana counted each shell as it left his gun. He wasn't trying to miscalculate how many shots he fired, because when it was all said and done, it may very well count.

"Santana!" Freezo called from the top of the steps.

When Freezo didn't get an answer, he called out again.

"SANTANA!"

"Yooo!" Santana replied as he attempted to look out the side of the curtain.

"Bruh, hurry up! They're advancing."

As soon as the words left Freezo's mouth, Santana saw four masked men running up the driveway.

Fuck . . . Fuck . . . FUCK! Think, nigga, think! Santana told himself as he watched the men split up, surrounding the house.

Without second thought, Santana took off up the stairs to an awaiting Freezo and Leek.

Both men had their guns drawn, looking out the windows stationed around the house. It was one thing about Zach and his family that Santana loved— they kept their house secure at all times. So he had no worries about the shooters gaining access easily. Their access would come with consequences, that was for sure.

"Where are they?" Santana asked, leading them into Zach's room.

He opened the closet and pulled up the wooden floorboard.

Leek watched on in awe. *This nigga just doesn't cease to amaze me*, Leek thought as Santana handed them each an AK-47 assault rifle.

It was obvious—Zach and Santana was ready for a war.

Santana stood at the top of the landing, daring someone to enter his residence. He was going to leave them where they stood.

He looked behind him. Freezo was stationed at one window, while Leek was stationed at another. They were as ready as they would ever be for the situation at hand.

Santana rested the stock against his shoulder as he looked through the sights.

Come on, nigga, bring ya ass in here. I fucking dare you, Santana thought, biting his lip in anticipation of stripping another nigga for his soul.

The sirens in the distance snapped Santana out of his reverie of violence.

Oh, shit.

"We gotta get the fuck out of here!" Santana finally exclaimed.

Leek took off, choppa in hand. Freezo followed suit.

"Follow me," Santana said as he opened the back door leading to the alleyway that sat adjacent to Chamberlain Court.

"What about the whip niggas drove up in?" Leek asked.

"Nigga, fuck that whip," Freezo said before leaping off the porch and following Santana into the alley leading to Kat's house.

Chapter 16

"Oh shit. You really killed this nigga," Peedi laughed out loud.

Simfany looked at Peedi, irritated at his sudden sense of humor.

"Nigga, if you don't stop playing. What the fuck am I supposed to do? I know this nigga told someone that he was coming over here. That's just how this paranoid ass nigga is."

Peedi couldn't do shit but shake his head from side to side. This was a mess, and he knew in his heart he needed to detach himself from the issue at hand—but he just couldn't.

"Love, I'm only here to help. I just find it funny that just yesterday we were shook about what this nigga would do regarding his daughter's death . . . and now he's lying dead in your living room. Shit crazy how the world work, shorty. That's all."

"That's obvious, P. What I want to know is where do we go from here?" Simfany said, hand on hip, annoyed at Peedi's immaturity.

"First we have to get this nigga out of—"

Buzzz . . . Buzzzzz . . . Buzzzzzz . . .

Carlos's phone began to vibrate, startling them both. Simfany gave Peedi a look that screamed *what should I do?*

"Answer it, Ma," Peedi stated simply.

"But what if—"

"You act like touching the phone is going to be damaging of some kind. That nigga was powerful, Ma, but that nigga wasn't *that* powerful. Man, fuck it, I'll answer it."

Peedi walked over to Carlos's lifeless body and wrenched into his pocket, taking his phone out and scrolling through his call history. The names he looked at might as well have been written in Chinese, 'cause none of them meant shit to him. It was that exact reason he told Simfany to grab the phone in the first place.

"What does it say? Who's calling?" Simfany asked curiously, with interest laced in her voice.

"Some nigga named Juanito. Do you know who that is?" Peedi asked.

"Yeah. He one of Carlos's most trusted friends and bodyguard. I think they grew up together in the Dominican Republic. Carlos employs him and his twin brother," Simfany explained, biting her nails nervously.

"Oh, okay. That makes sense. It says this number called 7 times in the last 30 minutes. Why would he be ca—"

They're coming, Simfany thought to herself as she ran to the window and looked out the blinds.

"OH SHIT! Peedi, we gotta go. NOW!" Simfany exclaimed, grabbing Peedi by his arm.

"Shorty, what's wrong?" Peedi asked, looking out the window himself.

The masked men rushing Simfany's home made it all clear—they had to go while they had the chance.

"Nigga, come on!" she shouted, grabbing Peedi's arm again.

This time, Peedi cooperated and ran behind Simfany in hopes of escaping with their lives.

Simfany ran to her back door and saw that it was impassable. Killers dressed in all-black blocked their exit.

"We blocked in," Simfany said nervously.

Peedi sighed heavily and looked up into Simfany's eyes.

"I got you, shorty. I'm gone try to make it out with you, but how it's looking, only one of us gone be able to make it. I promised to protect you with my life, and that's what I plan to do."

"But Peedi, this not—"

Peedi interjected before Simfany could finish protesting.

"Shorty . . ."

"Nigga . . ."

"Shorty, listen—"

"I'm not trying—"

"Simfany! Shut the fuck up and listen. Please. This is my choice. Let me do something right in my life. I fucking love ya hard-headed ass, a'ight? Let me get you out of here. No matter the cost. Okay?"

Simfany nodded as tears streamed down her face. Peedi took his finger and wiped away her tears.

"I'm good, Ma. We good. I got you."

"I love you, Peedi," Simfany replied as she leaned forward and kissed Peedi's lips. Peedi pulled away after a few seconds.

"I love you more, shorty. Never forget that."

Bang . . . Bang . . . Bang . . . Bang . . .

They looked up, awaiting their entry—but nothing happened.

Seconds later, the front door burst open. Peedi rose and fired at the first person that came through the door.

Boc . . . Boc . . . Boc . . .

"Go!"

Simfany got up to run but thought better of it and raised her Glock also. She took stance next to Peedi and fired.

"I'm not leaving you, P."

"Yeah, the fuck you are. I got this, Ma. Please. You got people who need you, Simf. Go!" Peedi yelled, awaiting the next set of niggas that tried to enter Simfany's home. "GO!"

Peedi yelled again, pushing Simfany to the stairs. The flash bang hit the ground near them, giving Simfany only seconds to make a move.

Without any further protest, Simfany took off up the stairs—but she didn't get the chance to escape the flash bang altogether.

Simfany stumbled up the stairs weakly before dropping against the steps. She tried to reach her gun, but she was too discombobulated to do so. Before passing out, all she saw was black figures surrounding her.

Santana . . . was her only thought before she succumbed to the darkness.

Coming Soon

For The Love of Blood 6

Till My Casket Drop

Lock Down Publications and Ca$h Presents Assisted Publishing Packages

Due to an increase in the price of services we have increased our prices. The prices below reflect the price increase as of 11/1/24.

BASIC PACKAGE **$699** Editing Cover Design Formatting	**UPGRADED PACKAGE** **$1000** Typing Editing Cover Design Formatting Upload eBooks to Amazon Upload Paperback to Amazon
ADVANCE PACKAGE **$1,400** Typing Editing (line editing/content) Cover Design Formatting Copyright Registration Proofreading Upload eBooks to Amazon Upload Paperback to Amazon	**LDP SUPREME PACKAGE** **$1,700** Typing Editing (line editing/content) Cover Design Formatting Copyright Registration Proofreading Set up Amazon Account Upload eBooks to Amazon Upload Paperback to Amazon Advertise on LDP's Amazon and Facebook Page

***

Other services available upon request.
Additional charges may apply

Lock Down Publications
P.O. Box 944
Stockbridge, GA 30281-9998
Phone: 470 303-9761
Email: lockdownpublications@gmail.com

Submission Guideline

Submit the first three chapters of your completed manuscript to ldpsubmissions@gmail.com. In the subject line add **Your Book's Title**. The manuscript must be in a Word Doc file and sent as an attachment. Document should be in Times New Roman, double spaced, and in size 12 font. Also, provide your synopsis and full contact information. If sending multiple submissions, they must each be in a separate email.

Have a story but no way to send it electronically? You can still submit to LDP/Ca$h Presents. Send in the first three chapters, written or typed, of your completed manuscript to:

LDP: Submissions Dept
P.O. Box 944
Stockbridge, GA 30281-9998

DO NOT send original manuscript. Must be a duplicate. Provide your synopsis and a cover letter containing your full contact information.

Thanks for considering LDP and Ca$h Presents.

NEW RELEASES

BLOODLINE OF A SAVAGE 1-3
THESE VICIOUS STREETS 1-3
RELENTLESS GOON 1-3
BY PRINCE A. TAUHID

THE BUTTERFLY MAFIA 1-3
BY FUMIYA PAYNE

A THUG'S STREET PRINCESS 1&2
BY MEESHA

CITY OF SMOKE 3
BY MOLOTTI

GET IT IN SLUGS 1 &2
BY B. STALL

STANDING ON HER BUSINESS 1&2
BY DG SANTANA

STEPPERS 1,2&3
THE REAL BADDIES OF CHI-RAQ
BY KING RIO

THE LANE 1&2
BY KEN-KEN SPENCE

THUG OF SPADES 1&2
LOVE IN THE TRENCHES 2
CORNER BOYS
BY COREY ROBINSON

TIL DEATH 3
BY ARYANNA

THE BIRTH OF A GANGSTER 4
BY DELMONT PLAYER

PRODUCT OF THE STREETS 1-3
BY DEMOND "MONEY" ANDERSON

NO TIME FOR ERROR
BY KEESE

MONEY HUNGRY DEMONS 1-2
BY TRANAY ADAMS

HUB CITY MENACE 1-3
BY J. WHITE

A THUGGISH PASSION 1&2
LAND OF DA HOOLIGANZ 1-4
KILLAZ ON STANDBY 1&2
BY IRA B.

FO'EVA ROLLIN 1&2
BY ASSA RAYMOND BAKER

THE LEVEL UP 1&3
BY LUXURY KING

Coming Soon from Lock Down Publications/Ca$h Presents

IF YOU CROSS ME ONCE 6
ANGEL V
By Anthony Fields

A THUGS STREET PRINCESS 3
By Meesha

CORNER BOYS 2
By Corey Robinson

THA TAKEOVER
By Keith Chandler

BETRAYAL OF A G 2
By Ray Vinci

SAVAGE FAMILY EMPIRE 1&2
SOULLESS GOON 1,2&3
THE DIRTY SIDE OF MONEY 1,2&3
By Prince

FOR MY ENEMY'S SAKE
AMBITIONS OF A SLIDER
FRESH OFF DA PORCH
By IRA B.

THE TRUCKLOAD 1-4
TIPPIN' THE SCALES 1-3
BAD BITCHES WIT GUNZ 3
PROBLEM SOLVED 2
By Christopher "Diesel" Hornezes

Available Now

RESTRAINING ORDER 1 & 2
By **CA$H & Coffee**

LOVE KNOWS NO BOUNDARIES 1-3
By **Coffee**

RAISED AS A GOON I, II, III & IV
BRED BY THE SLUMS I, II, III
BLAST FOR ME I & II
ROTTEN TO THE CORE I II III
A BRONX TALE I, II, III
DUFFLE BAG CARTEL I II III IV V VI
HEARTLESS GOON I II III IV V
A SAVAGE DOPEBOY I II
DRUG LORDS I II III
CUTTHROAT MAFIA I II
KING OF THE TRENCHES
By **Ghost**

LAY IT DOWN I & II
LAST OF A DYING BREED I II
BLOOD STAINS OF A SHOTTA I & II III
By **Jamaica**

LOYAL TO THE GAME I II III
LIFE OF SIN I, II III
By **TJ & Jelissa**

IF LOVING HIM IS WRONG…I & II
LOVE ME EVEN WHEN IT HURTS I II III
By **Jelissa**

PUSH IT TO THE LIMIT
By **Bre' Hayes**

BLOODY COMMAS I & II
SKI MASK CARTEL I, II & III
KING OF NEW YORK I II, III IV V
RISE TO POWER I II III
COKE KINGS I II III IV V
BORN HEARTLESS I II III IV
KING OF THE TRAP I II
By **T.J. Edwards**

WHEN THE STREETS CLAP BACK I & II III
THE HEART OF A SAVAGE I II III IV
MONEY MAFIA I II
LOYAL TO THE SOIL I II III
By **Jibril Williams**

A DISTINGUISHED THUG STOLE MY HEART I II & III
LOVE SHOULDN'T HURT I II III IV
RENEGADE BOYS 1-4
PAID IN KARMA 1-3
SAVAGE STORMS 1-3
AN UNFORESEEN LOVE 1-3
BABY, I'M WINTERTIME COLD 1-3
A THUG'S STREET PRINCESS 1&2
By **Meesha**

A GANGSTER'S CODE 1-3
A GANGSTER'S SYN 1-3
THE SAVAGE LIFE 1-3
CHAINED TO THE STREETS 1-3
BLOOD ON THE MONEY 1-3
A GANGSTA'S PAIN 1-3
BEAUTIFUL LIES AND UGLY TRUTHS
CHURCH IN THESE STREETS
By **J-Blunt**

CUM FOR ME 1-8
An LDP Erotica Collaboration

BLOOD OF A BOSS 1-5
SHADOWS OF THE GAME
TRAP BASTARD
By **Askari**

THE STREETS BLEED MURDER 1-3
THE HEART OF A GANGSTA 1-3
By **Jerry Jackson**

WHEN A GOOD GIRL GOES BAD
By **Adrienne**

THE COST OF LOYALTY 1-3
By **Kweli**

BRIDE OF A HUSTLA 1-3
THE FETTI GIRLS 1-3
CORRUPTED BY A GANGSTA 1-4
BLINDED BY HIS LOVE
THE PRICE YOU PAY FOR LOVE 1-3
DOPE GIRL MAGIC 1-3
By **Destiny Skai**

A KINGPIN'S AMBITION
A KINGPIN'S AMBITION II
I MURDER FOR THE DOUGH
By **Ambitious**

TRUE SAVAGE 1-7
DOPE BOY MAGIC 1-3
MIDNIGHT CARTEL 1-3
CITY OF KINGZ 1&2
NIGHTMARE ON SILENT AVE
THE PLUG OF LIL MEXICO 1&2
CLASSIC CITY
By **Chris Green**

A GANGSTER'S REVENGE 1-4
THE BOSS MAN'S DAUGHTERS 1-5
A SAVAGE LOVE 1&2
BAE BELONGS TO ME 1&2
A HUSTLER'S DECEIT 1-3
WHAT BAD BITCHES DO 1-3
SOUL OF A MONSTER 1-3
KILL ZONE
A DOPE BOY'S QUEEN 1-3
TIL DEATH 1-3
IMMA DIE BOUT MINE 1-6
DYING FOR LIKES
By **Aryanna**

A DOPEBOY'S PRAYER
By **Eddie "Wolf" Lee**

THE KING CARTEL 1-3
By **Frank Gresham**

THESE NIGGAS AIN'T LOYAL 1-3
By **Nikki Tee**

GANGSTA SHYT 1-3
By **CATO**

THE ULTIMATE BETRAYAL
By **Phoenix**

BOSS'N UP 1-3
By **Royal Nicole**

I LOVE YOU TO DEATH
By **Destiny J**

I RIDE FOR MY HITTA
I STILL RIDE FOR MY HITTA
By **Misty Holt**

LOVE & CHASIN' PAPER
By **Qay Crockett**

TO DIE IN VAIN
SINS OF A HUSTLA
By **ASAD**

BROOKLYN HUSTLAZ
By **Boogsy Morina**

BROOKLYN ON LOCK 1 & 2
By **Sonovia**

GANGSTA CITY
By T**eddy Duke**

A DRUG KING AND HIS DIAMOND 1-3
A DOPEMAN'S RICHES
HER MAN, MINE'S TOO 1&2
CASH MONEY HO'S
THE WIFEY I USED TO BE 1&2
PRETTY GIRLS DO NASTY THINGS
By **Nicole Goosby**

LIPSTICK KILLAH 1-3
CRIME OF PASSION 1-3
FRIEND OR FOE 1-3
By **Mimi**

TRAPHOUSE KING 1-3
KINGPIN KILLAZ 1-3
STREET KINGS 1&2
PAID IN BLOOD 1&2
CARTEL KILLAZ 1-3
DOPE GODS 1&2
By **Hood Rich**

THE STREETS ARE CALLING
By **Duquie Wilson**

STEADY MOBBN' 1-3
THE STREETS STAINED MY SOUL 1-3
By **Marcellus Allen**

WHO SHOT YA 1-3
SON OF A DOPE FIEND 1-4
HEAVEN GOT A GHETTO 1&2
SKI MASK MONEY 1&2
By **Renta**

GORILLAZ IN THE BAY 1-4
TEARS OF A GANGSTA 1/&2
3X KRAZY 1&2
STRAIGHT BEAST MODE 1&2
By **DE'KARI**

TRIGGADALE 1-3
MURDA WAS THE CASE 1-3
By **Elijah R. Freeman**

SLAUGHTER GANG 1-3
RUTHLESS HEART 1-3
By **Willie Slaughter**

GOD BLESS THE TRAPPERS 1-3
THESE SCANDALOUS STREETS 1-3
FEAR MY GANGSTA 1-5
THESE STREETS DON'T LOVE NOBODY 1-2
BURY ME A G 1-5
A GANGSTA'S EMPIRE 1-4
THE DOPEMAN'S BODYGAURD 1&2
THE REALEST KILLAZ 1-3
THE LAST OF THE OGS 1-3
By **Tranay Adams**

MARRIED TO A BOSS 1-3
By **Destiny Skai & Chris Green**

KINGZ OF THE GAME 1-7
CRIME BOSS 1-4
By **Playa Ray**

FUK SHYT
By **Blakk Diamond**

DON'T F#CK WITH MY HEART 1&2
By **Linnea**

ADDICTED TO THE DRAMA 1-3
IN THE ARM OF HIS BOSS
By **Jamila**

LOYALTY AIN'T PROMISED 1&2
By **Keith Williams**

YAYO 1-4
A SHOOTER'S AMBITION 1&2
BRED IN THE GAME
By **S. Allen**

TRAP GOD 1-3
RICH $AVAGE 1-3
MONEY IN THE GRAVE 1-3
CARTEL MONEY 1&2
By **Martell Troublesome Bolden**

FOREVER GANGSTA 1&2
GLOCKS ON SATIN SHEETS 1&2
By **Adrian Dulan**

TOE TAGZ 1-4
LEVELS TO THIS SHYT 1&2
IT'S JUST ME AND YOU
By **Ah'Million**

KINGPIN DREAMS 1-3
RAN OFF ON DA PLUG
By **Paper Boi Rari**

THE STREETS MADE ME 1-3
By **Larry D. Wright**

CONFESSIONS OF A GANGSTA 1-4
CONFESSIONS OF A JACKBOY 1-3
CONFESSIONS OF A HITMAN
CONFESSIONS OF A DOPE BOY
By **Nicholas Lock**

I'M NOTHING WITHOUT HIS LOVE
SINS OF A THUG
TO THE THUG I LOVED BEFORE
A GANGSTA SAVED XMAS
IN A HUSTLER I TRUST
By **Monet Dragun**

QUIET MONEY 1-3
THUG LIFE 1-3
EXTENDED CLIP 1&2
A GANGSTA'S PARADISE
By **Trai'Quan**

CAUGHT UP IN THE LIFE 1-3
THE STREETS NEVER LET GO 1-3
By **Robert Baptiste**

NEW TO THE GAME 1-3
MONEY, MURDER & MEMORIES 1-3
By **Malik D. Rice**

CREAM 2-3
THE STREETS WILL TALK
By **Yolanda Moore**

THE STREETS WILL NEVER CLOSE 1-3
By **K'ajji**

LIFE OF A SAVAGE 1-4
A GANGSTA'S QUR'AN 1-4
MURDA SEASON 1-3
GANGLAND CARTEL 1-3
CHI'RAQ GANGSTAS 1-4
KILLERS ON ELM STREET 1-3
JACK BOYZ N DA BRONX 1-3
A DOPEBOY'S DREAM 1-3
JACK BOYS VS DOPE BOYS 1-3
COKE GIRLZ
COKE BOYS
SOSA GANG 1&2
BRONX SAVAGES
BODYMORE KINGPINS
BLOOD OF A GOON
By **Romell Tukes**

CONCRETE KILLA 1-3
VICIOUS LOYALTY 1-3
BLOODY MONEY BAGS
By **Kingpen**

THE ULTIMATE SACRIFICE 1-6
KHADIFI
IF YOU CROSS ME ONCE 1-3
ANGEL 1-4
IN THE BLINK OF AN EYE
By **Anthony Fields**

THE LIFE OF A HOOD STAR
By **Ca$h & Rashia Wilson**

NIGHTMARES OF A HUSTLA 1-3
BLOOD AND GAMES 1&2
By **King Dream**

GHOST MOB
By **Stilloan Robinson**

HARD AND RUTHLESS 1&2
MOB TOWN 251
THE BILLIONAIRE BENTLEYS 1-3
REAL G'S MOVE IN SILENCE
By **Von Diesel**

MOB TIES 1-7
SOUL OF A HUSTLER, HEART OF A KILLER 1-3
GORILLAZ IN THE TRENCHES
OOPS CRY TOO 1&2
THE DAUGHTER OF A CARTEL BOSS
By **SayNoMore**

BODYMORE MURDERLAND 1-3
THE BIRTH OF A GANGSTER 1-4
By **Delmont Player**

FOR THE LOVE OF A BOSS 1&2
By **C. D. Blue**

KILLA KOUNTY 1-5
TENDER
By **Khufu**

MOBBED UP 1-4
THE BRICK MAN 1-5
THE COCAINE PRINCESS 1-10
STEPPERS 1-3
SUPER GREMLIN 1-4
A GANGSTA'S SON
By **King Rio**

MONEY GAME 1&2
By **Smoove Dolla**

A GANGSTA'S KARMA 1-5
By **FLAME**

KING OF THE TRENCHES 1-3
By **GHOST & TRANAY ADAMS**

BAD BITCHES WIT GUNZ 1&2
PROBLEM SOLVED
By "Christopher Diesel" Hornezes

QUEEN OF THE ZOO 1&2
By **Black Migo**

GRIMEY WAYS 1-3
BETRAYAL OF A G
By **Ray Vinci**

XMAS WITH AN ATL SHOOTER
By **Ca$h & Destiny Skai**

KING KILLA 1&2
By **Vincent "Vitto" Holloway**

BETRAYAL OF A THUG 1&2
By **Fre$h**

COUNTDOWN OF A KILLA 1&2
SEX, MURDER AND GOD 1&2
GUNS DOWN, BOTTOMS UP 1&2
By Lo-Life

THE MURDER QUEENS 1-7
By **Michael Gallon**

FOR THE LOVE OF BLOOD 1-4
By **Jamel Mitchell**

HOOD CONSIGLIERE 1&2
NO TIME FOR ERROR
By **Keese**

PROTÉGÉ OF A LEGEND 1,2&3
LOVE IN THE TRENCHES 1&2
By **Corey Robinson**

THE PLUG'S RUTHLESS DAUGHTER 1&2
By **Tony Daniels**

BORN IN THE GRAVE 1-3
CRIME PAYS
By **Self Made Tay**

MOAN IN MY MOUTH
By **XTASY**

TORN BETWEEN A GANGSTER AND A GENTLEMAN
By **J-BLUNT & Miss Kim**

LOYALTY IS EVERYTHING 1-3
CITY OF SMOKE 1-3
By **Molotti**

HERE TODAY GONE TOMORROW 1&2
By **Fly Rock**

WOMEN LIE MEN LIE 1-4
FIFTY SHADES OF SNOW 1-3
STACK BEFORE YOU SPLURGE
GIRLS FALL LIKE DOMINOES
NAÏVE TO THE STREETS
By **ROY MILLIGAN**

PILLOW PRINCESS
By **S. Hawkins**

THE BUTTERFLY MAFIA 1-3
SALUTE MY SAVAGERY 1&2
By **Fumiya Payne**

THE LANE 1&2
By Ken-Ken Spence

THE PUSSY TRAP 1-5
By **Nene Capri**

DIRTY DNA
By **Blaque**

SANCTIFIED AND HORNY
by **XTASY**

BOOKS BY LDP'S CEO, CA$H

TRUST IN NO MAN
TRUST IN NO MAN 2
TRUST IN NO MAN 3
BONDED BY BLOOD
SHORTY GOT A THUG
THUGS CRY
THUGS CRY 2
THUGS CRY 3
TRUST NO BITCH
TRUST NO BITCH 2
TRUST NO BITCH 3
TIL MY CASKET DROPS
RESTRAINING ORDER
RESTRAINING ORDER 2
IN LOVE WITH A CONVICT
LIFE OF A HOOD STAR
XMAS WITH AN ATL SHOOTER

www.ingramcontent.com/pod-product-compliance
Lightning Source LLC
Chambersburg PA
CBHW051541260626
47170CB00003B/1053
* 9 7 8 1 9 6 5 4 4 8 7 3 1 *